Who is this lovely destitute g[   ]
from entering a brothel?

His offer of employment to her sets their relationship as employer
and employee, but that does not stifle his curiosity. Curiosity about
Mrs. Olivia Williams grows to passion, returned by her only to meet
obstacles they only overcome with the aid of friends, family, a London
gossip and helpful servants.

Mrs. Olivia Williams realized she had reached a new low while stood
outside the salubrious establishment. Sir Edmond Linnington
watched as she grappled with her indecision and made a split-second
decision to help.

Olivia takes Edmonds offer to help renovate his London townhouse
for sale. Both rather reserved and polite, they struggle to find a way to
deal with their growing affection for each other while trying to
maintain a professional relationship. Olivia's past haunts her and
Linnington has his own demons to bear. Overbearing family
members, spiteful gossips and secrets strive to keep the two
separated. But a gentle, endearing love like theirs will surely survive?

From the busy streets of London to the calm and beauty of the Oxford
and Cornish countryside, Linnington and Olivia's one night of
passion changes the course of their lives - but will it be permanent?

A Reasonable Lady
Copyright 2021 by Janet Taliaferro
Digital ISBN: 978-1-68361-535-4
Print ISBN: 978-1-68361-562-0

Published by Decadent Publishing LLC

This book and its sequel are the direct result of the COVID19 pandemic.

After writing three novels, two collections of short stories, countless poems, and a memoir, at eighty-seven years old I thought I had hung up my spurs as a writer. Then along came the pandemic and I decided I could not knit or needlepoint enough to keep my sanity during the long days of isolation. The television was not an option and I decided if I had to fill the time with stories, instead of Netflix I would write my own.

The first chapters of a romance novel had been residing on my computer for years. Thus I took up those chapters, began to rewrite and write anew. The result is A Reasonable Lady. Growing up on Jane Austen, her works were my template but living in a much different era, I always wanted to follow Mr. Darcy and Elizabeth into the bedroom. This, Miss Austen left to our imagination. I plunged right in. After all, you don't forget how.

Although my novels and short stories are Main Stream fiction and deal with serious subjects such as addiction, rape and abortion, I have always had a soft spot for romance fiction. To quote a friend of mine who published romance novels, when asked why she wrote them she said, "Honey, I'm married to an engineer. You have to do something!" This is my something.

I am grateful to Decadent publishing for agreeing to give my work an airing. I call this "luck in the time of COVID." In addition I want to thank Decadent's patient publisher, Kate Richards and my editors, Caroline Hedges and Laura Garland as well as my careful and faithful readers Karen Clark and Courtney Taliaferro.

I hope you enjoy reading about Linnington and Olivia as I did in writing about them.

Janet Taliaferro

A Reasonable Lady

By

Janet Taliaferro

Chapter One

Good, God, she's not really going to do that, is she?

Sir Edmond Linnington was surreptitiously watching a slight and pretty young woman with abundant light-brown hair. She wore a pelisse and lovely bonnet, now the worse for wear, but once of excellent quality and style. Gripped between both hands was a rather large, shabby portmanteau.

A nervous hesitation on her part first caught Linnington's attention as he walked down the busy London street with James Talent, his dearest friend. He couldn't help but notice the woman's well-worn pelisse was of excellent quality but also somewhat out of style, the dark fur at the neck showing hard use. Curious, he purposely stopped at the corner, leaning his broad shoulders against the pleasantly sun-warmed brick of a corner building, in casual conversation with James.

The woman spent some time walking between the house on the opposite corner and a parapet blocking the end of the street. He had a fleeting worry she might consider jumping over the impediment into the Thames, but she turned away from the river toward a rather plain building across the street. Its white door with an oversized brass knocker was fronted by a discreet flight of stone steps with a hand railing of wrought iron. A Mrs. Taunton owned the building, and she was a notorious madam.

The young woman standing irresolutely near the entrance fascinated him. She did not have the demeanor of a "lady of the night," but her clothing would indicate she was in straightened circumstances. Her boots were worn almost to disuse.

Twice, during the time they stood there, she approached the house then retreated to the parapet on the Thames close by.

Just as he was wondering if the girl would perhaps consider the river a third time, she mounted the steps with determination. Alarmed at what she was about to do, on impulse he sprinted across the street, dodging a phaeton, and bounded up the steps behind her as she sounded the brass door knocker. A uniformed servant opened the door just as Linnington grasped her hand and tucked it under his arm.

"My dear, I think perhaps we have the wrong address." He smiled at the servant. "So sorry to disturb you." He descended the stairs, pulling the startled woman with him. The portmanteau bumped along the steps, and he paused long enough to take it from her with his free hand.

"Sir, what are you doing?" Her blue eyes widened with alarm, tears trembling at the edges. "Please, you must let me go. Let me return."

"Woman, do you know what sort of house you are approaching?"

"Yes, sir, I do." Despite the tears, she straightened to her full five-foot-three-inch height and raised her chin. Her tone was firm rather than defiant, quickly eliminating any sign of her earlier despair.

"Why in the world would you go in there?" he inquired in fully as forward a way as she used.

"For employment, sir, as I am now totally without funds."

They glared at each other until she swayed slightly, appearing somewhat unsteady on her feet.

"When did you last eat?"

"Two days ago."

By this time, James, curious about why his friend had intervened, crossed the street and overheard the conversation. He reached them just in time to take the girl by the other arm and prevent her from crumpling at their feet.

"Give me a hand here, Talent." Linnington dropped the portmanteau and grasped her arm with both hands.

"Steady there, miss." James set her on her feet between them.

"Come with us and we will at least obtain a meal for you," Linnington spoke firmly, hoping his tone brooked no argument.

James smiled at the girl. "Madam, since you know neither of us, I doubt if my word will carry much weight, but you may be assured you are safe in this gentleman's hands. I have never known him to do an untoward thing. Do you think you are steady enough now to proceed?"

"I believe I am able to make my way, sir. I thank you for your assistance." She straightened her shoulders.

"Then as for me, Linnington, if this young lady is right enough to seek a meal, I must be off. I need to get to the country. My dear wife is dealing with our newest who seems determined not to sleep. Good luck to you, Linnington, and good day, miss." He gave her another charming smile, tipped his hat, and walked away.

Linnington again tucked her hand into the crook of his arm and picked up the worn portmanteau. With military precision, he began to step forward to guide her down the street, but she resisted moving with him and withdrew her hand.

"Thank you for your offer, sir, but I am disinclined to accept it. I have no idea who you are or your purpose."

"Well, Madam, may I introduce myself. Edmond Linnington." He hesitated, adding rather diffidently, "Baron Linnington." A moment's irritation assailed him. He almost never introduced himself with the full title. What was he doing? Trying to impress this bereft and forlorn girl? She didn't seem overly impressed, so he hurried on. "To allay any fears you might have, may I assure you I am offering only a meal, without which I am quite certain you will soon faint away on the cobbles. And you are?"

"I am Mrs. Olivia Williams." She made a movement to proffer her hand, the way a lady might at an introduction but quickly tucked it into the sleeve of her coat. "I thank you for your kindness and I accept your offer." She hesitated then placed her hand on his arm for support.

They walked a few blocks down the street in silence. Linnington was conscious of the sounds of industry on the river, the occasional bell, the rattle of chains, and the dull thud of hawser as well as the shouts of the watermen at work. At least the autumn rains had washed away some of the perpetual coal dust of the city, leaving room for the fragrance of burning wood. Trees on the opposite bank were turned a pleasant combination of rust, orange, and gold.

They arrived at the rather nondescript public house where he and James had lunched earlier. This would make an excellent place to converse in private. They entered, and he took a table near the wall. The filtered light from a leaded window, inset with bottle ends, invaded the dark interior, but, even in the middle of the day, the table he chose needed a candle. The food was excellent, but the air was always heavy with stale barley ale and tobacco smoke mingling with smoke from the wide fireplace. The men considered it a friendly place

4

of dark wood, low ceilings with heavy beams, and good conversation. He was quite sure if nothing else appealed to this woman, the food surely would.

He waited until she had ordered a shepherd's pie before he questioned her. He asked for only a glass of ale.

She sat with her hands in her lap and would not meet his gaze. "It was quite uncivil of me not to have addressed you properly when we met, my lord. I should have recognized you. I believe you, upon rare occasion, accompanied your sister to my former place of employment, *La Boulangerie*. Your sister used to visit regularly to purchase *croissants* and *tartan* and occasionally have tea. The establishment was a small bakery and teashop off Milbank Street."

He stretched out long legs and crossed one polished boot over the other. "That's quite all right. I don't recall being there." He wasn't sure why he lied. Perhaps it was to spare her embarrassment. He certainly had no memory of this woman. *I visited the teashop once and vowed never to return.*

The waiter brought her food, and he withheld conversation as she ate. Something was amiss. Shopgirl somehow didn't fit her any more than prostitute did. Mrs. Olivia Williams delicately ate the homely dish before her. The way she held the utensils and, indeed, the manner in which she spoke did not fit the lowly position, either, nor did her precise pronunciation of the French words. He had interrogated dozens of French officers when they were taken prisoner in Spain. His ear was attuned to nuance, particularly the Parisian pronunciation of "r" which the English never seemed to be able to master.

Linnington was, by nature, a cautious man, and his actions on behalf of this young woman were a mystery even to him. He had rueful thoughts about the last time he attempted to help a damsel in distress. She turned out to be much more than he bargained for, and he was in the process of cleaning up the trail of disaster she left in her wake. Thankfully, at least he was rid of the harridan. His predicament gave him an idea.

He took a deep breath and waded into water he had been contemplating since they entered the alehouse. "So, you know you were about to ask for employment at a house of ill repute?"

"I do, my lord."

"Regardless of the fact Mrs. Taunton's establishment is of good reputation among gentlemen of the Ton, I suppose you do know what activity goes on there?"

"Sir, I am a widow, so not unfamiliar with men."

Man rather than men, I would wager. Much of what would be expected of you in an establishment like that would not be pleasant and quite beyond your knowledge. "And your husband?"

"He fell at Corunna, my lord."

He looked away. "I was there." The horrors of the Peninsula from Corunna to Salamanca were never far from his thoughts. A soldier by training, Linnington had never expected to hold his father and brother's title. Only the untimely death of his unmarried elder brother, Giles, had brought him home from the wars and given him the title. "I'm sure your husband was a gallant soldier." Curiosity prodded him. "His regiment?"

"He served under Paget, and he was indeed a proud soldier."

"I was with the King's Own."

"Oh, you were there when Sir John Hope fell." It was more statement than question.

"I was." He had helped carry the fallen commander's body for burial.

"I have often thought had Sir John lived, perhaps he would have handled Paget's advance differently." She fiddled with her fork for a moment. "Not so many of my husband's comrades fell as the King's Own, but perhaps the outcome would have been different, and David, my husband, would have survived if the command was different."

A momentary silence engulfed whatever private thoughts each of them had about the war. Linnington was impressed the lady knew her battles.

"And the teashop?"

"Closed. I had known Mme. Dufour, the owner, from childhood, and after my husband's death, she kindly asked me to come live with her and assist in the shop. There were lodgings above the shop with room enough for two women. Some unfathomable problem with my widow's pension made me most grateful for a gainful employment."

"And Mme. Dufour?"

"Tragically, she died." She blinked away tears, taking a handkerchief from her sleeve to dry her eyes. "I had expected to simply continue to operate the shop after her sudden and untimely death just this past week, only to discover the debts on the business were much more than could be afforded. I wonder if the owner of the building did not secretly wish to let the space to a friend for an increase of rentals," she mused. "The sheriff came the day before yesterday and left me only my personal belongings."

"And now?"

"It does not seem I have any alternative but to return to the house after you have been kind enough to buy my meal. I'm sorry if it disappoints you, but the only other thing would be the poorhouse where I have no means of escape or a life on the street, and I prefer the comforts of a roof and fireplace."

Said in a different tone, her statement could have been insolent. To Linnington, her declaration only sounded as though she had thoroughly assessed her plight. What was there to say about a society where a woman with even some modest refinement was reduced to this? And what was the difficulty with a widow's pension? Even though the amount was minuscule, it would have given her something to subsist on until she found employment.

He frowned at her, more in curiosity than censure.

Olivia glanced up. "I assure you I searched for other employment." Words tumbled from her lips in rapid succession. "I tried the milliners and the dressmaker. I even tried the pawnbroker, but he would give me so little for the one thing of value I own, I was loath to part with it. All I wanted in any circumstance was to earn enough to obtain passage to Cornwall where I grew up."

"You have no other friends to whom to apply?"

"Only one and she is out of the city. I wrote, but when I tried to deliver the letter, the house was shuttered and no servants seemed to be on the premises."

Sad resignation coupled with determination settled on her pretty face. Linnington had seen this particular expression hundreds of times on the faces of women in Spain, fleeing the depredations of war. This woman was a survivor.

"I should be glad to advance you the sum."

"Oh, thank you, sir, but no. I have no way of knowing when or if I could repay you."

An idea occurred to him, perhaps far-fetched and rash, but he voiced it anyway. "May I offer an alternative of my own?"

Her eyes widened with question. "My lord?"

Good God. I don't want her to speculate I want her for the same purposes she would have performed at the bawdy house. "First, I would like to inquire if, other than the management of the shop, have you any experience in the management of a household?"

To his surprise, a wry smile lit her face. "I have, my lord."

"Excellent. I have a small house here bordering Five Fields, or Tothill Fields, as it is now known. It is near my city residence in Mayfair. The house is not grand, I'm afraid. It is a townhouse close to the mews where I stable my horses. It is not new, probably built some fifty years ago, but commodious enough for one or two people and a small staff. For a time last year, I kept a...tenant there but have not done so for several months. Two of my superannuated retainers, a butler and cook, now man and wife, are also housed on the premises. They keep the place for me, but it is mostly a quiet retirement for them. The former tenant left in quite a rage, I must admit, and did some damage to the house and furnishings, and her sense of décor was...um, extraordinary. I am anxious to repair what needs reparation and get the property on the market to sell. I am hopeless with paint and fabrics. Would you be interested in occupying the house and overseeing its renovation, for compensation, of course?"

"And what sum would you consider fair for such a project, my lord?" Beginning with a note of enthusiasm, her voice acquired a slightly wary tone. "And my duties exactly?"

What a practical girl and no fool. Yes, he had let slip the pronoun "her." He described some of what needed doing, promised a list of vendors for construction, renovation, and décor, offered a wage, and waited for her answer. Olivia heard him out, not exactly with an expression of skepticism or calculation, as one of assessment.

"And would my wages be paid monthly or at the end of the contract?"

"The other servants are paid at the end of the month. However, in your circumstances, an advance seems proper."

"I would very much appreciate your generosity, my lord." Her face relaxed in nearly palpable relief, and she smiled, revealing small, even white teeth and the hint of dimples.

She mentioned her trunk, left at the now-abandoned teashop, and he assured her he would dispatch Jeremy, his footman, to retrieve it.

The meal finished, they rose to leave. "My lord, if I may ask, when you saw me on the street, with whom were you talking? What was the name of the other kind gentleman?"

Odd question." My old friend from Sandhurst, Mr. James Talent. Why?"

She had donned her bonnet so he could not see her expression, but her voice showed no particular interest. "Only so I might someday thank him for his kindness, too, should I chance to meet him."

Chapter Two

Linnington, carrying Olivia's portmanteau, hailed a hackney. It was nearly four when they drew up before a narrow brick townhouse with a green door surmounted by a three-paned transom of plain glass with white stone steps leading up to it. To the right of the door were two six-over-six windows painted white. On the second floor was a matching pair of windows and a single one above the door. Two dormers marked the attic quarters. There was nothing grand in the house's facade, but it had a familiar, welcoming appearance to which Olivia instantly grew attached.

Linnington's description of the age of the house seemed to her to be correct. The Flemish bond brick bespoke the Georgian style made so popular by Sir Christopher Wren. She found it odd there would be this small cluster, perhaps two blocks long, of residential dwellings sitting rather forlornly away from the city. However, London was growing at a pace disquieting to many of its residents. She had no doubt this part of town, so convenient to much of the city, would soon give the little house some company. She speculated the house might have belonged to one of the shopkeepers on York Street, just a few blocks away.

Olivia liked the quiet appearance of the place and the nearly deserted street. As they entered, she was gratified the place didn't have the mustiness some older buildings had, denoting they were not tightly built.

The thought of a real bed for the evening made her almost giddy. The food had at first stimulated her, but now lethargy was pushing away any energy she had gained. His lordship opened the door with his own key and called, "Partridge?" loudly from the hall.

After a moment, a slight, elderly man emerged from what must be the kitchen stairs rising at the end of the hall. He quickly shrugged into a black coat then hastily arranged his shirt collar. The sight of shirtsleeves was not, Olivia was sure, what any well-trained butler would like to display.

"My lord. We did not know... We received no message..."

Linnington waved away the protestations. "I sent none. This is all much on the spur of the moment, Partridge. This is Mrs. Williams. My butler, Partridge."

The introductions were terse, and Olivia made a slight nod in recognition of the older man.

George Partridge made just as slight a bow to the lady as though he was not sure quite how to address her, as gentility or tradesperson. Olivia returned his effort with a smile and a tilt of her head. "May I call you Partridge?"

"Indeed, madam."

"You may call me Mrs. Williams."

She was next introduced to a round, bustling woman, whose dress, apron, and cap were immaculate. Her face was impassive, but her eyes shown suspicion and disapproval.

"This is Mrs. Person," continued his lordship.

"Mrs. Person," echoed Olivia, with the same nod she had given Partridge, recognizing the status of the woman, not just as cook but housekeeper. Mrs. Person made a small nod in return, without a hint of a smile.

"Mrs. Williams will be staying here overseeing the renovations. I apologize for the lack of notice, but I'm sure the bed will be acceptable, and you both have done your usual fine job of keeping up the house."

"But the dust covers are on, my lord," asserted Mrs. Person with perhaps the faintest hint of asperity as if to say, *"If you had let me know..."*

"That's of no consequence." Linnington handed his hat to the butler and shrugged out of his coat. "Mrs. Person, will you take Mrs. Williams's bonnet and pelisse? I'm going to take her on a tour of the house. Oh, and the portmanteau, in the front bedroom if you will, Partridge. And send Jeremy for Mrs. William's trunk." He turned to her. "The address, madam?"

Olivia obliged, giving Partridge directions to the shop. She reached into a reticule and handed him a key. "I hope, Mr. Partridge, the lock has not been changed. And please tell Jeremy there is no need to return the key to me." She smiled at him and was gifted with a genuine smile in return.

Olivia had removed her coat and bonnet. "Thank you, Mrs. Person." She handed them to the woman. From Mrs. Person, there was no answering smile.

From the hall, she could see into the drawing room, still barely lit by the late fall sunshine. Pale squares of light made a pattern on its wide plank floor. Just as suggested by the exterior, the room was nicely trimmed with a well-turned, if not elaborate, cornice, chair rail, sturdy four-paneled doors with the panel repeated on shutters, now folded into the window reveals. A lovely Adams mantle surrounding the fireplace dominated the room. It had been converted from a wood-burning grate to a stove accommodating the alternate use of coal. She would discover this to be true of all the fireplaces on the main and bedroom floors, the only updating the house had ever received, she surmised. A simple wreath of pargetting adorned the plaster ceiling, surrounding a brass, eight-branched chandelier. She could see a small portion of another room finished in a similar treatment, separated by what she assumed to be pocket doors.

Olivia shook some of the wrinkles out of her plain lawn dress then followed Linnington on a tour of the house.

The entire edifice was so small, the hall in which they entered was nearly taken up by the stairway rising to the second floor. Another lay below, leading to the basement. There was one above it to access the attic rooms. To her right was the drawing room. As they entered, she observed a dining table in a cozy space beyond double doors. She would discover the same arrangement obtained on the second floor, a generous bedroom with a smaller dressing room beyond. In the basement kitchen, the smaller area served as larder and cold room, since it lacked the corner grate as in the dining area and dressing room above. The main rooms were served by fireplaces, rising directly above the kitchen ovens and hearth. The kitchen floor opened into the small garden space.

If the bones of the house were quite charming, although its style dated, the décor was a horror. The drawing room was painted a peculiar shade of purple, and the Georgian mantle, the chair rail, and the molding around the ceiling had been picked out in a garish orange, perhaps to simulate gold. The dining room was similarly decorated. Olivia was grateful the hall was a simple white, although its wood trim could stand some color.

As Linnington stripped the Holland covers from the furniture, Olivia had to steel herself from either laughing or regarding his

14

lordship with wonder at the taste of his "companion," for she assumed it was indeed the woman's taste ruling the choice. She was afraid to reveal her feelings in case the man had actually done the choosing. Two large wing chairs in the style of half a century ago, covered in floral fabrics better suited for draperies than furniture, flanked the fireplace. A sofa and armchair of a much better style had been placed here and there. They had equally bizarre coverings, a mix of stripe and pattern, none of which complimented the other and detracted from their basic design. To her dismay, all the upholstery had been slashed in places.

She hazarded a glance at Linnington, and although he was not smiling, amusement lit his eyes.

"Now come, madam, don't you think the furnishment of this salon to be just the thing?"

She smiled in return. "My lord, I think it atrocious! In fact, quite an affront to taste in any quarter."

"Good. Now tell me, what would you do to this room?"

He appeared quite serious, so she took a turn around the small, drawing room. "First, sir, there is the matter of color and paint. I am not fond of the faux gilding, although I am sure it was costly to devise. I think a good, warm white, and perhaps yellow walls? It will take a deal of paint to overcome the purple, but I believe, since the room faces north, it would be a help on dark days. Then I don't see much in the way of furnishings needed, except for new covers. Perhaps one more chair, to go with the Queen Anne's style couch, in a smaller size. Enough to accommodate less than a dozen people."

"Excellent. Now the dining room."

There, Olivia discovered a lovely mirror above a serviceable sideboard made of cherry wood. The gold-leafed mirror, and this time real gold leaf, reflected the garden beyond French doors opening to a landing and a short flight of wooden stairs leading to the garden. Well kept, the plot showed the signs of the impending winter dormancy but would become a charming vista in spring.

A hedge defined the edge of the garden itself, leaving a footpath from the kitchen door to the alley and the gate behind the house. The railing on the stairs was lovely, in the Chippendale style but now sat in sad need of paint. The table in the dining room was quite fine, a pleasant surprise, but the heavy, ugly chairs were too large for the space and of a much earlier period, with high backs and rush seats. They were quite out of style with the rest of the furniture.

"I think the same color in here, and other than simpler chairs, not much should change."

He met the suggestion with approval.

The appearance of a gangly young man with her trunk on his shoulder in the hall interrupted their planning.

"In the bedroom above, Jeremy," Linnington directed.

"Yes, milord." He mounted the stairs.

"Jeremy calls every morning to help Partridge with the heavier work and has acted as courier between the houses. He is quite at your disposal for any needed errands."

"I'm just glad my poor belongings were not pilfered."

"Come sit down, madam." He called to Partridge and bade him bring paper, pen, and ink.

They sat in the pair of wing chairs in the living room, a small, Pembroke table between them onto which Linnington gestured for Partridge to put the writing utensils.

Olivia assumed they were there for her to take notes just as he had assumed, she could read and write.

"As for your duties, your first challenge is to redecorate this place from top to bottom. I will send around two tradesmen on whom I rely. Mr. Hackman will see to any repair or carpentry you desire and see to the paint. Mr. Taylor will bring pictures and examples of furniture and fabric. Do not ask the price of anything. I have always admired this old house and would dearly love to see it renovated. Mrs. Person will guide you as to anything needing to be done in refurbishing the kitchen, and Partridge can inform you of any structural needs. I rely on what you have already shown me of your taste to take care of the bedroom above. However, I do ask you to leave the dressing room in its present state. Again, please do not inquire after the expense. I want it done properly. I am anxious to get the property on the market and would like to do so as quickly as possible. It should fetch a decent price if the premises is offered completely furnished. I leave tomorrow morning for a week or more at my estates. The fall work is already underway. I shall spend most of the winter in town and promise not to hang over your shoulder as you do your duties." Linnington gazed thoughtfully out the window.

In the brief silence, Olivia was aware she would rather like for him to remain in town and help with the planning.

Mostly, she was as giddy as a child just given the most beautiful of dolls to dress up and play with. "Indeed, my lord."

He took an unused sheet of paper and the pen from her. He carefully wrote out a document complete with a place for two signatures. "I am no barrister, but read this and see if it approximates our agreement, Mrs. Williams."

Olivia carefully read the contract. Seeing no need for amendment, she took the pen from its well. "I believe this is in order, sir. Should I sign and date it?"

"If you would, please."

When she was finished, he retrieved paper and pen and signed his name in a bold hand. He then folded the instrument and tucked it in his pocket.

"If you trust me to do so, I shall have my clerk make a copy of this for your use."

"Thank you. That would be most satisfactory. And what can you estimate about the duration of this project, sir?"

"With the delays of the Christmas season not far off, I anticipate about six months work. You should be on your way to Cornwall by spring." He rose as to take his leave.

"I'm deeply grateful, my lord."

He gave her a calculating appraisal from level gray eyes, stepped away, and called for Partridge to bring his hat and coat. He paused at the door. "Goodbye, Mrs. Williams. I look forward to your reports of progress. Do not hesitate to contact me at any time if you need assistance with any of the tradesmen."

"Thank you, my lord. I shall keep you apprised by correspondence of everything as it is done."

He nodded but then turned around. He opened the purse below his waistcoat and counted out some coins. "Your advance, Mrs. Williams, as we agreed." After a moment, he added an additional one or two silver coins. "Perhaps a new pair of boots?"

"Thank you, sir, but it is quite unnecessary. I can purchase some from the wages you have generously advanced."

"My pleasure, Mrs. Williams. I am sure your industry will earn this sum and more." Then he left the house.

She stood a long time in the darkening living room, deeply grateful for his generosity. However, she didn't know whether to be chagrined or flattered he had noticed her boots. It had been years since she had given her wardrobe a thought. Perhaps she could take a little of the money and purchase some fabric. She had always been a skilled seamstress. Her mother taught her both the basics and the finer arts of embroidery. When her mother had been a little girl, living in Paris, the nuns had taught her.

In six hours, her life had completely changed course. But it had done the same twice before, once after her father's death and then when she returned to England after her husband was killed. She had been fortunate the first time when David offered her marriage. Mme. Dufour rescued her the second time. And though wary, she was determined to enjoy this experience while she had the chance. When she returned to Cornwall, she might once more be dependent upon the charity of friends.

Exhausted from the emotional and physical toll of the day and not in need of food after the late lunch, she shook off her ruminations. Halfway down the stairs to the kitchen, she called to Mr. Partridge, inquiring if he could provide her a chamber stick. As he gathered up candle and flint from a sideboard, she descended the rest of the way to save him the trip upstairs, his knees seeming to make his trips up and down a struggle.

He gratefully handed her the now-assembled chamber stick with a small packet of lucifers. "Good night, Mrs. Williams. I know you must have had an arduous day. Sleep well."

"I have, Mr. Partridge, and I wish you both the same."

Mrs. Person did not respond, so Olivia retired to her chamber for the night. She pulled off her clothes, donned a nightgown from the portmanteau, and climbed into bed. However, unable to stop herself from going over what might have been, sleep did not come. Lying awake, she reviewed the day.

Just this morning, Olivia had sat on her worn trunk in the abandoned teashop, gazing around sadly. Where there had once been small tables with pretty tea services and delicate lace tablecloths, only bare planking and dust remained. The Limoges teacups had been boxed and taken to auction an hour earlier. The ovens sat cold which added to the chill of the place. No perfume of baking bread and pastries wafted from the kitchen where there was nothing to mix and pour or knead, nothing to decorate with sweet fondant or ganache. The trunk in the corner of the room appeared as forlorn as her spirits. It held all her worldly possessions, except for the few things of value or necessity she had tucked into a portmanteau. She had a vision of the teashop without even these personal items remaining, just an empty shell where she had hoped for a placid but busy life. She remembered thinking her hopes were scattered like the bits of refuse left to litter the dusty floor.

Pushing away her regrets, she slipped to her knees by the bed to count the real blessings she had and to thank God for this miracle of where she was this very moment.

Assessing the past was a bad habit she had carried from the trauma of childhood. The memory of the greedy eyes of the pawnbroker came to her. She had gone to his shop, hoping to gain enough money from the string of finely matched pearls that had been her mother's, to pay for passage home. The sum he offered had not been enough to get her to Exeter, let alone beyond Launceston. The pawnbroker loudly expressed his doubt the pearls were genuine. Nettled, Olivia had refused to be bilked, even in her extreme circumstances, especially since the sum would still leave her short of her goal.

At the time, she considered these options the only the ones available to her if she wanted to stave off immediate starvation. Perhaps the workhouse was the better option, but Olivia had believed her chances of saving enough to get herself home were better at Mrs. Taunton's. Knowing nothing of the business arrangements there, her only information came from stories the wives and camp followers told at the various bivouacs to which she had traveled with David before he went to Spain. The stories might have been overdrawn, but it seemed some of the women made quite good money. Anything was better than the street, which she refused to consider. The river would have been her watery grave first.

Here she found herself, not only in a comfortable bed but with the promise of a decent wage and the real prospect of getting home. Even though she had already knelt and said her prayers, before closing her eyes on this momentous day, she whispered another one of thanks.

Chapter Three

George Partridge glanced at his wife across the kitchen. The sour look on her face drove his attention back to *The Times* and the article he was reading concerning a veteran's measure before Commons. His usually sunny dispositioned wife was decidedly cross. He could tell the level of her irritation by the amount of banging about she did with the crockery.

Standing at the deal table that doubled as workspace and their dining table, she was measuring flour, sugar, and salt for tomorrow's baking. It was her habit to have all but the ingredients from the cold room in order so that she could begin the mixing and kneading early the next day. Tomorrow morning, she would scald the milk and fat as she made morning tea. Her husband marveled at her energy and efficiency.

George knew much of her displeasure simply came from change. Emma hated change. When they married, she had insisted on being called Mrs. Person. "If I change, it will just confuse the staff since we will still be employed by his lordship at the other house. The staff will fumble about trying to remember how to address me. Let's leave things as they are." She was so definite in this decision, George decided to let things be. Perhaps if they ever got to the country in their own house, she would use her married name.

The staff of both the Mayfair townhouse and the Linnington country manor, Crossfields referred among themselves to Mr. Partridge and Mrs. Person as The Ps. The unlikely pairing as a couple was a surprise to all concerned, since like Jack Sprat and his wife, they agreed on absolutely nothing. Superannuation and marriage had not changed the situation.

George decided to break the silence. "I wonder if his lordship took heed of this article about the veteran's bill?"

The silence breached, Mrs. Person ignored the question and started in on the subject which interested her more.

"Well," harrumphed Mrs. P, "*I* wonder how quickly that little piece of baggage upstairs will get her claws into the master?" She began to set aside the prepared ingredients and cleaned the table in preparation for their light supper.

"I'm surprised at your words, Emma. She seemed a young woman of some refinement."

"A ruse, I'm sure." She set the cutlery on the table with more force than necessary.

"I'm quite prepared to give her the benefit of doubt."

"You are entirely too kind and trusting, George. I'm sure she has acquired that veneer of refinement. Perhaps she is now an unemployed lady's maid, out to better her station."

"Well, I, for one, will allow myself to reserve judgment." He folded the paper and laid it on the cozy settle that occupied the inglenook next to what had been an old-fashioned fireplace and bake oven, now equipped with a stove.

He rose and filled each of the two tankards on the table with ale from a pewter pitcher.

"I won't," she countered.

"At least, Emma, she is not foreign and seems a quiet sort. I believe if I had to endure another bout of being shouted at in some foreign tongue and in words, I am sure I would be reluctant to utter in

English translation, I would ask his lordship to send me out to the country."

"Then you should hope she does just that, George Partridge. I know how you would like to go to Crossfields. You and your rabbits."

"Now, Emma, don't start. The little creatures cause you no trouble, and I have promised not to let them breed."

This old bone of contention between them put both in the mood to eat their cold mutton and cheese in silence. Emma stared at her plate. George concentrated on the bright pots and pans hanging from the ceiling reflecting the glow of tallow candles in a five-armed brass fixture. The low-beamed ceiling and stone walls took on a look of warmth and security to him. It was almost the only place in London he felt comfortable.

For George, his precious rabbits were as close to animals as he could be. They were quite spoiled by his petting and cosseting.

He cleared his throat. "I shall go feed the rabbits." With no more conversation, he gathered scraps in a pan and went out the door.

The upper two stories of the house were at street level. The basement kitchen, accommodating to the slope of the land, opened directly onto the footpath leading to the alley behind the structure. Across the alley, the doors in the rear of a row of shops could be seen.

He kept the pair of rabbits in a hutch by the door onto the footpath during most of the year, but his spouse did allow him to bring them inside when it was too cold, providing they not make a mess on her kitchen floor or be let loose to run. He fed them scraps from the kitchens of both houses. Jeremy named the animals Punch and Judy, perhaps with a sly reference to their owner and his wife. The pair were round, floppy-eared creatures with incredibly soft fur.

***

After Partridge had gone, his wife sat scowling at her plate. "The only place for a rabbit's in a stew!" she mumbled.

As she gathered the supper dishes to wash, she allowed her real feelings to surface.

Regardless of their differing tastes, she would never confess to her husband she had begun to understand his desire for quietness and country air. As she washed the supper dishes, she thought how ridiculous she and her partner were. He was London born and adored the animals and the country air. He found the soot and fog of the city abhorrent while treasuring every plant and flower at Crossfields, especially the massive oaks that stood in front of the house since Tudor time.

She, of course had been reared a country girl. London and its shops, its sights, and smells, the hurrying carriages and lazy drays, fine horses as well as the draft horses, the fashionable and the plainly dressed kept her endlessly entertained. She was happy to be within the sound of bells from more than one church and the odor of London's hundreds of chimneys rather than the odor of the farms. Never one to be afraid to change her mind, she often hated to admit the fact.

Part of being peeved by the new lady above stairs was Emma secretly hoped his lordship would leave the renovation in the hands of his man of business and could find for them some sort of accommodation in Oxfordshire. She was certain his lordship had a plan for them once their London duties were at an end.

Instead of returning to the country by Christmas, this situation would make it necessary for them to keep the house open through the holidays for some strange woman and with no holiday visit to the country at all. Spring would come before the project would be finished. And even with the woman gone by April, George would insist on setting the garden to rights, which meant they would not get to the country until June.

Perhaps poisoning the woman's tea would bring about a more agreeable scenario. She envisioned such a plot but then shook her head. No, the idea would never work. She set the bowl of baking ingredients back on the cleared table and draped a cloth across the top. There were other ways to encourage the woman to leave.

Chapter Four

Olivia awoke shortly after first light. The chamber stick had been insufficient to give her much of a sense of her surroundings last night.

Her first impression elicited a giggle. The bed hangings were a particularly nauseating shade of green coupled with clashing bright-blue paint on the walls. The bedstead, a plain four-poster bed with a sturdy tester and an unadorned broken pediment headboard, was quite adequate. A rather ornate but serviceable armoire stood next to the fireplace, a dressing table with a bench in front of the windows, and a washstand in the corner. There was one chair with velvet-upholstered seat and armrests. Thankfully, the velvet was a much more subtle blue. It sat before the small fireplace faced with a white Adams mantle plainer than the one in the parlor.

If she ignored the garish colors, she could imagine being quite at ease during her stay. The table and chair were all she needed as a place to read and sew. And the bed was surprisingly comfortable. *A good thing, given its former use.* She had to laugh at herself. There was absolutely nothing about Edmond Linnington suggesting a romp here, especially with any woman with the temper its occupant surely had.

She smiled at something the daylight had revealed. On the wall opposite the fireplace, there was enough of a gouge to allow the white plaster to show through. What had caused that? The mark was approximately the same distance from the floor as Lord Linnington's head. Perhaps a bit of china thrown with purpose? She couldn't help but giggle at the image, especially since the plain mantelpiece had nothing ornamental on it, save a pair of utilitarian candlesticks.

Steps on the stairs resounded in the quiet house, and she rose from the bed. Jeremy, evidently, was already aiding in the household duties. He let out a loud harrumph as he set a heavy object outside her door. Waiting until the footfalls descended the stairs, she opened the door to a welcoming unadorned ewer of hot water, which she carried to the washstand. How very nice to have a good, warm wash.

She smiled at herself. In her present state, this was absolute luxury.

Olivia dressed then opened the trunk to unpack her things into the armoire. The previous occupant had left a few scattered garments. Not only did the color palette remind her of the décor, but the diaphanous quality of the dresses left no doubt about the place in the household of the woman who wore them.

How very strange. His lordship seemed a most sober man, almost terse in his command—much in control of his words and actions. The fact he had been in military service fit him, but somehow the passion associated with these objects did not. She put the dresses and petticoats on the bed.

Olivia lay away her own clothes. Compared to the opulence and extravagance of the previous tenant's attire, her clothes were pitiful. None of them new, most of her dresses were plain cotton ones she'd sewn in the last few years, along with three aprons. All were utilitarian things she'd worn while tending the shop.

She had one good walking dress in gray, sadly out of style, she wore to church. The best things she owned were a pair of paisley shawls and another of wool, all of quite attractive colors, principally the greens, blues, and rosy pinks that flattered her complexion. A couple of summer frocks in nice pastels finished off her inventory, except for the one item she prized the most. A miniature, not of David but of a beautiful woman. At the bottom of her portmanteau it lay, among the few things she kept from her old life other than the pelisse, which although worn, kept her warm on the coldest day.

She also kept her white silk wedding gown, now more of a cream shade. She had worn it on the few occasions she and David attended a ball given by his commanding officer or some such event. There was also the fine lawn petticoat trimmed in a narrow band of Belgian lace she had worn under it.

As she placed the garments into the armoire, she laid her only pair of long white kid gloves on top of the silk dress. Whether she would ever wear them was uncertain, but she could not part with such memories of her time with her husband. Then she carefully stacked her everyday gowns, aprons, and the walking dress in a more accessible spot in the cabinet, along with her good black shoes and winter boots. Her stockings, ribbons, and other accessories she could put in the dressing table.

The dressing table drawer contained a few discarded items, a comb with missing teeth, and perhaps a clue to the woman, a broken Spanish fan of ebony and black lace. Intrigued by the lace, which was quite beautiful, she carefully separated the delicate demi-lune of fabric from the ebony guards and gorge. Such beautiful lace should not be thrown away.

On top of the dressing table was a powder box with a cracked lid, which had once been quite a pretty piece of blue porcelain with white flowers. Olivia decided to use it; her own rice powder currently housed in a tobacco tin. The other items she relegated to the dustbin.

Into the drawer she put the red leather box of pearls and the small miniature of her mother. She took a long look at Amelie Forret Constant. Olivia had inherited her father's light-brown hair of no distinction, in her opinion, but she luckily had her mother's curls. Her own eyes were blue, like the Constant family, but her mother's showed the French heritage of her own father's eyes, a dark and lustrous brown. Those eyes had gazed upon her so lovingly, unlike the indifferent glances of her father. The softer eyes were the same ones she reached over to close after the agony of whatever malady had taken her mother after her third miscarriage. Olivia had been twelve at the time. She shook off the sad memories and began to put the room in order.

She took some time to ponder the decoration of this room, since it was the only one other than the public rooms on the first floor she was charged with redecorating. The blue was all right but certainly in a shade lighter than the one chosen by Mistress Whomever. Possibly more of a Wedgwood blue of the color pottery makers were now using. She would love to see some sort of pattern at the windows and on the bed, but plain white would do here and be much less expensive than chintz or printed linen. His lordship may not mind the expense, but she was determined to mind the pence.

As for the abandoned pieces of feminine clothing, she folded them and put them in the corner of the top shelf of the armoire. The only garment worth notice was an embroidered black silk dress made to be worn by a woman of some height. The fabric was heavy and costly with a garland of chain-stitched silk embroidery bordering it, also in black, creating a pleasing pattern of relief and preserving the monotone effect instead of the distinct contrast white or a color would have made. Admiring the fabric, she laid it gently folded on top of the other garments. It seemed in sharp contrast to the other brighter dresses. When and for what occasion had the woman worn it?

Her own few items, of both winter and summer wear, took up less than half of the space. She pushed the empty trunk into the corner opposite the washstand and sat down to repair what she could of her appearance. Her curls she tied up with a ribbon then pinned the ends of her hair into a knot. The addition of a clean apron covered almost all her dress and finished her outfit. After another glance in the mirror, she was ready to meet the day and take up her duties.

When Olivia arrived downstairs, she found a single place set in the dining room. *As though I am the lady of the house.*

On the small sideboard was tea, toast, what she took to be Wiltshire honey, jam, some cold meats, and boiled eggs. Olivia's mouth watered at the sight of the English breakfast. For the past four years, her breakfast had consisted of a croissant and French coffee. The *café au lait* she would miss, but she would forego the yeasty taste of the roll for the salt of savory ham. As for the condiments, she hesitated between the prospect of the sweetness of thick honey or the tang of marmalade. She chose the honey, filled her plate, and sat down.

Mrs. Person had set out the silver from the sideboard drawers, and the table was covered by a proper, snowy cloth and matching napkins. All this gave her a moment of nostalgia. When she was Lady Olivia Constant, the lady of the house, she had become used to dining in such a manner. All such advantages were in the past. Now, she was just like Mr. Partridge, Mrs. Person, and Jeremy—the hired help. She would not ever again be the mistress of a home, and she was no longer a lady.

She smoothed the linen napkin in her lap and fought the rising feeling of an old resentment. Her father had taken all she had possessed away from her, the house, the title, and even any subsistence. Had it not been for dear David, coming to her rescue, she would not have been wife or widow, either.

Shaking her head as though to chase away an annoying gnat, Olivia hoped she was long past digging about in the tragedies of yesterday just as she had pushed away last night's ghosts. The room was filled with the comfortable and familiar aroma of freshly baking bread. This must be Mrs. Person's day to bake. The yeasty smell helped her concentrate on today's needs.

She ate quickly but lingered over her tea. The teacup was Spode, more ornate than was to her liking, but the feel of the smooth glaze on her fingertips brought a memory. She remembered the day Linnington came to the shop. Harriet Woolley entered first, and Olivia was immediately put into a temper. She despised the sort of woman Harriet was, with a sense of entitlement, bent on making life miserable for anyone she considered her inferior. *If you only knew,* she used to think. This day, in addition to Harriet's compliant husband, there was a tall man and she heard Harriet refer to him as "brother." Olivia put on a welcoming smile since any new visitor was appreciated during the wars with the French. Englishmen seemed to consider it disloyal to support anything French. Linnington appeared to be in as foul a temper as she. Olivia was the one who poured the tea, brought the sandwiches and cakes, but he never once glanced at her. She assumed he was as high in the instep as his sister. So much for quickly judging people.

As she sipped the aromatic tea, her thoughts turned to her employer. What a strange man. His manner was aloof but not exactly cold. He seemed more guarded than antagonistic and certainly businesslike. She appreciated the propensity, as she was nothing if not forthcoming, herself. *Well, I have known many a commanding officer with such traits, not unappreciative of his men but loathe being too close, and mindful of being in command.*

She allowed herself mentally to assess his appearance. He was tall, well-built, and handsome, with a finely chiseled profile, full dark hair, and gray eyes. But somehow, as she had observed last night, if there was any passion there, it was well hidden. In fact, there was a distinct air of melancholy about him. This she had observed in many of the men returning from war. If he was with Lord John, he had seen more than his share of carnage. Those unforgettable pictures could never, she was sure, be erased from the mind of the observer. And some men were so traumatized, they lost all savor for life.

The thought of the garments upstairs crossed her mind. Clearly, her employer retained some vestiges of feeling. Or perhaps such apparel was the only things able to arouse his senses.

She turned her thoughts away from such speculation, grudgingly admitting to herself the clothing intrigued her.

Of no matter. He's hardly the man for me, even if I were in a position to accept the attentions of anyone.

Staring out at the fall asters in the garden, she took a last sip of tea.

So, his best friend is a gentleman called James Talent. There cannot possibly be two men of the same name and approximate age, even in London. He didn't mention the name of his wife, but it must

33

be Sophie. She was surely at her time of confinement. Coincidence piled upon coincidence meeting him on a London street, just as she happened upon Sophie at the bookstalls two years ago. They had not seen each other since they were eighteen when Sophie's parents forbade her to have anything to do with Olivia. Friends from girlhood, they'd been inseparable until the situation with her father. It broke her heart and Sophie's.

And then there was James Talent. Not at all the sort of person she'd believed would have appealed to Sophie, let alone stolen her heart. With his square face and apple cheeks, he had the muscular yet compact physique Olivia had come to associate with practical men of boundless energy. She had imagined Sophie attracted to a pale-skinned poet, with a penchant for books. In truth, she found it difficult to see Sophie, with her fair hair and oval face, blue eyes always behind spectacles so she could read whatever book was constantly in her hand, as wife of this gentleman. Nevertheless, although Sophie had said little of her husband in the frequent times over the past two years they'd had tea together, she could tell by the way Sophie talked about him she loved him dearly.

A thought flashed through her mind. Linnington had, in all probability, stood witness when they married. She had been forbidden to attend, but if things had been different... A vision of the four of them standing at the altar of All Saint's Church, Tinston, with the Reverend Mr. Williams officiating of course, flashed through her mind.

She laughed out loud in the empty room. *Oh fate, you can be so droll!*

A pang of nostalgia for all that was lost overwhelmed her

momentary merriment. She shook crumbs from her apron onto the now-empty plate. Today, there was no time for sad thoughts.

Olivia arose and gathered her dishes, piling them on the sideboard for Mrs. Person to take to the kitchen with the uneaten food.

She went to the top of the stairs, leading to the basement kitchen. "Mr. Partridge?"

The butler, impeccably groomed but in shirtsleeves, slowly mounted the stairs. "May I help you, Mrs. Williams?"

"Would you be good enough to show me about the house? His lordship indicated you were the one to acquaint me with any necessary repairs to the building."

The two of them spent the next hour examining the house, starting on the attic floor and working down. She hated to invade the private quarters of the couple, but Partridge wanted to apprise her of the leak near the corner grate in their apartments. On the bedroom floor, they discovered the damage had also allowed rain to seep around the fireplace in his lordship's dressing room. This was the first time Olivia had seen the room, which resembled nothing so much as the cramped quarters of an officer's billet—a narrow bed, chest of drawers, plain washstand and shaving mirror, one straight chair, and a serviceable table with a smaller one next to the bed. *This is what he did not want disturbed? So be it, but it will probably require a coat of paint, white, of course, once the plaster is repaired.*

Partridge thought in all probability Mr. Hackman would not find much more amiss to the property than repair of the roof and sealing around the chimneys. Olivia made a mental note though. The plaster repair would have to be done before the painting and would take some extra time. In her experience, the thing taking the longest was upholstery and hangings.

Nevertheless, all could be accomplished, including a hiatus over the Christmas holidays, by February or March if weather cooperated. She wouldn't mind staying a week or two longer into April to see the little garden set to rights.

Gazing pensively out of the dressing room windows, she could imagine daffodils in May and the wonderful fragrance of lilac later in the summer. The rose bushes, now bare, would be fully in blossom, and it would be a treat to discover their color. She hoped yellow and perhaps the wonderful color of orange ice on the climber rose roaming the trellis next to the alley gate.

Instead of the delightful odor of roses, the air would be filled with the not-so-pleasant paint fumes for the several weeks it would take to accomplish the decorating. In the damp of winter, it would take some time for the paint to dry sufficiently for a second coat, and the dark purple might necessitate a first coat of white to keep it from changing the color of the final paint. No matter. The windows would bring in some cold, brisk air to dampen the fumes. They would all survive.

Partridge interrupted her thoughts to inform her the first thing to be done, in his opinion, was to have all the chimneys thoroughly swept. The former occupant, as he referred to her, had objected to the soot, so the chore had not been completed in a timely manner.

"Would Mr. Hackman oversee the task?"

"No, madam. If you wish, I will contact the people we use for the Mayfair house. It would be wise to do it before the weather is more inclement."

"Indeed, Mr. Partridge, if you would be so kind. Let me know how soon they can come as well as their charges. In the meantime, if you have Mr. Hackman's direction, I will write asking him to come and estimate the roof repairs."

She sat at the dining table with pen, paper, and ink, and wrote the first of many lists of things to be done and, as time went by, things accomplished. She had separate pages for the accounts, which would accrue during the project. At the end of the week, she would make a habit to gather all the information together in the form of a report for his lordship, and either have Jeremy transport it to the townhouse if Linnington was in London, or address them to Crossfields, ready for Partridge to post, if the gentleman was in the country.

Getting this project planned on paper was the perfect task to take her mind off her father and his cruelty.

Chapter Five

Nearly two weeks later, Olivia sat at the dining table, assessing the papers on which she had made all her notes. Included in these were the two notes from Linnington she received in answer to her weekly reports. The writing was firm and fine, the letters formal and businesslike. More and more, she allowed herself to speculate on what lay behind the words. She told herself it was a desire to know whether he considered the job she was doing exemplary or merely adequate. In her quieter moments, she openly wondered what he thought of her.

Olivia pulled the paisley shawl closer around her shoulders. Today was the day the sweeps were expected, so no fires were laid, except for an early heating of the fire in the kitchen to boil tea water and some eggs. Luncheon and supper would probably be cold, too. Without the warmth of the fires, the house was only just bearable. Olivia was glad for her shawl and hoped Partridge and Mrs. Person were not too uncomfortable in the kitchen.

Christmas was only six weeks away, so she was pleased Mr. Hackman had not found anything major concerning the house. His men would start tomorrow to patch the roof, unless rain prohibited it. Hackman estimated a week or two should suffice to do the repairs and replace the few rotting pieces of window frame, which would necessitate painting the trim on the outside of the house. And though time consuming and costly, the suggestion was probably a good idea to make the property fresher and more appealing to a buyer.

The little house was not very prepossessing, just comfortable appearing from the street, but the place had its simple charms. A buyer would need to venture inside to appreciate those charms. And her job was to enhance them as much as possible.

When the kitchen door opened, she rose to accompany the sweeps as they prepared the floors, laying canvas to catch any soot falling into the rooms. They began with the corner fireplaces in the dining room, dressing room, and servants' quarters. She let them work alone as they started in the attic but accompanied them on the bedroom floors. In the dressing room, the two sooty men lifted his lordship's chest of drawers.

"Take care," she called out as they tipped the bureau and the drawers slid out, the contents threatening to end on the floor. Just in time, one of the men caught the drawers, and the workmen set the thing down rather hard yet sufficiently away from the fireplace so they could work. The older man sent the climbing boy to the roof with his brushes while he stayed waiting for his workmate to call down to him.

Olivia stood guard, watching over the rather poor job they did cleaning up once they were through sweeping. They replaced the chest of drawers but not without tilting it sufficiently to once more disturb its contents. She sighed but said nothing. They still had the lower floors to do, and she did not wish for them to make more mess.

As they went below to the dining room, Olivia remained behind to straighten the things in the dresser. Perhaps his lordship would never notice, but he gave the appearance of a military man used to the strict order in his belongings. She began at the top drawer and found to her surprise a brace of pistols, powder horn, shot, and patches, along with handkerchiefs, stockings, and one cravat.

How very odd. Why pistols in a townhouse? Was the woman so violent, his lordship considered it necessary for protection? Had he been involved in a duel? None of this seemed plausible, and the firearms were not for dueling but the sort military officers would carry.

David had just such a one. In fact, he'd owned two and had her practice with one of them during the few short weeks she was in Portugal before he departed with the regiment. He left a pistol with her when he went. He had not wanted to go to battle and leave her entirely defenseless in a foreign country. Before she departed Portugal, she sold the gun to another officer.

The rest of the articles in the dresser were unremarkable male gear. She straightened all the personal items first.

Touching the firearms made her shiver. It was not that she was unfamiliar with them. David's tutelage was only to refresh her technique. From the time her mother died when she was twelve until she was eighteen, her father took out on Olivia his frustration at not having a boy. He insisted she improve her riding and learn to shoot. The riding and horses she loved. The shooting she was less eager to engage with but learned to handle long guns and pistols with equal ease. She was never terribly fond of it, especially when it involved killing things, particularly the grouse, whose rustling wings always thrilled her when they rose up out of the fields. However, these pistols were similar to the ones she had grown up with, one of which she had removed from her father's dead hand.

Refusing to get drawn into the past once more, Olivia returned the pistols to the drawer. If she had been on better terms with the other members of the household, she could have spoken to them about why the pistols were here. Were they connected to the former occupant?

A loud bang sounded from the dining room, and Olivia shook off her speculations and spent the rest of the day seeing the sweeps did their job with a minimum of damage to the rooms. When they were through, Mrs. Person brought cleaning supplies to rid the rooms of whatever leftover soot the sweeps had failed to remove.

The woman silently began her business.

Olivia interrupted. "May I help? If you sweep, Mrs. Person, I will gladly dust."

A look of surprise supplanted the habitual disapproving countenance Mrs. Person always gave her.

"Thank you, Mrs. Williams, I can manage." She stopped a moment, giving Olivia a serious appraisal. "But it would make a quicker job with the two of us." They spent until supper setting things to rights.

With no fires burning and the evening drawing in, the house had grown quite cold. The only fireplace working was in the kitchen; Partridge had laid a fire to heat supper.

Mrs. Person hesitated at the top of the stairs. "If you like, Mrs. Williams, you can join us in the kitchen until bedtime. The house will be cold until Jeremy lays tomorrow's fires." Unsmiling, she descended the stairs, carrying her equipment. Olivia followed gratefully.

The evening was a quiet one. Mrs. Person prepared a simple evening meal of soup and bread while Mr. Partridge and Olivia sat at the deal table. Partridge was courtly and kind, asking about the renovations and then seemed at a loss for conversational subjects.

Olivia gestured toward the newspaper at his elbow. "So, Mr. Partridge, you have *The Times*. Is it recent?

"It is. Yesterday's. Each morning, Jeremy is kind enough to bring me the newspaper from the townhouse after everyone there is finished with it."

"May I ask about the news from France? Are troops still there?"

"The news is not specific, but with the nasty little emperor secure on the Island of Elba, all should be home shortly, if not already."

"My fervent hope for them is we might soon have other places like Chelsea Hospital for those who have wounds to treat. It is unconscionably overcrowded."

"So I hear. His lordship visits there occasionally just to cheer the troops, and Jeremy often accompanies him. Jeremy says it can be deplorable. Of course, the government never counted on the influx of patients when it was built last century. They could not foresee the casualties from the Continent."

"Quite true, but it pains my heart to see some of the men relegated to quarters never meant for wounded. I go each Sunday to a place called St. Stephen's House and spend some time there after services with troops housed for the time being. It is a house Westminster parish has let for just such a purpose."

"How admirable. And what do you do?"

"Often I read and write letters for them. Many are illiterate. But most of the men there are sufficiently ambulatory to take care of their own personal needs. Sometimes, I think they linger because there is nowhere else for them to go."

"Supper is ready," Mrs. Person broke into their conversation, setting steaming bowls on the table, along with slices of bread.

For a few minutes, they ate in silence.

Olivia dabbed her lips with her napkin. "Mrs. Person, your bread is excellent. And I assume the scones we sometimes have you also make. I mastered Mme. Dufour's *croissants* and *brioche*, but confess my scones are quite wanting. I should love to know your method if it is not a secret."

The woman's demeanor thawed a slight bit.

"Not at all."

The two women entered into a discussion of baking which became more and more involved. They were soon exchanging methods with each other like old friends. Mrs. Person remembered the baked goods from the shop Linnington's sister, Harriet Woolley, brought home to their mother. Mr. Partridge wisely retreated to his newspaper.

Thus began a routine the three of them practiced through the ensuing months. Olivia fixed her own breakfast tray and carried it up the two flights to the bedroom, saving old knees from climbing stairs to the dining room. She usually ate by the fire in her bedroom. Luncheon was with the P's, often with Jeremy, teatime was catch-as-catch-can with workmen in the house, and whatever light supper they desired was eaten communally at the table in the basement just as they would have done in any servants' hall. They retained the façade of civility by keeping the more formal, Mr. and Mrs. address. If the surface formalities were retained, the relationship slowly evolved, at least for Mrs. Person and Olivia. Mr. Partridge maintained his nearly fatherly oversight of Olivia. He seemed to consider her one more thing to give loving attention besides Punch and Judy.

Both women shared everyday duties of the house and the naturally ensuing casual conversation that altered their attitudes. Mrs. Person's stopped treating Olivia as an alien presence, and Olivia discovered Mrs. Person had a romantic heart approximately as hard as a marshmallow.

Sundays, Olivia went her own way to Westminster, and the P's went to services at St. James's with the household from the townhouse and took their noon meal there, for a welcome gossip with old friends and relief from the small quarters of the Tothill Fields house. Many of the townhouse servants inquired about Olivia, wanting to know more concerning the Mrs. Williams their lordship had employed.

They were always amused by the P's differing accounts of whatever had transpired at the house. Still, they were aware, to their amusement, the young woman had gained the approval of both Mr. and Mrs. P.

Had she known she was the center of staff gossip, she would not have cared, since her comings and goings were innocent and straightforward enough. At the moment, Olivia was determined to do her job as professionally and efficiently as possible. This professionalism compelled her to sit at the dining table each week, laboriously writing to his lordship. Her letters detailed every conversation with the tradesmen he had recommended, and always included a careful accounting of estimates and expenditures she had authorized. She folded then sealed the missives.

During her early rummaging about the house, in the corner of the parlor, she discovered a little table. It was the only piece of furniture she found small enough to fit the space in the front hall and be available for such things as mail and packages.

There, she placed the outgoing letters on the table for Partridge to post.

Chapter Six

The day after Linnington left Olivia in charge of the Tothill Fields house, he departed London for Crossfields. As he often did, instead of taking one of the carriages, which were more suited to town anyway, he had his big roan gelding, Maximilian, saddled and made the journey on horseback. This gave him the freedom to make the trip at his own pace, stopping as he wished to view a vista or have a conversation with a passerby. However, such a sense of freedom was only an illusion, a reminder of life before the responsibilities of title and lands had descended on him.

Riding alone meant leaving Owens, his valet, and any other attendants in London, but with his mother usually in residence at Crossfields, there was plenty of help, and the army had made him self-sufficient enough he required little. Owens suited him because the man seemed to know exactly when Linnington needed help and when he preferred to be left alone. Traveling on Maximilian, he could leave early in the morning and reach the estate lying just inside Oxfordshire within a day. It would be rather late when he arrived, stopping only at a convenient inn for a bite of lunch and ale.

There was a row of hills at the edge of the shire, and once you crossed them, the wide valley below was checkered with rich fields and hedgerows. He loved this vista. He always conjured this image in Spain, when he prayed to be home or was terrified he would never return. Today, the copper disc of the sun hovered over the hills on the other side of the valley as he approached, turning the valley a smoky blue.

One couldn't see the house because of the distance, but just the sight of the countryside and the streams marking the property lifted his heart. Linnington always experienced a sense of anticipation descending from the hills, especially when he turned into the byway leading to the long drive and the house. He eagerly anticipated seeing a glimpse of warm-toned, yellow stone before a copse obscured his view. It was a short ride to the gatehouse, now rarely occupied, except for occasional staff if they had visitors. The gatehouse included a small cottage once housing the gatekeeper, when there had been the need for one. His father deemed the countryside safe enough to permit those who approached to come to the door and allow Benson, the butler, to decide who should be admitted. The gatehouse remained as an attractive entrance adornment.

The last gatekeeper, Whitten, had been a favorite of the boys. Even though their father instructed them on firearms, it was Whitten who'd imparted all the lore needed for the successful hunting of rabbits and squirrels. He shivered, remembering the high squeal of a wounded hare. He hadn't known at the time he would have a chance on the battlefield to compare the sounds of dying men to the cry of a wounded animal.

Linnington halted his horse and regarded the gatehouse. Way too small for a dower house, he would have to inquire of the estate manager if the cottage was in any condition to house the Ps when the London property sold. If so, he must ask them if it would be suitable.

As Linnington turned up the long drive, lined with plane trees, the house dropped in and out of his vision, tantalizing him but never enough for a good, clear view. Not until he was three quarters down the drive could he see the full beauty of the place.

The original Tudor structure grew considerably from the simple original hall. The first house was only a rather unimpressive two-story building consisting of a central hall and stairway with chambers above. The plain symmetrical front was pierced on the second floor by three casements glazed in lead with diamond-shaped panes. On the ground floor, a massive oak door was flanked by similar fenestration. Somewhere between the time of King Henry and when the Linningtons acquired the lands along with a title, two matching wings flanked the hall, more than doubling its size. At the time, the roof was probably raised to give the house more presence. Finally, Linnington's grandfather had brought some semblance of order and modernity to the house during the time of George Third. He embarked on an extensive restoration rather than tearing down the original home to build a grand country home in the Georgian style.

It was a credit to the baron's taste he had kept to the same locally quarried stone for additions to the two wings extending from the house. He preserved much of the charm of the original building while combining it with a myriad of improvements, updating fireplaces and adding the convenience of closets and interior trim to fit a more modern time. A magnificent terrace sloped away to the formal gardens toward the valley. Paths forming a grid of fine gravel bound the orderly rows of flowering fruit trees. The central space was laid out in conforming beds of herbs and low plants to preserve the vista to the riverbank and its natural assortment of trees. In the central area was also a small pool with an ornamental fountain. The boxwoods were carefully trimmed, if not in topiary style, into geometric shapes to complement the layout of the garden.

The only addition his grandfather made to the front of the house was the construction of a narrow walkway stretching all along the façade of the original house and its first two symmetrical additions. This flagstone surface was set upon a two-step rise, so the entrance to the vast oak door did not open directly on the gravel drive. To the left of this porch was the original English garden, with its wonderful welter of plants. Blooming from spring to fall with everything from tulips, daffodils, violets, and hollyhocks in spring through the summer riot of homely plants like pinks, lupine, daisies, day lilies, phlox, and lilacs. In addition, he had been fond of wildflowers so one could also find cornflowers, primroses, larkspur, and a host of plants flowering into autumn with its chrysanthemums. The garden complemented the additions to the house, extending behind the original dwelling. In contrast, the rose garden on the right was laid out by the baron in English boxwood, in an orderly rectangle enclosing two paths of fine gravel bordered on each side by rows of rose bushes. Linnington often regarded the boxwood with amusement. Planted by his grandfather, they were now shoulder high. By the time his children were close to his age, they would be above head height and provide a beautiful little private space.

Nearly at the end of the drive was the vista Linnington most loved. In front of the house where the baron left the original natural approach, the drive bent around a small lake, fed from one side of the road by a tiny stream, a run coming from the hills and passing under a small bridge into the lake, which in turn, dammed by a few rocky shoals ran on to join the larger stream marking the furthest edge of the estate and then to the Thames. The little lake offered its hospitality to families of canvasback ducks and mute swans. A great blue heron with stunning plumage made its home there when he was a child. Numerous bream swam both in the lake and in the water just below the shoals.

Today, with the sky so evenly overcast, the lake appeared as a smooth gray mirror, clumps of still-green rushes lacing the edges. The surface reflected the few bright leaves left on the trees opposite the place where he stopped on the little bridge. Near the outlet of the lake, the willows stood bare of their leaves, their long, drooping branches nearly touched their reflection in the water. The tableau was completely still giving the illusion the tree had a perfect, upside-down twin. A faint aroma of burning autumn leaves and field gleanings filled the air.

His eye caught a movement at the casement windows in the original hall with their leaded diamond-shaped panes. The one in the upstairs sitting room hung open. His mother watched from the casement, so he waved a cheery hello with his hat. In answer, Lady Linnington's arm, clad in dark red, drew her pale hand in a lazy wave through the window.

***

Elizabeth Oliphant Linnington was a tall woman. She and Edmond's father, William, were married for thirty years. It had been a relatively happy union. There had been no grand passion, the prospect of love an expectation she had only imagined as a child. Marriage brought stability, children, and perhaps most importantly, a commingling of resources. She'd had a substantial dowry.

Nevertheless, she and William found themselves surprisingly well suited. The only cloud on the union was the delay in the arrival of children. She was plagued by a series of miscarriages and had nearly given up when, at almost thirty, she became pregnant with Giles. The pregnancy was blessed and, two years later, Edmond was born, quickly followed by two girls, first Harriet and then Amelia.

She could still feel tears pushing at the corner of her eyes when remembering Amelia. She was a laughing toddler of almost two when Giles then Edmond and Harriet, and finally Amelia came down with measles. The three hardy older children survived with no issues. Her precious Amelia died in her arms. Elizabeth kept a little pencil sketch of her brown-eyed angel on the wall by her dressing table so she could say good morning to her every day.

It was true the family still had one daughter, but she never felt the same about Harriet, and the fact brought her pangs of guilt sometimes, as though she rejected her daughter just because she wasn't Amelia. On rare occasion, she voiced the feelings to one of her sons, the response always the same. "No, Mother, it's because Harriet isn't remotely like Amelia." Where she suffered guilt over her feelings concerning Harriet, her husband William compensated by spoiling the girl outrageously. Whatever the cause, his spoiling or her own unspoken rejection of the child, Harriet grew into a shallow, devious woman often at odds with her mother.

Whenever just she and Edmond spent time together at Crossfields, she was healed, heart and soul. She was overjoyed at his arrival ten days ago. His presence at the house released the irrational fear she often suffered at the thought of losing this last male child of hers and being left completely alone at Crossfields or being dependent on Harriet. In addition, she enjoyed his company.

Giles had always been the incandescent one, constantly in motion, stimulating, and great fun but, for her, exhausting. However, something about Edmond's self-containment reassured her. The weeks between Giles's untimely death and when Edmond arrived home from the war had been agony for her. She could not keep herself from imagining his dying in battle before the summons home could reach him, or the ship foundering on the way, even perhaps a carriage accident between South Hampton and Crossfields.

Edmond's melancholy had been a worry for her during the last year and a half he had been home. At first, she fretted over his drinking, and then six months later, the Spanish woman, Mrs. Fernandez, appeared, and he'd kept her at the house he'd purchased on the edge of town. The drinking gradually abated as his grief over Giles lessened and his activities with his friends increased.

James Talent, with his sunny disposition, and his lovely wife Sophie were a Godsend. They fortunately lived close enough in Berkshire to visit often. It wasn't close enough for a daily call, but the Talents, and just as often she and Edmond, would make the trip between houses. Leaving in the morning gave them plenty of time to have a lovely visit, spend the night, and return the next day. She always encouraged Sophie to bring the children. She loved having them about, and they seemed to give life and spirit to the old house.

Then there was the crux of her present disquiet. Edmond was close to accepting he must marry. She was torn. She longed for grandchildren, but she was not impressed by any of the young ladies he escorted. She particularly disliked Sybil Trent and wondered whether the girl deserved her disfavor or if her reluctance about the girl was because Sybil was a close friend and confident of Harriet's. Elizabeth found Miss Trent insipid to the point of boredom. True, Sybil was a classic beauty, with fair hair, nice teeth, blue eyes, and the rosy complexion often compared to an English tea rose. Her only detraction was the undeniable fact she had no figure. To be kind, women called her willowy. Among the young men, Elizabeth overheard her simply referred to her as flat chested. Her appearance or demeanor did not put Elizabeth off, but something about the girl was disquieting. In truth, she suspected, underneath the bland, "I'm such a lovely, innocent girl who never has an evil thought about anyone or anything" simpering exterior, might lie a mean and conniving woman.

Since Elizabeth and Harriet were not close, she longed for Edmond to marry someone with whom she could have a warm relationship. She feared her feelings were selfish since what she really wanted was to be part of a growing family with lots of grandchildren to fuss over. She doubted if Miss Trent would be open to any interest she took in the family. Elizabeth would be consigned to the role of lonely dowager.

Then there was that Spanish woman, who made her doubt Edmond's discernment as to women. At first, she'd believed he was only being kind to a poor war widow and decided to provide shelter for her temporarily. However, it soon grew apparent the woman had marriage on her mind while Edmond remained content with her role of mistress. She held no brief for her son. The liaison was ill advised, and he should have been smarter about the wiles of such creatures, but the woman's tantrums, some of them quite public, put *finis* to the relationship. It had been her misfortune to meet the woman once. Edmond had the poor judgment to bring her to the opening of the Royal Academy of Arts last Season. She could not believe the garish creature had a place anywhere near her son and certainly not in his heart. Fortunately, this had been nearly at the end of their liaison.

All these thoughts ran through Elizabeth's head while her maid,

Rose, dressed her—once long and dark, but now nearly snow white—thick hair. She screwed up her liquid brown eyes, making a face at herself.

"Oh, Rose." She sighed. "I can't help but be peeved that when white hair was the fashion, I had either to wear an insufferably hot wig or a pound of powder. Now the fashion is one's natural color, and I long to look as I did instead of as if I had donned one of those wigs. I suppose I'm never satisfied."

Rose, her maid for twenty years, smiled. "Your hair is lovely, milady." She didn't have to add "for someone your age" for Elizabeth to understand.

"It reminds me of my grandmother Oliphant. She used to say God would give you anything in the world you wanted, just not at the time you wish and never all at once."

"And right she was."

They both laughed.

Elizabeth breakfasted each morning in her bedroom and preferred to sit in the upstairs drawing room most of the day. The windows faced east and caught the glorious morning sun on clear days. The space was cozy in winter, and the assortment of furniture in their floral colors always cheered her mood.

The casements opened out on the gardens and the drive where she had seen Edmond when he arrived. The room was wide and relatively shallow, having been created from two chambers in the original hall just above the entrance. In the renovation, wainscoting had been added, along with other trim, including the addition of interior shutters folding into the deep reveals of the original windows. Elizabeth had added the paint and furnishings when she and William came into the title and inheritance. She'd painted the woodwork in what was often called French blue, but to her, depending on the quality of light from the windows, the color would change from blue to green. She sometimes wondered whether it was truly the light, or was it her mood had changed?

She'd furnished the room with a huge Aubusson carpet in subtle shades of rose and yellow with touches of the blue and green. The furniture, covered in complementary fabrics, was the styles of her era, Chippendale and Hepplewhite.

Knowing her preference, Harding, the under butler who tended to her needs when the rest of the staff was in town, always left the post on a silver salver on the table in the room. Elizabeth idly leafed through the stack of letters. There was a note from Harriet to her, and, for the second time in a week, a letter addressed to her son in what was distinctly the fine handwriting of a woman. The earlier letter he had opened, read, smiled, and shaken his head then requested the footman put it in the library with his other mail.

Elizabeth picked up the missive, tapped it on her thumbnail, and acknowledged to herself that curiosity was about to triumph over her better judgment. She was about to open it, when an appreciation for her son's sense of privacy prevented her from doing so. She carefully laid it on the tray.

Shortly before luncheon, Edmond came inside dressed in riding clothes. His boots were dusty from riding Maximilian, checking the fields and the progress of preparing the flocks for winter.

He picked up the letter, gave his mother a kiss, and sat down to read it. His reaction was much the same as before. Something about the contents elicited one of his rare smiles. She was forced to inquire.

"Good news, it seems?"

He glanced up, a definite sparkle of delight in his eyes. "I'm always entertained by a letter from Mrs. Williams."

"And whom might she be?"

Edmond tossed the sheets of paper from the letter on the couch beside him and briefly told his mother about his employment of Olivia.

"So, what is so amusing?"

"Here, see for yourself. You will notice how meticulous she is in reporting on the renovation of the Tothill Fields house to ready it for sale."

What Elizabeth read was a respectful and careful account of the business this woman had conducted in the past week. Appended, in neat figures, was a list of all expenses she had incurred and estimates of future expenditures with notations of how certain choices would result in this or that savings. The detailing seemed quite in order. The only thing of note was the unmistakable use of cultured language and the extremely fine hand in which the letter was written. Nowhere could she read anything that could be construed as amusing.

"It appears to me simply as an exceedingly careful accounting. I thought it was possibly a personal letter, since you seem so amused by it. I see nothing unusual, except it is obviously a lady's writing. I suppose Harding thought it was personal rather than a letter of business."

"Oh, Mother, my amusement comes from the fact that, from the beginning, Mrs. Williams is determined to keep me out of the poorhouse, no matter how often I tell her to spare no expense."

"You seem lucky to have found her. She sounds mature and

sensible."

"I find her quite reasonable and easy to deal with, especially for a woman her age." His tone was carefully casual.

"And what is that?"

"I'm not at all sure, but I would guess younger than Harriet. Perhaps Sophie Talent's age?"

He stared at the letter, thankfully missing her astounded expression. She had pictured a gray-haired matron, not someone young enough to be her daughter. When he turned to her, she smiled.

"I think I shall leave for London on Monday. Are you planning to come to town at all this winter?" he asked.

Elizabeth had, in fact, thought she would winter in the country. She enjoyed her friends in town and relished short visits but soon tired of the frenzy of society, especially in spring when the Season approached. Something made her say, "I shall certainly stay here through Christmas, and I expect you and Harriet to join me, but I shall probably come in January and stay until near when the Season opens."

"I'm glad. Town is always more pleasant with you there."

Curiosity about what was going on in London, specifically at the townhouse, was the real cause of her suddenly reconsidering her winter plans.

Chapter Seven

After Monday's return to town, Linnington spent Tuesday taking care of business affairs, leaving Wednesday free for him to meet James for some fencing in the afternoon, a good supper at Whites, and a game of whist. Talent and his family were in residence for a few weeks before returning to White Marsh Manor for the holidays.

After the hands were finished, James Talent also remained at the table now abandoned by their usual evening's partners, good friends Gavin Freeman and John Canning. He watched as Linnington sat at the card table, idly fingering the cards from the games just played.

Talent gave a sigh. "So, what is it, Linnington? You've hardly said three words and I've seen only two smiles." Talent turned his compact body in the chair in order to comfortably cross his legs and face his friend. His hazel eyes sparkled. "Surely this dispirited mood cannot be the result of me quite besting you this afternoon." The two men often fenced, Talent's athletic ability matching the longer reach of the larger man.

"Jamie, I've either made an excellent bargain or a disastrous blunder." Linnington rubbed a hand over his jaw. "I've taken a new tenant in the Tothill Fields house."

Talent groaned inwardly but sat patiently, knowing his friend would continue without prompting. He and his beloved wife, Sophie, often expressed amazement someone as fastidious as Linnington could keep any sort of company with such a garish and unsophisticated a person as the woman who followed him from

Spain. The one time he and his wife discussed the matter, they were agreed the attraction lay in only one mutual interest between the man and the woman. On Sophie's part, she offered the thought the lust on the part of the woman in question was also heightened by pecuniary desires. They were terribly glad when the Spanish woman finally left Linnington's life. Now, here he was in the clutches of another woman.

At Linnington's continued hesitation, he ventured, "Not another bit of muslin, Edmond?"

Linnington did laugh at this. "No, no, my friend. This lady is no Carmelita and there is the source of my doubt. It's the young woman we rescued from entering Ms. Taunton's establishment. Do you remember?" James nodded warily, "She is peculiarly well bred, even though the only thing I know about her is she was the shopgirl in *La Boulangerie*, a bakeshop and tearoom where Harriet on one occasion dragged Malcolm and me for tea and where my mother often had the servants purchase baked goods. Did you happen to go in there ever?"

"I don't believe I did. You know my bookish Sophie is not one much for more small talk than is required for visits to balls or dinners and the obligatory calls on family and friends. She quite avoids the sort of place your sister Harriet would find appealing. At any rate, Harriet must have blackmailed you to make any occasion for you to drink tea and eat cakes at such an establishment?"

Linnington laughed and took a sip of brandy. "Mrs. Williams has a quite extraordinary story. It seems the shop owner, her employer, died several weeks previously and the shop was closed because the debts exceeded expectations. This dashed her hope to keep the business going. She sought employment elsewhere and finding none, as a last resort, resigned to sell herself. I simply made her a better offer and moved her into the house to oversee its renovation. By spring, she should have enough saved to return to her home in Cornwall. And I assure you, no part of the business proposal was to ask her to behave as she would at Taunton's."

"Good God, Edmond. What You've done is rather like the rescuing of a stray puppy. I suppose it an admirable thing to do, but now what? Is she up to the task?"

"Her suggestions for décor seemed in good taste and she is quite reasonable and able. As a matter of business, I believe I have made a wise choice. Although I have not been by the place and will most likely be too busy this week, she sends detailed reports of her progress weekly. I was especially glad her availability makes it possible to get the house on the market by spring. Tothill Fields is building up rapidly, and I think the property should appeal to some young merchant and his wife, wanting to better themselves without spending a fortune, especially if it is offered completely furnished down to the last teaspoon."

He sat musing awhile. "Yet, there is something about the woman that does not seem to fit. I cannot discern why I am uncomfortable about her history."

"Do you suspect she is hiding some felony?"

"She does not seem to be of a criminal mind. In fact, she is a widow whose husband fell at Corunna. This background of marriage, she believed would equip her to withstand whatever was required at Mrs. Taunton's. You and I know it is not the case at all, so in a sense, she is far better off in my employ. What I find curious is the fact she is obviously well brought up and her French pronunciation is impeccable. I keep thinking perhaps she is a clergyman's daughter fallen on hard times, but there is something more."

"Is this the only thing disturbing you? If so, I see no problem. Her business is hers and yours is yours." He had the disquieting feeling Linnington was not being wholly honest about his intrigue with the woman. Yet, any thought of romance seemed hardly plausible. They had only met the young woman once and afterwards, James assumed had nothing but correspondence on which to base any interest. Yet, Talent knew women could make Edmond act very uncharacteristically. He tried to remember the young woman they aided all those weeks ago. There was nothing outstanding about her other than she was pretty and impoverished. He shrugged off his disquiet.

Talent rose. "Well, you are into it now. I'm afraid I have no better advice than to let things come to pass as they will, since she quite fits the job." The men shook hands and Talent called for his carriage.

He paused when he arrived at the front door of his townhouse, handing his coat and hat to his butler, Johnson. It was quiet. No crying daughter. He smiled at the thought of the cherub his wife had delivered just six weeks ago. But the young lady, Miss Eugenia, had an obstinate streak and had given them little rest. The older two children, Robert and Caroline, were dutifully asleep, he was sure. He was at least glad to have them all in town with him.

When he entered the bedroom, Sophie was still awake, reading by candlelight, her fair hair in an attractive nightcap above her oval face. Talent kissed her before he went to the adjoining dressing room to divest himself of evening coat, breeches, hose, and shoes with the help of his valet. He waited until his man had gone before he joined his wife in her bed where he pulled the book from her hand, marked the page, and set it out of reach on his side of the bed. Her spectacles followed. He wanted to talk.

"Still awake so late? Interesting book?"

"Eugenia woke an hour ago but went quickly to sleep after I fed her, thank goodness. Did you have a pleasant evening?"

"Pleasant enough. Linnington and I soundly beat Canning and Freeman at whist." He paused. "Then Linnington decided to confide in me."

"Good Lord, don't tell me he has acquiesced to his importunate sister and gotten engaged to that vile Lady Sybil she wants him to marry?"

"No, but it does have to do with his personal life. I thought he had taken a new mistress."

His wife groaned at the news as sincerely as he had done.

"But not so, and there lies the puzzle." Talent proceeded to tell the tale just as Linnington had related it to him. He was sitting propped up on the pillows beside his wife, nuzzling the charming cap, so he missed the sudden astonishment when he mentioned the name of the teashop.

Taking his wife's silence when he finished as disinterest, he blew out the candle. Beside him, Sophie lay awake, her mind racing over all James had told her and wondering how she could move forward with this disquieting news. She was overwhelmed with the baby and preparations for Christmas. She would wait a while for more information from James as to the exact identity of this person. Mme. Dufour sometimes employed other young women than Olivia. In any case, after the holidays, she must seek out Olivia and be sure she was all right. She willed all the tumbling thoughts away. She needed the sleep.

***

The next morning, Linnington decided he should drop by the Tothill Fields house to see for himself how the work was going. Perhaps he wouldn't see much, since the only tasks completed so far were the preliminary work, most of which didn't show on the surface. He was perfectly content with Mrs. Williams' account of the progress and could simply leave the entire enterprise in her hands and go by when it was finished to see if there was anything needing further attention. Possibly it was in truth curiosity about her drawing him there, but he told himself it was due diligence for any task he undertook.

With other pressing business left from his sojourn out of town. By midafternoon Thursday he made his way to the house.

He opened the door and called, "Partridge?"

Instead of the butler appearing, Mrs. Williams' called to him.

"Mr. Partridge and his wife have walked into town as it is their day off, my lord. May I help you?" Her voice came from the dining room, so he stepped into the parlor and walked toward her.

Evidently, she had been working at the dining table and rose at the sound of his voice. Olivia stood silhouetted against the light of the French doors. The light penetrated the thin fabric of her dress and petticoats and since she was not wearing the usual apron, it gave him a fair outline of her body. He could discern the slender waist and the shape of her hips usually concealed by the gathers of the empire-style dress. He was not prepared to be stirred by the sight and momentarily could not answer. He had always been curious about her background, but it had not consciously occurred to him to be curious about anything more intimate in her person.

"Is there anything I can do for you?" she persisted.

"Yes, Mrs. Williams. I forgot it was the staff day off, but as you are here, I can accomplish my purpose anyway. I came to see any progress for myself." Somehow, instead of standing and staring at the delightful image, he willed himself to continue to approach in a businesslike manner.

"I'm afraid there is not a great deal to see, but I am glad to show you about." She had been holding a paper, perhaps with items for her report to him. She laid it on the table. "If you will follow me." She walked toward the hallway where the shadow erased any vestige of the earlier scene. She was once more merely an attractive young woman in a simple day dress.

They began their tour in his dressing room, where she pointed out the repairs and informed him similar ones were made in the servants' quarters above. "As you see, sir, the plaster in here has been repaired. I know your instructions were not to alter this room, but I have ordered it repainted with the rest of the house. I understood you did not want anything done to this chamber but thought paint would meet with your approval. I hope I have not presumed."

"Not at all, madam, the room could certainly use refreshing."

They returned to the dining room to view the repairs there. "I'm afraid there is nothing more to see. I can report Mr. Partridge quite pleased with Mr. Hackman's repairs to the chimneys. That should prevent any further water damage as what we have just seen."

"Thank you. Mrs. Williams. If he has told you he is pleased, I have no need to check further."

They stood rather awkwardly, the slight bit of real business disposed of.

"My lord, it is tea time. May I offer you some? There are always supplies of Mrs. Person's delicious scones."

"Thank you. I believe I should like tea. May I assist you?"

"Not at all. Mrs. Person always leaves a kettle on the hob for me on Thursdays. Please sit down and I shall return shortly."

She disappeared below stairs, and Linnington went to the parlor and sat in one of the wing chairs as he had on the first day with her. The time it took before she brought the tea tray gave him ample chance to think about the other times he had been in this room. Most of them were not pleasant and many accompanied by shouts and curses. He found he was anticipating the change in atmosphere with a quiet tea in the company of this young woman.

For a brief moment, his mind strayed to the fact he was sitting directly below the bedchamber. He preferred not to think about the former activities in the room, given the present company. There was no way he could reconcile those actions with the endeavors of a much more gently bred employee. Perhaps the fact of her occupying the space above might cleanse it of some of the tawdriness he associated with it, as she seemed to do sitting in this still disreputable room.

Olivia returned with the tray. She picked up the pot. "How do you take your tea, sir?"

"Milk and two sugars, please."

She prepared the cup and with the pitcher still in hand, regarded him with a questioning glance.

"That's lovely, thank you," he responded.

She sat opposite him, her hands moving in graceful motions as she prepared her cup. What in the world could he talk about with her?

"So, my lord, if you don't mind, I know you keep up with the actions in Parliament. Can you tell me anything about bills pertaining to veterans to be presented when next they sit? The newspaper tells us little."

Given this opening, he was grateful to relate details on everything he knew for certain as well as all the rumors heard concerning the issue. Her questions were pertinent and he answered them as well as he could. A small chime from the mantle clock announced the hour, and Linnington realized if he did not leave now, the Ps would return to find him alone with her. He pled business elsewhere, thanked her for the tea, and rather hastily left.

He walked to St. James Street where he intended to stop at Whites for conversation and supper. Why had being caught alone with her caused him guilt? While he'd been there, he had not given half a thought to whether it was proper or not to be alone with her in the house. Perhaps his guilt stemmed from the need for the Ps not to draw any odious conclusions. Part of him wished they could when he remembered her standing in silhouette before the windows.

Olivia took the tea tray to the basement, replaced the few uneaten scones in a tin, and washed the cups. Then she went into the dining room but was in no mood to return to her bookkeeping. She sat and stared out the doors at the winter garden. The afternoon had been more pleasant than any time she could remember in ages. When they were sitting in the parlor, as he discussed the pending legislation, all she could think about was how lovely it would be to spend some time with him in a half-civilized room. She was anxious to set this place to rights. There was something about the incongruity of its décor that set her teeth on edge. She didn't want to be reminded of speculation about things that happened in this place. She could picture the two of them sitting in the refurbished room quite comfortably. She chided herself for being silly. Should the day she imagined ever come, it would mean she would be on the cusp of leaving the house forever. She didn't particularly relish either idea.

Chapter Eight

The following Sunday was the First Sunday in Advent. Olivia returned rather earlier than usual to the house from St. Stephen's House. She and the Ps had their own keys and used the front door, since they were the only occupants in the house, rather than the much longer way around through the alley to the kitchen or servants' door. Jeremy still came in and out from the rear, since it was closer to the muse where he lived in rooms above the stalls and he had no key.

It was still light, so she didn't bother with a candle but went straight to her bedroom to be rid of her woolen shawl and winter bonnet and to lie down for a while. It had been a long week for her.

Olivia had no more than lay down when she thought she heard a noise in the direction of the garden. She lay still and listened. Nothing. Then there was a definite scratching. Perplexed, she considered perhaps an animal had gotten through the fence. Sitting a moment on the side of the bed, unsure what to do, she rose and walked quietly to the windows in the dressing room. Nothing could be seen from her vantage with the stairway blocking the view, but she was still concerned. She considered opening the window and leaning out when there was the distinct sound of breaking glass then the scrape of wood on wood. A wave of terror assailed her. Someone was breaking in! She considered shouting at them but by then was sure whoever it was would have made their way into the house.

Pushing down the rising panic, she went to his lordship's dresser. She took out the pistols, and with shaking hands utilized powder, patch, shot, and ramrod on each of them. The action was automatic even though her hands were trembling. Gradually, her hands steadied; something about handling the weapons calmed her or rather numbed her to any danger. She tiptoed to the head of the stairs. Whoever the intruder was, they were still in the kitchen, so she quietly descended to the front hall. The Ps would return very shortly. Her hope was the person would spend enough time rummaging in the kitchen until the couple might come home and the three of them could confront him together. Some of the fear crept up her spine. She considered slipping out the front door and trying to find a constable.

Instead, a bearded head with a dirty cap appeared from the stairwell. No time to run.

"Stop there!" she cried out in what she hoped was a commanding voice and didn't show the terror gripping her heart. The pistols in each hand were hidden behind her skirts.

The man had an astonished look on his face turning slyly to a grin.

"Well, missy. I didn't think to find something like you in this house."

"Leave now, sir!"

His answer was to mount two more steps. Hers was to raise the pistol in her right hand and aim it straight at him.

The man hesitated and then took one more step. "A girl like you wouldn't..." He had no time to finish the sentence. She aimed the pistol at the floor well in front of him and fired. The explosion splintered a plank, filled the hall with the acrid smell of cordite, and stopped the man in mid-step. The din also covered the sound of Partridge opening the door and Mrs. Person's accompanying scream. For a moment, all four stood rooted to the floor and stared, the man at Olivia and the other three at him.

The intruder turned and fled, the earlier grin firmly removed from his face. Olivia ran behind him, not so much as to get another shot at him as to be sure the man was truly fleeing. The Ps descended right behind her. His coattails were soon seen disappearing over the fence into the alleyway.

The horror of the last few moments forced Olivia to sink into the settle, shaking uncontrollably. Partridge went directly to the kitchen door to be sure the man was nowhere to be seen. Mrs. Person sat next to her and put her arm around Olivia's shoulders "Are you all right, luv?"

Olivia nodded. "I must get rid of these things." She was somewhat in a daze, staring at the loaded pistol in her left hand.

"Let George do it, dear."

"No, I'm all right. I'll put them away and then perhaps some tea?"

Mrs. Person appeared to want to say more but instead glanced at George, silently asking him to take charge. The shock of the intruder was too much for her sensibilities. George unfortunately was in no better a state than she.

"Of course, missus. I'll get the water on."

Going directly to the dressing room, Olivia unloaded the one pistol and cleaned each with a patch, not knowing where to find the proper oil. She carefully arranged everything just as it had been in the drawer. Before she shut it, she stared at the guns with distaste. They reminded her both of her unease by herself in the Spanish camp when David went off to battle and the more disquieting thought of how alike they were to the one her father used to take his own life, the one she had first pulled from his desk in the library at Newington Hall. Yet, she couldn't deny without the weapons here, something terrible could have just happened. She shut the drawer with a bang and went down to tea.

***

The story was much too good to be kept within the three of them for long. Jeremy first carried it to the townhouse in a much-glorified way, and it became quite a topic of conversation among the staff. They were extremely eager to meet Mrs. Williams, a sharp-shooting mystery of a woman. The only member of the staff who contrived to do so was Mrs. Hendrix. She called on Mrs. P, ostensibly to share a new recipe. Instead, she received a kind and thorough lesson from Mrs. Williams on the method of making choux paste.

Mrs. Hendrix returned to the townhouse with nothing but good things to relate and assure all the present resident of the formerly infamous house was more than acceptable.

At the next Sunday luncheon, Mr. Partridge got his turn to tell the tale, interrupted, amended, and corrected at every turn by Mrs. Person. Quite used to this, the servants sorted out for themselves later an approximation of what happened.

As the Ps were about to leave Owens, Linnington's valet pulled Partridge aside. "Partridge, do you intend to tell his lordship?"

"I hadn't thought to worry him."

"I believe he should know. Do you think there is any chance the man will return?"

"I rather doubt it. He appeared to be one of those ruffians and pickpockets who inhabit Five Fields at night."

"Nevertheless, I think his lordship should know his property was in the process of burglary."

"Do as you think best, Mr. Owens."

Owens thought it best to tell the gentleman.

Chapter Nine

Linnington was peeved at himself. He had procrastinated even to go by the property for more than a week, contenting himself to answering promptly Mrs. William's detailed and careful notes to him on the progress of the project. In truth, he wondered if his reticence had anything to do with his attraction to her on the previous visit. He really should go check out the damage from the attempted robbery.

He had business the next day but resolved to go by before retiring to his club. He declined a supper party he didn't want to attend anyway and made arrangements to meet Jamie and their partners for an extra game of whist later.

He let himself into the house and called for Partridge. The Ps both bustled up the stairs from the kitchen, and he was aware Olivia hesitated at the head of the stairs from the bedroom floor.

"Mrs. Williams?"

"Yes, my lord." She slowly descended the steps.

"Mr. Partridge, Owens tells me you had an intruder?"

"We did, sir."

"And the man was repelled by an armed Mrs. Williams?" He glanced at Olivia who demurely concentrated on her hands nervously clasped in front of her.

"He was, sir."

"I would like to survey the damage." He spoke briefly in a decidedly businesslike way.

Partridge indicated the stairs to the lower floor. The three followed their employers down the stairs in silence, noticing his hesitation before he descended to inspect with his fingers the splintered plank where a ball had buried itself. He and Partridge examined the now empty window frame, boarded up to keep out the weather. Jeremy had removed the entire sash to repair the mullions and glaze the window. The men went into the yard to assess the fence and the outside.

Olivia stood in the shadow of the stairs. Her face reflected she would rather be on the moon than in the house.

When the men returned and shut the door, Linnington turned to her. "How fortunate, Mrs. Williams, you knew where to find a firearm, and, from the gouge in the floor above, it seems how to load and fire one." He really wanted to laugh at the situation but hoped he had put on a stern face.

In a rush of nervous words, Olivia hastened to explain. "Oh, my lord, I assure you I did not find the firearms by invading your privacy. The men who came to sweep the chimneys moved your dresser and clumsily handled it until the drawers flew open. I discovered the pistols when I was setting things to rights. Please believe me, I would never go through your things from mere curiosity." Her tone begged to be believed. He pressed the issue to see how she would react.

"And evidently you have had some practice at handling weapons?"

"Oh, sir, I'm a country girl. My father, not having a boy, taught me when I was young, to fire and care for all sorts of firearms. He was quite a..." She hesitated, and Linnington almost thought she was going to say "sportsman" when she added, "an excellent shot. Then when I went to Portugal to be with my husband in the camps, he insisted on my being able to use a pistol. He left one with me when he went into battle. I assure you I cleaned your pair quite thoroughly before I replaced them in the drawer."

Linnington smiled, letting the girl off the hook. "Well then, I count myself quite fortunate you were in position to defend my castle."

Her face betrayed her relief, not unmixed with a sidelong glance telling him she wasn't sure if he was being honest or just teasing.

Linnington was not the least put off by her discovery of the guns, only grateful the incident had resolved itself without accident, injury, or bloodshed. What caught his ear was her reference to Portugal. This she had not mentioned when she spoke of her husband. The delightful odor of Mrs. P's cooking reminded him he hadn't eaten since breakfast and was famished.

After glancing at the table already set for three, Linnington stepped back. "Very well then, I shall take my leave. I've delayed your supper. Mrs. Person, my nose tells me you have been making your excellent meat pasty." He wanted to give Olivia a chance to be reassured he was not angry with her. "Mrs. Williams, when we were boys, we often used to sneak away to the kitchen to sit at the servants' table and let Mrs. Person stuff us with whatever she was making. Pasties were always a delicious favorite." He smiled at Mrs. P who puffed up like a proud hen and, to his and Partridge's surprise, said, "You're most welcome, sir, to stay and have some." Then she added, sheepishly aware of the rather inappropriate invitation, "I'll set a place in the dining room."

Why not? In the last years, I've dined often with a less genteel crowd than these three. "No need, I shall be quite comfortable joining

you at the table here." He shrugged out of his fine brown coat. The
waistcoat with its patterned weave and cravat followed, all of which
he put on the settle by the hearth, and Partridge pulled up a fourth
chair while Mrs. Williams set a place. Soon, the four of them, with
almost no conversation and a good helping of awkwardness, sat
across from each other. Linnington broke the silence. "Mrs. Person,
this does remind me of Giles and myself taking refuge in the kitchen
at Crossfields after we had stolen Mr. Harris' horse to ride to the
village. We thought we would be on bread and water for a week, but
you came to our rescue. I'm sure, Mrs. Williams, both Partridge and
Mrs. Person could tell you stories of how naughty my brother and I
were."

After this gambit, all he and Olivia had to do was listen and laugh
at the stories, told as usual from two vastly different viewpoints. They
talked of boyhood adventures and pranks, including one involved tale
of the brothers abandoning Harriet in an apple tree. Linnington
found the stories gave him time to study the woman sitting across
from him without being noticed. Olivia was once again her composed
self, unlike her earlier chagrin at having found the firearms. He
judged her quite pretty in a rather simple way with a small but lovely
figure under the plain dress a fact he had already assessed. With the
bulky linen apron she habitually wore removed, he could see her in
detail. She had glorious hair always pinned up with a ribbon. For the
first time, he considered her not as an employee nor something
abstract as she appeared upstairs with the light behind her but as a
woman. Although he perceived the first time they met she had the
demeanor of a survivor, the experiences had not removed a certain
vulnerability and softness about her. The more he observed her the

more appealing she seemed. He cautioned himself about any thoughts of replacing the notorious Mrs. Fernandez with this estimable woman but reasoned knowing her better would do not harm.

When it was nearly time for Linnington to go, he changed the subject. "Mrs. Williams, you followed your husband to Portugal? Not many wives did."

"I was there only a short time, sir. We were childless, so there was really nothing to keep me in England. I was only there a few short weeks before Corunna."

"I see." He rose to put on his waistcoat, tying the cravat with quick expertise. Partridge hurried to help him on with his coat. He turned to Olivia. "I hope you are not afraid to stay alone in the house now, when the others are not here."

"Oh, not at all. It was only happenstance I was even here when the man broke in. I returned early from St. Stephen's House."

"What, pray, is St. Stephen's House?"

"Westminster parish has let a house nearby to be used as a hospice for wounded veterans who cannot be accommodated at Chelsea Hospital."

"What do you do there?"

"Simply visit with the men who want for company. Many of their families are too poor or too far away to visit. I often read letters and write answers for those who cannot do it for themselves."

"How good of you." She really was an extraordinary woman.

They had been moving towards the front door during this conversation, and, after taking his greatcoat and hat from Partridge,

Linnington turned.

"Thanks to all of you for a pleasant evening."

The door closed behind him, and he began his walk to the club. The new gaslights made the dark street quite inviting. Linnington had thoroughly enjoyed himself. Since returning from Spain, he silently chafed under the restrictions of a title and the constant demands of society. He missed the companionship of the army. He missed being free of anything except following the discipline of a soldier. It was true he loved Crossfields and found its management to be most satisfying, but for him, it was the stultifying atmosphere of London society he found a burden. An evening with plain people seemed to refocus his perspective on the world he lost sometimes in the rush of business and society.

Thank God for his friends like Jamie. He could hardly wait to get to the whist table and relate the entire tale of the Amazon who defended his house. He found himself laughing aloud. Mrs. Williams continued to surprise him. Maybe he should spend more time at the townhouse. In addition, he was intrigued by the reference to St. Stephen's House. He should check it out since he was interested in veterans' affairs. His new interest had nothing whatsoever to do with possibly visiting at the same time as Mrs. Williams.

Chapter Ten

The following Sunday, Linnington attended services at St. James's even though his mother was not in residence. He lunched at home alone and by midafternoon found he was bored and restless, unable to even settle down with a book. He remembered what Olivia told him about St. Stephen's House. He and Jamie had often discussed the overcrowded and really deplorable situation many returning veterans found if they were disabled. Even the healthy had little help from Parliament despite their service to the nation. He was passionate enough about it to consider standing for a seat in Commons. The thought of serving in Lords was repugnant to him.

It wasn't much of a walk from the Mayfair to St. Stephen's House if it was near Westminster Cathedral.

Perhaps an outing and change of scene would do him good. The day was cold, but a greatcoat should keep him comfortable.

There had been light snow two days before but relatively mild since and the walks were fairly clear. One needed to avoid the gutters full of slush but he had on boots, so it was not really a problem. He walked down St. James Street then around St. James Park to York Street. The establishment had to be somewhere in the area.

The walk cleared many of the cobwebs from his head. The air was just cold enough to make his breath visible in small clouds. His nostrils stung pleasantly. He was always curious when he visited the wards at Chelsea to see if any of his comrades were there. This would give him an entirely new venue to discover any old friends. And if she was there, it would be pleasant to see Mrs. Williams. His step quickened.

The house let by the church was easy to find. The sign for St. Stephen's House was lettered in formal, old English script. The door opened straight into a large room in which perhaps a dozen narrow beds had been set up with a small table separating the beds and a box or trunk at the foot for personal belongings. Another part of the room was full of mismatched chairs, pulled up before a generous fireplace where a coal grate warmed the room. Some of the beds were occupied, but the majority of men were in chairs by the fire. He noted the orderliness of the place. Linnington was impressed even though there was the usual welter of bandages and supplies for the afflicted. The iron beds were covered with the familiar military blankets. He wondered if some of them belonged to the occupant and had warded off snow in the Pyrenees. The place was free of the usual odors associated with sick rooms. All appearances assured him it was well run by the parish.

There was a scattering of women, some there to take care of the needs of the men who were quite possibly relatives, and the others, mostly well dressed, were probably visitors. Olivia sat in the far corner, pen in hand, talking to a man whose eyes were covered in clean bandages. Her expression was serious as she waited for him to speak. Dressed in a simple gray walking costume, she leaned forward, her scarf slipping to reveal the smooth, fair skin and softness of her décolletage. A stirring occurred in Edmond he had not experienced since the departure of his previous tenant.

A man in shirtsleeves and waistcoat who seemed to be in charge interrupted Edmond's reverie.

"May I help you, sir? Are you seeking anyone in particular? I'm

Mr. Selkirk, and I oversee the house for the parish."

Linnington introduced himself simply as Edmond Linnington. "I was in the King's Own and I heard about this house. I'm in the habit of visiting Chelsea upon occasion. Veterans Affairs is of great interest to me.

The two men discussed the situation facing the returning wounded, especially those without family or funds.

"I'm always happy to know there are men like you, sir, who return to civilian life and retain their interest in those who are unable to do so. As you know, the parish established us for an overflow from Chelsea."

"They do as estimable a job as they can considering the circumstances. When it was built, who could foresee the number of victims produced by the European wars? It is a blessing to have the Church interested enough to lend a hand."

"It's what we were once established to do." A note of frustration tinged Selkirk's voice.

"I wanted to see your establishment for myself and also wished to inquire if there was anyone from the King's Own here perhaps?"

"I believe there are one or two here. You are most welcome to visit with our patients." Selkirk waved an inviting hand.

They parted ways, and Linnington took the opportunity to chat with the veterans nearest him, inquiring of their postings during the war. One very young man had seen nothing of Spain but been recently conscripted and sent to France.

"How long were you there, soldier?"

"Only weeks, sir. It was my misfortune to be injured by a defective caisson. I feel mighty guilty, sir, bein' with these men who saw battle."

"No need for guilt, Private. Many more men served behind lines than at the front and they were crucial to all of us who survived."

The boy was cheered at the words. Linnington also thought with youth on his side and the sort of care he was receiving at St. Stephen's, he would probably mend enough to gain employment.

As Linnington worked his way nearer to Olivia, the blind man she was tending turned at the sound of his voice. It was difficult to see the man's face below the bandage surrounding his head, but he looked familiar.

"Capt'n! Capt'n Linnington?" a raspy voice rang out. "That you?"

"Higgins?"

"Yes, sir. It's me."

If Olivia was surprised to see him there, she hid it well and rose to give her seat to Linnington. "Here, my lord, do sit down."

"My lord?" scoffed Higgins.

Linnington laughed. "I fear so, Higgins. I left Spain because my brother was killed in a fall from his horse. Thus the title."

"Well, I apologize for all the times Geoff and I made fun of the gentry. Never thought you would one day be part of it. Wouldn't have thought it would suit you."

"Sometimes, I confess, it doesn't. I miss the army and its ways. Now tell me about yourself. You and your bad-tempered friend Banks were still hale and hearty when I left and just ready to go into battle."

"We wondered what happened to you. We thought Wellington had gotten smart and put you on his staff permanently when you was called to headquarters. And old Banks still comes by to see me now and then."

"I was on staff but had very minor duties, I assure you. I mostly was a liaison between our troops and the Spanish and interrogated my share of French prisoners."

As Olivia went off to talk to other patients, Higgins told of his last battle in the Peninsular War, a mere skirmish, leaving him blind. Higgins was his usual optimistic self despite his wounds. Linnington was sure Banks made up for his lack of complaining by making the overseer, Mr. Selkirk's life a misery. A subsequent conversation with Selkirk confirmed this opinion.

"What brought you here, Capt'n?"

"A conversation with Mrs. Williams. She was telling me about visiting the veterans here and, since I'm interested in seeing if I have any influence with the powers in Parliament, I came to see for myself."

"Well, it ain't Chelsea here, but they are kind and we have angels like Mrs. Williams who come by regular. I might know you would end up with a girl like her instead of that Fernandez doxy, if you don't mind me sayin'."

Olivia returned to the bedside in time to hear this last remark. A distinct blush colored her cheeks. "Oh, Sergeant, Lord Linnington is my employer, I assure you."

"More fool he." Higgins gave a loud guffaw.

"I really must be going," Olivia interrupted, ignoring the remark. "I just came to say goodbye and I will see you next week, Sgt. Higgins. By then, I hope you have some mail for me to answer."

"I should be off, too. Good to see you, my man." He took Higgins' hand and shook it.

"Glad you're well, Capt'n." Higgins was not going to use the honorific. What was of importance to him was the rank.

Linnington and Olivia left the hospice at the same time. "Allow me to accompany you home."

"Oh, no thank you, sir, it's but half a mile, as you know and quite out of your way."

"Not at all. I'll simply walk with you and then it is a but few steps to York Street and the Park."

They walked in companionable silence across Dean's Yard for a while.

"Thank you for mentioning St. Stephen's. Had you not, I would never have known what sort of fate Higgins met. Of all the men in my company, he was the closest to Geoff Godfrey, my batman. I was extremely fond of Geoff. One becomes unusually close to one's batman when you are engaged in a real war. Geoff was killed in the first skirmishes at Salamanca."

"Oh, I'm so sorry. It must have been a sore loss."

"It was." For some reason, Linnington began to talk about Geoff and the days in Spain. He rarely mentioned any of this even to Jamie. Seeing Higgins had made all the memories of the war flood back and he had to talk about it to someone, and this young woman who was acquainted with both the Army and the peninsula seemed to allow him the outlet to do so. She listened respectfully, merely nodding and smiling, leaving him to open up in a way he had never done so previously.

When they reached the house, he changed the subject. "I assume from your notes the renovation is going as planned."

"It is. The plasterwork and minor repairs should be finished this week, before everyone is busy with the holidays. I believe the painters may even begin the work before Christmas, although Mr. Hackman says they will not finish until mid-January. He has a previous commission which must be done before then, so we may be in something of a shamble for the holidays."

"You mentioned in your last note the possibility of having Jeremy take you to the shops in Stepney, where you thought you might sell the present chairs from the dining room and be able to find replacements."

"If such a trip is to your satisfaction. Although it is always a chance, Stepney is where one can often find the best bargains."

Linnington smiled. Here she was, once more being frugal with his money.

"Would Thursday be convenient unless there is rain or snow?"

"It would, sir."

"Then plan on it. Good day, Mrs. Williams."

As he made his way home, Linnington determined to accompany them. He secretly loved the hurly-burly of the markets. At least that was what he told himself.

Chapter Eleven

Thursday dawned gray and threatening but without precipitation. Olivia was relieved. She really needed to get away for a while, and the thought of visiting shops and a ride in the open air lifted her spirits. She was feeling quite cooped up in the little house, regardless of the amity in which she now found herself concerning the Ps. The prospect of shopping without the need to assess her own meager funds excited her. She assumed Linnington would join them when they arrived at the shop in Stepney. In her last report to him, she gave directions to the block of shops in her estimation worth visiting.

Jeremy drew up before the house with a small wagon and loaded the eight heavy chairs in it. She wasn't sorry to see them go and hoped she could find acceptable replacements.

She put on her old pelisse. "Jeremy, I'm going to need a little assistance getting up on the box if you wouldn't mind." She reached up for his hand.

"Oh, no, missus. His lordship is coming directly with the brougham. He said you should ride with him."

Her blue eyes widened in astonishment. "He did?"

"Yes, missus."

At that moment, Linnington appeared in a brougham drawn by two finely matched gray horses. The one thing she could say in her father's favor was he bred fine horses on the estate. She found herself staring at this beautiful pair. His lordship had an excellent eye for horses, she concluded. And they appeared well fed and loved, another mark to hold him in high esteem.

"I hope, Mrs. Williams, the team meets with your approval. I assure you they are quite well trained."

"And they are also quite lovely, sir."

He leaned down to give her a hand mounting the carriage's step. His grip was firm and as soon as she was settled, the coachman started the carriage. Olivia took a deep breath and fought the urge to sigh in ecstasy. It had been so very long since she had ridden in a proper carriage drawn by a first-class pair. She reveled in the breeze on her face despite its chill. The lap robe was warm and luxurious, and the seats smelled of good leather. It reminded her not only of riding in a carriage as a child but the familiar odors of the stables at home, leather saddles, harness and reins, even the sweat of horses, hay, and manure.

What a spectacle. This well-turned-out gentleman in his lovely equipage with this shabby, out-of-fashion companion. At least I will not see anyone I know, and I hope no one he knows sees us. I'm glad we are not in a barouche and not so exposed to every passerby.

She leaned against the squabs and reveled in the sounds, the squeak of a good leather harness, the rumble of well-sprung wheels, and the disciplined ring of the feet of a matched pair of horses on gravel. She had no need of conversation and apparently neither did his lordship. They rode the way in an easy silence.

She was also conscious of the solid presence of the man seated next to her. Without touching, she sensed the heat from his body. Olivia missed David, yet there was no gainsaying this man disturbed her peace more than David ever had. There was a hint of the familiar scent of wool, tobacco, and shaving soap. She willed herself to concentrate on the patches of countryside between clusters of buildings on the way. He did not seem inclined to speak, and she didn't know how to open a conversation, given their circumstances.

Jeremy, already at the block of shops, patiently waited for instructions on where to offload the chairs. It took about thirty minutes before Olivia spotted a set of chairs she liked. They had been in and out of a dozen establishments, and she hoped Linnington wasn't becoming bored with her dithering.

The replacements were a set of eight shield-back chairs, their slip seats well-worn, but it would be a small matter to recover them. She inquired of the cost and asked if the shopkeeper would consider taking a reduction in price for an exchange of the chairs from the house. She described their dark, Queen Anne style and woven seats. He heard her out and turned, deferring to the gentleman at her side, making his counter proposal to him and ignoring her.

Linnington shrugged and folded his arms. "I have nothing to do with these negotiations. Deal with the lady."

The shopkeeper frowned in puzzlement but turned to Olivia, and after some earnest haggling, they settled on a price and the exchange. In the meantime, Linnington had wandered away, roaming about through the man's wares.

"Mrs. Williams, you mentioned the need for an additional chair for the parlor. What would you think of that one?" He pointed at a small, armless chair. "And perhaps the escritoire just beyond it? The chair would service the desk, and I have noticed you use the dining table for all your business. Wouldn't the desk be more convenient and the chair serve two purposes?"

Olivia studied the desk. It was a lovely piece of furniture, but one of the tambour doors was damaged. When she pointed this out, Linnington confirmed he liked the lines of the little Hepplewhite desk with its satiny, honey colored finish, and added Jeremy could repair anything having to do with cabinetry. Thus encouraged, she drove a bargain with the owner to take it also "as is."

Jeremy set about unloading the old chairs and loading the new wares. After settling the bill, Olivia and Linnington left him to it and wandered down the row of shops toward the carriage, appraising the window displays.

When they passed one shop, Linnington announced, "I loathe those things," indicating a pair of pottery dogs on a table.

"Really? Why, sir?"

"They remind me of crotchety old ladies and their spoiled pets. And besides, I much prefer my own full-muzzled hounds and spaniels."

Perhaps it was the casual day and open air, but Olivia felt contrary. "I must say, I find them rather charming with their flat-faced ugliness. And many ladies think their décor quite incomplete without them."

"But you do at least also find them ugly?"

She laughed. "To be honest, my lord, I do find them to be quite ugly, but I still insist they are charming in their own way."

"Then since you do think them ugly, I challenge you. There are a number of pairs here. Which is the ugliest?"

She put her hand to her cheek, considering the assortment. "This pair has particularly flat faces."

"And these appear to have a decided squint, although it is hard to tell, since to me the eyes all resemble frogs more than canines."

Thus ensued the discussion of each pair until they both conceded a particular one was quite the ugliest. They were a rather nondescript duo of brown spaniels with very flat faces and bugged eyes.

The couple headed towards the carriage, noticing Jeremy was finished loading the wares. Linnington handed Olivia into the brougham and turned to him.

"Wait up for a moment, Jeremy." At this, he reentered the market.

Olivia and Jeremy exchanged glances. What was his lordship up to?

In a short time, he returned, whispered to Jeremy and got into the carriage.

"I'm pleased with the purchases, Mrs. Williams, and I think I was wise to leave the bargaining to you."

"I'm glad you are satisfied, sir. I was hesitant at the damage to the desk."

"Jeremy can repair it. His father was a cabinetmaker, and he hoped to be one, too. It seems the fellow drank away the business, so Jeremy went into service. It's a shame young men like him find it so hard to start a business. With his skill and discipline, he would have been a success, but he could find no backer. I've often thought I should make it possible for him to do so."

Olivia marveled at the man next to her. It was not unusual for a lord to care for their servants, but stumping up a stake for a business venture was going beyond the by.

The snow came down in huge, fluffy flakes. The coachman drove swiftly, and they soon arrived at the front door. Linnington bade her goodbye and waited for her to enter.

"Thank you for your help, my lord, and thank you for the lovely carriage ride." She gave him a brilliant smile as she went inside.

A week later, Jeremy returned, set the beautifully repaired desk in the parlor in front of the window where Olivia had cleared a place for it, and brought in the chair. On it sat a package wrapped in brown paper and straw. Olivia pulled away the string and wrapping to find the pair of Staffordshire dogs.

So, his lordship could be a tease. She laughed and set them in a prominent place on the left side of the mantle, moving the square brass parlor clock and the candlestick to the right to make, what she considered, a rather attractive grouping.

Chapter Twelve

Elizabeth Linnington anticipated supper tonight with particular satisfaction. Edmond was once more in residence and would be staying through Christmas and until after the New Year, she hoped. Perhaps it was the approaching holidays, or just the passage of time since Edmond had returned to Crossfields from Spain, but his mood was noticeably lighter. Perhaps, also, it was a feeling of being of service to his old comrades at arms. He had told her about his visits with a wounded member of his company at a hospice. He made it a habit recently, he informed her, to go there each Sunday after luncheon.

Tonight should be a happy one for all concerned. She very much preferred to dine *en famile*. Harriet and Malcolm were coming, but she had also invited James and Sophie to dinner before all of them became caught up in the rush of family Christmas. The couples would be spending the night, so no one had to hurry. She admitted to herself, even though she considered James and Sophie nearly family, the addition of the Talents was partly to keep her from having to listen to Harriet gossip all evening after the meal or to make a fourth at whist. Rose had put the finishing touches on her toilette. Pulling on her gloves, she made her way down the broad oak staircase.

Elizabeth stopped at the dining room to be sure all was in order. Even though this was a family affair, she had taken her usual interest in the details of food and table. The long, beamed room with its massive fireplace contained a dining table now covered in Irish linen. The demilune ends of the table had been removed and set next to the sideboard more for convenience than necessity, since there were only six people to serve at table.

Benson as well as all the personal staff from the townhouse were in residence for the holidays, and the butler and his footmen laid the table with her exquisite Spode china with its simple pattern of green leaves scattered around the center of the plates and narrow band of the same color bordering the slightly rococo rims. The Belgian crystal sparkled under a line of tall, silver five-branched candelabra. They were quite tall and the festive greenery of fir, holly, and ivy was low, arranged to weave around the base of the candelabra the length of the table. She preferred to be able to see her guests when they dined, and the simple rope of ivy not only complimented the china but also did not obstruct the view of the guests. The flatware had been laid out by Benson's own meticulous hand. Quite satisfied, she continued to the drawing room. Her expectations of a delightful evening lifted. The only fault would be if Edmond and Harriet got into one of their habitual spats.

Edmond was already in the drawing room, standing by the fire.

"Good evening, Mother. You look lovely, as usual." He bent to give her cheek a kiss, and the pleasant odor of his cologne mingled with redolence of oaken logs in the fireplace.

This evening, in a gown the color of spring violets in a damask pattern, one of her favorites, she let a bit of pride and vanity arise. This was her domain, this ancient room, with its beamed ceilings much too low for modern taste complemented by warm-colored Turkish rugs and the space between filled with comfortable furniture arranged to enhance conversation. The occasional tables each held some picture or treasure from her nearly forty-five years as its mistress.

They spent the few moments before the Woolleys came downstairs, in idle chatter. Harriet swept in with her usual air of authority, dressed in a teal gown her mother thought much too ornamented with ruching and ruffles. The ever-patient Malcolm waddled after her. Having not seen her mother since arriving in the afternoon from their own estate beyond Oxford, Elizabeth was immediately commandeered by Harriet to be the recipient of the latest news and fashion in London. The Talents thankfully joined the rest of the party five minutes later. When informed by Benson supper was ready, Edmond escorted Elizabeth to the table, and the men led their wives through.

Conversation during the meal was convivial and rather soon the dessert was brought in, a lovely apple *tartaine.*

After taking a bite, Harriet exclaimed, "This is excellent, Mother. I vow Mrs. Hendrix didn't make it. It is much like the ones I used to purchase at Mme. Dufour's teashop I used to frequent. Now closed, sadly. Where did you obtain it?"

Sophie glanced up with particular interest at the mention of the shop. Elizabeth noted her attention to the matter. She wasn't aware Sophie even knew of the place.

"No, I didn't purchase it. Mrs. Hendrix did indeed make it."

"If Mrs. Hendrix made it, her baking has improved since last I was here."

"As a matter of fact, she has gained some skills. It seems Mrs. Person has mastered the art of the *tartaine* and improved her methods with quite a number of baked items. Mrs. Hendrix has also benefitted from the knowledge and has provided several very nice bakery items since the staff arrived."

"Then I suppose Person had plenty of time on her hands to learn such things, now there is no one living in Edmond's little *abode*." She drew the last word out for emphasis and tossed a disapproving glance at her brother.

When he answered with the flash of angry glance, Elizabeth thought to settle the thing and avert any more discussion. "I believe she has acquired some skill from the woman Edmond hired to refurbish his house. He is in the process of advertising it for sale, as you know."

"Indeed? Do tell us, brother, you are selling the little, shall we call it, hideaway?"

Edmond slowly lowered his dessert spoon and fork. "I am. I intend to sell it furnished if possible. So, I hired a woman to oversee the renovation. The work is going along well."

James followed the conversation with an approving nod. Elizabeth surmised he knew something of the arrangements. Sophie, on the other hand, had said nothing, but Elizabeth noted a quickening of interest and knitting of her brow when Harriet had mentioned the teashop being closed. This entire conversation was causing her some distress and only increased when her husband spoke up. "And there's a story in itself."

"Really? Do tell all." Harriet was quick to press for more.

Edmond broke in. "No reason to belabor this subject, James."

"Oh, come, Edmond. It's much too good a story to hide." He began to regale the entire table. "Actually, Edmond and I came upon this poor woman, quite by chance. She was widowed by the war and destitute, since she had worked in the shop, and from what Edmond tells me, she hoped to keep it in business, but the debts were too much for her to do so. Anyway, Edmond came up with the clever plan of employing her. It seems all she needed was to earn enough for passage home, somewhere in the west, I believe."

Sophie put down her fork and spoon and clasped her hands in her lap, staring at them. Elizabeth eyed the girl. *What is wrong with her?*

"Cornwall," Edmond interjected tersely. "Shall we retire to the drawing room, Mother?"

Edmond clenched his jaw, marking the end of the discussion. There was an angry flash in the gray eyes. He was upset at Jamie's revelations, or he never would have usurped her place as hostess to adjourn the dinner. He wasn't the only person at the table discombobulated. At James's rendition, Sophie continued somewhat stricken and confused as they retired to the drawing room.

Harriet would not let the subject go. "So, brother, you have moved another poor war widow, or should I say tenant, as you call them, into your little house?"

"I assure you, Harriet," he said evenly through gritted teeth, "my relationship with Mrs. Williams is merely a professional one. She is a female of good sense and a reasonable disposition."

At the mention of the name, Sophie went white.

When Harriet opened her mouth to continue the conversation, her mother cut her off.

"I think we have delved into Edmond's business quite enough for this evening, and I don't want to spoil our enjoyment over a lovely tart."

Elizabeth didn't know whether to laugh or cry over Edmond's

and her own inadvertent use of the words "profession" and "tart." *Oh, please stop,* she admonished herself. *He's happy with things and that's that.*

However, she made a couple of mental notes. It was Mrs. Williams, he told her, who first mentioned the hospice at St. Stephen's. Had they both gone there, or had Edmond simply taken the suggestion and gone to see for himself? And Sophie? It was obvious she was aware of something concerning the matter but not of the connection between the woman and Edmond. The only thing of relevance Elizabeth could think of was Sophie had grown up in Cornwall, near Launceston somewhere. She met James when she came to London for her coming out and the Season and had rarely gone home to visit. Perhaps Sophie was acquainted with this Mrs. Williams from her childhood there. It was all most peculiar.

The ladies withdrew for coffee as the men went to the library for brandy and cigars. Harriet was bent on continuing the subject broached at dinner, but her mother adamantly changed the subject. Sophie gave her a look of profound relief.

When the men returned, Harriet joined them at playing whist since her mother was in no mood for gossip. This left Elizabeth and Sophie by themselves.

After a bit of chat about the children, Elizabeth made what she hoped wasn't too flagrant an attempt at some information.

"I was sad to hear of the closing of the teashop Harriet mentioned, Sophie, but I must admit I'm grateful for the lovely croissants Edmond sends to me every once in a while. Did you ever order from the establishment? Rose used to fetch me things from there, although I don't recall its name."

Sophie regarded her warily and proceeded in a careful tone. "If it is the one I think it is, I believe it was called *La Boulangerie.* Occasionally, I would take Caroline in for tea. She was very fond of the *petite fours,* and a French woman who was very kind to children ran it. I was unaware it had closed, as I haven't been there since before Eugenia was born."

"Did you know anything about the woman who worked there?" Elizabeth knew she was pushing too hard but probed anyway because, Harriet, restless as usual, was about to rise from the card table, abandoning the men to play three-handed.

"I believe she employed a number of young women during the years she operated it."

"Oh, come now, Sophie." Harriet, having overheard, injected her remarks into the conversation. "The girl was always there. A mousey nondescript little thing I grant you, but the only employee I remember being there with any consistency. I don't recall her name if such creatures have names."

Real anger flashed on Sophie's usually serene face. "I'm sure I don't recall anyone in the shop of such a description."

Sophie hadn't really answered the question. In addition, the girl was a very bad liar.

Chapter Thirteen

Christmas was fast approaching. After an autumn of color, the shortened days and rain cast a gloom over the little house. For Olivia, the daylight hours now had a rhythm to them, keeping her in good spirits. She did wish for a bit more snow to make their modest street take on the festiveness of Christmas and hide for a short time the soot from London's coal fires. The black grains seeped into the crevices between the brick pavers. Each Sunday, when she walked to Westminster for services and then home from St. Stephen's House, she imagined the layers grew thicker. The flocks of sparrows, pecking about for whatever they could scavenge, didn't seem to mind. It didn't deter a stray cat or two chasing the sparrows, either.

Olivia enjoyed Sundays and the occasional afternoon out when she was not occupied with workmen. It was her time to take a brisk walk, perhaps poke about a bookshop or just enjoy the open air, although it hardly had the fresh scents of the country. After being in the city for nearly five years, it would be a joy to walk the lanes and moors of her home. Only a few more months before she had enough funds to arrange her travel home to Cornwall. Her heart lifted at the thought, but she couldn't ignore the pang of sadness at the prospect her time with her employer would soon come to an end. She had come to enjoy her time with Lord Linnington and his surprising ways.

Her days were filled with overseeing workmen as they patched and pointed around the chimneys then chipped away and repaired the damage to the walls in the house. Mr. Hackman's crews were efficient, always on time, and careful to clean up when they left. They were remarkably diligent, making them on schedule to begin the first coats of paint on the woodwork before the holidays.

She did, however, need to turn her attention to the Christmastide. Olivia was certain such a conscientious employer as hers would observe Boxing Day even for those retainers left in town. She needed to think about something to give to the Ps and a small gift of appreciation for Linnington. She found nothing, or at least nothing she could afford for any of them in walking about the few shops on her rambles. Even so, she still enjoyed wandering about Piccadilly and Jermyn Street. His lordship might live in Mayfair, but she was decidedly in different circumstances, and since she was still unsure what the final cost would be to get her all the way to Tinstone, she was saving every penny. She would need to be creative in her gifts for them.

One of the most important things Olivia had salvaged from her earlier life was a small box containing two pairs of scissors, one large and one for embroidery, her embroidery hoops, the silver thimble her mother had given her on her tenth birthday, various threads, and a paper of needles. She considered them her tools of the trade and reminded her to write two letters to Tinstone, one to The Reverend Mr. Thomas Williams, her father-in-law, and one to Mrs. Mary Hastings, who owned the millinery shop.

Tinstone was more than a village but somewhat small for a town, albeit large enough to have its own parish church. The hat shop was also a bit of an oddity. Mrs. Hastings was so talented, often gentlewomen from as far away as Launceston made the trip to her shop. At times, a few even came from Exeter to purchase bonnets. She would write to the vicar inquiring if he could secure lodgings for her to rent when she returned to Cornwall in the spring, and to Mrs.

Hastings to see to gaining employment there. Since there was no market for a teacher of French, a skilled pianist, or a passable artist in the area, her needlework skills were all she had to sell. She was sure the reputation of her family would preclude any thought of procuring a situation as governess in the town or surrounding county. Mrs. Hastings and Mr. Williams had been almost the only two people who had not outright shunned her before her departure or at least found themselves uncomfortable in her presence. She would be quite happy with a quiet life of creativity. She loved bonnets.

His lordship said, at one point, he hoped to make inquiries concerning her pension and resolve whatever the problem was. If he prevailed, she would be quite comfortable in the small town. The income would be marginal, but it should be adequate to sustain a single woman.

Olivia began by searching the armoire. She dug to the bottom of the small pile of clothing and found there the keepsakes she had preserved, her white silk wedding dress and the fine linen petticoat edged in Belgian lace. She could not bring herself to consider doing anything with the dress, but the petticoat would suffice to make lovely handkerchiefs. She carefully cut out six squares from the material, two small ones and four large ones. She also picked the lace from the hem of the garment.

In the evenings, by the fire in her room, and whenever she had time on her hands in the day, she set about hemstitching the four large squares. Then she rolled the edges of the two smaller ones and finished these by carefully edging them in the salvaged lace. She then took the smallest hoop and in satin stitch, embroidered a "P" into the corner of two of the larger squares, and the cypher EL into the other two. By the last Sunday in Advent, she was finished.

On Sunday, she went by herself to St. Stephen's House, Linnington having already departed for the country to spend the holidays with his mother. He would be gone until after the New Year. Thus, she didn't expect him personally to bring gifts to the house on Boxing Day, but she was sure things would be delivered to the Tothill Field House. She would send her small gift via Jeremy with a note of thanks.

Walking to the St. Stephen's House from Westminster, she was in an uncharacteristic depression. Her usual attitude of stoically accepting life's challenges, indeed, expecting them, had abandoned her. With a start, Olivia was suddenly aware she missed having Linnington with her. She had come to eagerly anticipate their private, although brief, conversations on the walk to the Tothill Fields house. They would remark on all sorts of things, public affairs, books, the arts, and always observing the building projects in the changing neighborhood. Idle conversation and far from intimate, but she had come to cherish the walks. During their walks, to her they were equals rather than an employee.

She admitted secretly to herself, each time he bid her goodbye at the steps, she wished he would ask leave to come in to eat a cold supper with the Ps as he had done once in the fall. Instead, he always kept a courteous distance, a gentle reminder of their different stations in life.

Olivia straightened her shoulders and resolutely concentrated on the sound of church bells marking the end of service. Their toll usually gladdened her heart and reminded her of All Saint's in Tinstone. The tolling stopped, and only the barking of dogs some streets away remained. She forced herself to put on a pleasant face as she walked up the steps to St. Stephen's House. The men had come to anticipate her visits, and she was resolved to make the Sunday attendance as pleasant as she was able. She wouldn't mar it with her miserable thoughts.

Higgins smiled his usual ebullient smile, but today, his dour friend, Banks, was also visiting.

"There's the lady," called out Higgins.

Lady no more. Pulling off her shawl, she made her way to Higgins's cot. His rather odious friend was gentleman enough to rise and offer her the chair. "Good morning, Sergeant, and to you, Mr. Banks."

Higgins reached out a hand to take hers and give it a friendly squeeze. Banks grunted something.

"Seeing you and the capt'n on Sundays makes my week."

"His lordship won't be here today, Higgins. He is with his family at his country estate for the holidays. He probably won't return to town until mid-January. You will have to make do with me, I'm afraid."

"His lordship," grumbled Banks. "Ain't he the lucky one? In Spain, he was just another damned cocky officer in a ragtag army."

"Watch yer language around the lady." Higgins turned his attention to Olivia. "And he was never cocky, just confident, and that's what we needed. We could depend on him."

"Depend on him to do the wrong thing."

Olivia broke in. "Now please, both of you, we don't have enough time to waste the afternoon in a quarrel. Have you received any mail,

Mr. Higgins?"

She spent some time perusing the letter he had received from a brother while the men gossiped. Banks took his leave, and she busied herself with taking dictation from Higgins. When she attended some of the other soldiers and she was about to leave, she returned to Higgins.

"Mr. Banks certainly has a poor opinion of Captain Linnington." She would try in the future to remember to address him this way with the men, since "his lordship" seemed to be so very off-putting to them.

"Well, you see, Mr. Banks still has a straw up his nose because the capt'n broke him in rank."

"Really? Surely with cause."

"To be sure with cause. Capt'n found him cheatin' the men at cards. Banks was a clever one with a deck."

"Oh, I see."

"Don't get me wrong. Capt'n could have cashiered him but didn't. Banks was too good a soldier. Some men are just born killers, and I think he's one, although he's harmless enough in regular society, 'cept for his tongue. Then earlier there was that last battle, at Corunna, too. It was when Sir John fell." Higgins seemed to drift off into thought. Olivia was sure he was reliving some of the nightmare of war.

"And?"

"Banks had taken his men farther ahead than the capt'n had ordered, and the capt'n really tongue-lashed him good, in front of his men. But I know it wasn't really what got the capt'n. See, he really looked up to Sir John, and Sir John, I always thought, favored the capt'n, even though he was a fair man with all his men. Anyway, the capt'n was right beside Sir John when he took the hit. He even helped carry the general up the hill out of the way of the battle where he died. Him and Banks just never got on a right foot after that. I thought it might heal some once we lost Geoff. The only thing the capt'n 'n Banks agreed on was Geoff was the finest fellow ever was."

"Geoff? I remember Lord Linnington mentioning him. He was his lordship's batman, I believe."

Higgins nodded. "And he was a lovely man, Geoff. The capt'n's batman and a favorite of us all. As sometimes happens, I think the capt'n and Geoff become close as brothers. Anyway, in the melee of the very first day of battle at Salamanca, Geoff was killed. A cannonball took his legs right off and he died in the capt'n's arms. Upset him good, it did. Wept right there on the battlefield. Not that it's so unusual. Everyone gets emotional, especially when it's over. Only time I ever seen him cry, except when Sir John was killed and he was helpin' carry the body." Higgins's head nodded. He was drifting off to sleep.

"I see, Mr. Higgins. Thank you for telling me this. It certainly explains Mr. Banks, and the captain, too, I think."

On the lonely way home, Olivia willed herself to stand up straight and walk with purpose. She wanted to slump with depression. The only thing stirring as she crossed Deans Yard to Orchard Street was a flock of chattering starlings rising in a cloud of winter birds, acting as if they were a single unit. She hated starlings but admired their behavior denoting a dedicated unity of purpose. She would try to keep her mind on her one and only purpose.

The birds reminded her also of the discipline of the army and its tight-knit cadre. She had been around soldiers for the few years she and David were married, and around their wives, in barracks and in camps. She suspected there were things rarely shared with the women, but often, word of the horrors made their way into housewives' gossip.

Yet the men never talked about them. When they talked of the battles, they talked of daring deeds and argued over which maneuver was correct and, sometimes, either praised or excoriated their senior officers, but they never spoke of the smoke, noise, confusion, and blood of real battle.

So, there was a lot behind the formal façade of Lord Linnington. The first time he walked her home from St. Stephen's House after seeing Higgins, he had opened the door on those memories just a crack. Olivia had been grateful for the little Linnington shared on their first walk, and it made her feel helpful to him, even in so very little a manner.

Hearing Higgins talk about Linnington made her wish to push the door of intimacy further open. But she feared he might want her to be as candid about herself to him. If she were, it would change their relationship, and she was unsure what she wanted to do. By the time he returned from Crossfields, she would be halfway through the project.

Best to leave things as they are.

***

Christmas passed quietly in the little house. Everyone at the townhouse had departed for holidays at Crossfields. With Jeremy gone, Olivia fetched her own hot water and put coal on the grate each

106

morning to keep Partridge from climbing the steps. It was the best she could do for the couple, since she was sure they usually accompanied the personal staff to the country for the holiday. Mrs. Person had intimated Linnington requested they remain in town so she would not be in the house alone for more than two weeks, let alone having no company for Christmas. She hoped her help and her small gifts would make up for the loss.

Linnington had a basket delivered to the house with a goose to cook and several other treats. The three of them made as much of a feast as they could. Olivia even insisted they eat in the dining rooms and she set the table with china and plate from the sideboard. She bought some holly and greens for the table, and decoration along with candles made a festive scene. They had gone to Christmas Eve services at Westminster the day before and walked to the house in a light snowfall. The snow managed to make the streets with wreathes on doors and candles in the windows festive and enchanting. At dinner, they exchanged the small gifts they had for each other. Mrs. Person had made Olivia a plain but nicely sewn apron of good pale-blue cloth so she could have something better than her faded ones to wear. The Ps were delighted with the fine linen handkerchiefs, and Mrs. P went on at length about the beautiful lace and Olivia's skill with a needle, particularly about the cypher on Mr. P's kerchief.

In the afternoon of Boxing Day, Jeremy arrived with their gifts from Linnington. Even the Ps had not expected his lordship to come in person. The three of them were glad to see the boy, and he happily ate cold goose with them. In the evening, he informed them the family would not return until a week from the coming Monday. A pang of disappointment stabbed her. There was a sudden realization, or perhaps acknowledgment to herself, she sorely missed his physical presence. He aroused something in her she believed either long satisfied or dormant. She chided herself mentally for being fanciful and silly.

She gave Jeremy the small package of handkerchiefs for him to take, along with a note of thanks for all Linnington had done for her and telling him she had left Higgins in good spirits, which wasn't exactly the truth.

"Are you retuning to the townhouse, Jeremy?"

"No'm. I'll pass the night above the mews and ride to the country tomorrow."

She was glad Linnington would have them before two weeks passed. She was proud of her embroidery and wanted him to know she appreciated what he had done for her.

Olivia took her box to her room to open. In it, she found a dozen lengths of different colored ribbon. She was touched he'd noticed she always tied up her hair with a ribbon and hers were sadly worn. In the bottom of the box, she found a guinea. His thoughtfulness and generosity made up a little for not seeing him in person. She folded the ribbons away in her drawer, put the guinea in her purse, and the box in the armoire.

With this, she declared to herself that Christmas festivities were over, regardless of the fact the season would last until Epiphany.

Chapter Fourteen

Sophie could hardly wait to return to town from the holidays. She was as fussy as her youngest child until the first Wednesday came after they arrived. Wednesdays, Jamie and Edmond reserved for themselves when they went into town for sport during the afternoon then supper and an evening at the card table. When Linnington was not in town, James attended these functions alone.

On Wednesday morning, she called her maid, Hannah. If the servants knew all the gossip about their employers, the employers knew at least some about the servants. Hannah and Jeremy spent a lot of time together whenever the two families were at either Crossfields or White Marsh Manor, the Talents' country home. She suspected they availed themselves of frequent occasions in town to see each other since the townhouses were but a few blocks apart.

"Hannah, first I must pledge you to absolute secrecy. Not a word to any of the staff or certainly to Mr. Talent."

"Yes, mum. I promise." The girl was frankly curious.

"You know who Lord Linnington's footman Jeremy is?"

"Yes, mum." She blushed furiously.

"Do you think you could contact him this morning?"

"I believe so."

"Then go and find out from him the direction of Linnington's house in Tothill Fields. Do you think you could do that?"

"Oh yes, mum," Hannah assured her with certainty.

"As soon as you know, call for the carriage for two o'clock. We shall go shopping this afternoon. Do you think you can be prepared by then?"

Hannah assured her she could.

After lunch they were soon on the way, and Sophie instructed the driver to let them off on York Street, near the shops. They would walk the rest of the way to the residence.

"Remember, Hannah, not a word of what is about to happen."

"Yes, mum."

When they arrived, Sophie rapped loudly with the doorknocker. An astonished Mr. Partridge soon opened it. "Mrs. Talent!" He stepped away so she and Hannah could pass.

Mrs. Person and Jeremy, both their mouths agape, stood in the hallway. Jeremy's expression was decidedly mixed with delight.

Olivia—occupied in the parlor holding paint swatches Mr. Taylor had prepared for her—was equally as surprised. She instantly dropped them on the couch, and she and Sophie fell into each other's arms, not without a few tears.

"How did you know I was here?"

"I have my ways." She then turned to the staff. "If Mrs. Williams and I could have some privacy for a while, I would appreciate it."

"Of course," said Partridge, "but let me take your shawl and bonnet, madam."

Sophie removed them, after which Mrs. Person announced, "And since he didn't offer, Mrs. Talent, I shall bring tea to the parlor." She gave her husband a disapproving glance, which he ignored. Both were professional enough not to show any curiosity at how Mrs. Talent and Mrs. Williams were acquainted.

Jeremy and Hannah had already headed down the stairs, to

spend the afternoon on the settle by the fireplace, holding hands. He only left her side to deliver the tea and scones to the ladies.

Olivia and Sophie sat in the chairs before the fire, and Olivia related as much as she deemed necessary of the time since Sophie was last at Mme. Dufour's.

Sophie had only known Olivia was at the teashop for about two years. After Sophie discovered where Olivia was, she would often go to Mme. Dufour's, sometimes taking Caroline and Robert for tea at the shop so they could get to know their "Aunt" Olivia. The women were quite used to seeing each other surreptitiously because, after the earl's scandal and suicide, Sophie's socially ambitious mother refused to let the girls meet. She even forbade Sophie from including Olivia in her wedding party. Conveniently, at the time of the ceremony, Olivia and David were billeted far in the north. Even correspondence was prohibited. The two women occasionally were able to make contact or see each other in person, and not at all for a year before Olivia followed David to Portugal. They reestablished relationships only when Olivia came to live with Mme. Dufour and the two women happened to meet by chance at a bookstall near the river.

"Olivia, why didn't you apply to me after Mme. Dufour's death? You know James and I would gladly have taken you in, either in town or at White Marsh. Or at least given you passage to Tinstone."

"I did write to you, Sophie, and carried the note to your townhouse but found it closed and no one answered the door. The situation could not wait for a post to Berkshire and back. I was being evicted the very next day. It was simply a stroke of incredible luck his lordship happened along to rescue me. And even more of a coincidence James chanced to be with him. I could hardly ask his lordship to contact you without disclosing all. Besides, you were still in the country with the baby."

"I've never exactly thought of Edmond as a knight in shining armor."

Olivia laughed. "He's hardly that. But I will admit I must have been born under some sort of fortunate star to have David rescue me once and then Lord Linnington at this juncture."

They turned their conversation to family gossip, Olivia eager for details about all the children, especially the newest she had not yet met. The tea and scones took their attention after Jeremy brought it up, and post tea, they fell into a discussion of paint colors and choice of fabrics.

After an hour, Sophie said, "So, do you want to reveal all to Edmond, or do you want me to do it?"

Olivia was quite adamant. "Neither. I really want to keep things as they are. To him, I am Mrs. Williams and he is my employer. Let's leave it there."

Sophie was skeptical. She could tell Olivia was still living under the cloud of her father's scandal and surmised she was concerned Edmond's good opinion of her might suffer. "Well, I suppose we can swear the staff to secrecy. I'm not at all sure how long such an arrangement will last. No problem with Jeremy so long as he can anticipate Hannah and I may call on a regular basis. He would never jeopardize the opportunity. Partridge has always been the soul of discretion, particularly caring for this household during the last year, but I wonder about Person?"

"Sophie," Olivia whispered, "tell me about the creature who lived here? It seems so unlike his lordship."

"Indeed, it was. Edmond spent a short time on Wellington's staff before the news of Giles's death reached him. During the period he was there, he often served as liaison between the Spanish forces as well as interrogating French officers when they were captured, because he spoke both languages. It seems one of the Spanish officers was married to this woman. He was unfortunately killed soon after Edmond arrived at the headquarters. Edmond had known the Spaniard for some time, having been used as a liaison while with his regiment also. Having known her husband, Linnington was kind to her and spoke her language and she quite attached herself to him. I blush to say I believe he was probably more than simply kind to her at the time, but I don't think he gave it another thought after he left Spain until she turned up. She became one more thing he had to deal with in the wake of Giles's death. On her own, this woman, Mrs. Fernandez, followed him to England some six months after his return. She was insistent his attentions to her in Spain portended a more permanent alliance. I think Edmond was distracted by his duties, somewhat lonely in London society and homesick for the army, which made him vulnerable to her charms. She was quite a beauty. And, it turned out, a termagant. I assume she is the one who slashed the furniture? Anyway, her bad temper and tantrums, some in public, soon wore thin with Edmond, who, as you know, leans toward the fastidious. When he gave her walking papers, she left making it known to whomever would listen he was a person of very low character. Not many paid her much attention, and I assume she left for Spain or found another victim to leech onto. All this was shortly before he chanced to meet you."

"Thank you, Sophie. I have been curious about the details." The two of them went to the hall where Olivia called the staff. She let Sophie take over things when they had all assembled.

"I must ask each and every one of you to keep this meeting secret. We do not want either Mr. Talent or his lordship to be aware of it. In explanation, Mrs. Williams and I have known each other since we were children. Circumstances intervened where we lost touch for a few years but reestablished our friendship, under very different circumstances, a couple of years ago. I rely on your discretion, but I also ask you swear to abide by our wishes. Are you agreed?"

Each of them mumbled their assent in different ways.

"You can expect I shall visit as often as I can during the months Mrs. Williams is here. Hannah will accompany me, and it will always be Wednesday, since the gentlemen are occupied at sport and cards each Wednesday."

Mild mannered, Sophie could assert herself with the best of chatelaines. Her tone brooked no discussion and no deviation from what she required after they had agreed to their terms.

The women exchanged a farewell kiss on the cheek, and Sophie and Hannah departed.

Chapter Fifteen

A few days after the Woolley's returned to London, Harriet sought out her bosom friend, Miss Sybil Trent. The two were inseparable but certainly a contrast in appearance. Harriet, just younger than her brothers and quite the spoiled baby of the family, had taken on a matronly plumpness after the birth seven years before of her son, Simon. Elizabeth thought the weight might have to do with eating more than was good for her daughter, a habit of the rest of the Woolley family, since Malcolm and Simon could kindly be referred to as portly. Miss Trent, on the other hand, was tall and willowy.

For the past year, the two ladies conspired to have Miss Trent catch the eye of Harriet's brother. They had only modest success in this endeavor and chalked part of it up to Edmond's well-known alliance with Mrs. Fernandez. The news of the acrimonious departure of the Spanish woman was common gossip in London. Her leaving England raised the hopes of the two plotting to snare Edmond.

They met for tea at a fashionable shop.

Harriet arrived first and chose a table by the window where she could anxiously watch for Miss Trent. When Sybil came in, Harriet greeted her with the sort of enthusiasm years of separation would imply rather than simply being apart over the holidays. They then went through the obligatory flurry of compliments about what good taste each showed in the gowns they were wearing. After a liveried waiter brought tea and a tiered tray of cucumber and chicken sandwiches, along with lemon cake and tarts, Harriet got down to business.

"Sybil. I have some news I think is not good, although Mama disagrees with my assessment." She paused dramatically.

"Please, tell all," Sybil urged.

Harriet reached for the first of several sandwiches. "You recall the teashop and bakery we used to frequent? The one owned by that Frenchwoman?"

"Indeed. I dearly miss it. If the atmosphere was less elegant than this, the pastry was decidedly superior," complained Sybil Trent, with a petulant moue on her face any close acquaintance would instantly recognize as habitual. She poked a fork at her pastry with disgust. Miss Trent skipped the savories and went directly to the sweets.

"Well, James Talent let slip at dinner one night at Crossfields, Edmond has hired the shopgirl from there to oversee the renovation of his love nest. I can hardly credit it!"

"What in the world would a shopgirl know about décor?"

"Exactly. Do you remember her at all?"

"I'm sure I never paid attention. I do seem to remember a nondescript little thing with brown hair, I believe."

"I, too. Nothing to be of interest to a gentleman." She plucked another cucumber sandwich from the tray.

"So, what has this to do with Edmond?"

"I have been thinking. Mama tends to disagree with me when I brought up the subject the next day, but I believe she is a replacement for the infamous Spanish woman."

"You mean...?"

"I do."

"Oh, surely Edmond has better taste than a shopgirl if he was going to replace a mistress."

"Who knows? He certainly ended up with Carmelita."

Sybil started to say something then stopped.

"What is it, Sybil?"

"You know how anxious I am to attach your brother's interest. This is the second year I have put off other suitors just to try for the chance."

"You can't be having second thoughts." Harriet decimated the sandwich tier.

"I believe I am. I know men often have their bit of petticoat on the side, but is he going to keep mistresses all the time?"

"Now, my dear, don't let such a thing bother you in the least. As a married woman, let me tell you, a mistress on the side takes a bit of burden off a wife. I know you understand what I'm saying."

"I do, and I appreciate it. I suppose a mistress might be a good thing, and perhaps I wouldn't mind. It's simply right now, when I am trying as best I can to have his attention, I would just as soon he not be otherwise engaged."

"So, what is the solution?" Harriet gazed out the window, pondering. "Of course, we could begin a rumor casting doubt upon the woman."

"What can you say about a shopgirl that would be credited? The rumor of such a woman would hardly bear repeating? Besides, she is a widow, so nothing in that vein would be of interest to anyone, given what you believe to be Edmond's interest in her."

"He says she speaks French like a native. We could put it about she is suspected of being a spy." Harriet attacked the sweets.

"But Boney is safe on Elba, and people are tired of the war anyway even though we still have troops on the Continent."

"There I think you are wrong. People still loathe the French, and there is talk Bonaparte is not secure on Elba. Fear of him makes some people a bit irrational in their discernment."

"Still, who would believe an English shopgirl had the wit to be a spy?"

"You remember Mme. Dufour? She was decidedly French and evidently rather well educated, in spite of being reduced to running a little bakery. And by the by, you are right about the pastry in this place." The remark didn't deter her from finishing off the last tart.

"So, what does a dead Frenchwoman have to do with this?"

"What if we also put about the woman is not dead, but instead, arrested on suspicion of treason. All very hush-hush of course. After all, the shop was certainly closed down by the authorities, or at least someone in authority."

"But wouldn't such a tale cast doubt on Edmond? Surely, we wouldn't want any hint he might be in the least involved."

"The addition of his own story of a very chance meeting should accompany the charge, with the suggestion he had no idea what the woman was up to and thinks he has simply hired her to oversee the renovation, while on her part, she was seeking cover for her activities, and catching the interest of a man above suspicion was a convenient boon for her. The people we would begin the rumors with should not be close enough to Edmond to alert him about this. I'm sure he would scoff at such an idea and scotch the rumor immediately, but properly planted, it can grow in secret and then, given the pace of rumors in town, blossom, we hope, just in time for him to be sure she quits

London as is her announced plan." Harriet finished the last sweet and took a sip of tea.

"Perhaps it might work. I would dearly love to have all his attention. Even so, you know Edmond doesn't care much what is said in polite society."

"So he maintains, but I believe the scandal of Mrs. Fernandez was much more embarrassing than he would let on. After hearing anew rumors about himself, he may not be eager for even the breath of a repeat."

"I suppose it is worth a try."

"Good. I'm glad you approve, Sybil. We shall plant the rumor where I know it will be only a few weeks until it is known not only by Lady Whitworth and her circle but the entire Ton. You can pretend to be shocked, but sadly acknowledge you understand there is some truth to it. Society will suspect this might be a cause for his failure to come up to the mark with you. The more speculation the more likely to cause a ruckus Edmond would be loath to have."

The women wiped their mouths delicately with tea napkins, pulled on their gloves, and ended their cozy session in complete agreement.

Chapter Sixteen

Linnington was feeling decidedly unwell. He had been suffering from a slight cold, and recently, it had worsened. Now, he was developing a deep cough. He was anxious to return to town and not be caught in the country if he was to be down with ague for a few days. His mother planned to return on Tuesday, but on Sunday, deciding to skip services, he had Maximilian saddled. He was eager to be on his way. With the townhouse staff still in the country, he intended to stay at his club. He asked Owens to pack a light bag for him and charged him to follow on Monday with whatever equipage he deemed necessary.

He went to bid his mother goodbye.

"You can't intend to ride into London today?" she admonished. "It will probably rain, and you are not well."

"I shall be fine," he insisted, "and I'll be safe at Whites before dark if I leave now. That way I also hope to miss the rain. Forgive me for skipping church and luncheon." He left with her protests ringing in his ears.

Crossfields, barely into Oxfordshire, was more than half a day's ride from the outskirts of London. Late in the afternoon as he approached the town, he encountered fog. It became denser the closer he got to town, and the heavy smell of acrid coal smoke burned his lungs. He was sure he was running a fever and his bones had begun to ache. Instead of going directly to the club, he went instead to Tothill Fields.

He would catch a hackney from there, but, in the all-enveloping fog, it had grown harder and harder to see ahead. He also wanted to make sure Mrs. Williams found her way home safely from St. Stephen's House, if, indeed, she had even gone on such an inclement day. He left his tired horse at the mews and walked the short way to the house with a small valise.

He let himself in the kitchen door. Mrs. Person was gathering the evening meal, and Partridge sat at the table with *The Sunday Times*, his treat each Sunday after services.

Without preamble, he inquired, "Partridge, did Mrs. Williams return after services or go to St. Stephen's House?"

"I believe she must have gone to the House, my lord. We are expecting her any moment."

"I hope she has not lost her way in this terribly thick fog. I'm going to see if I can find her between here and there."

Without another word, he set his valise in the hall and went out the front, starting toward St. Stephen's House. Perhaps it was his training as a soldier, but Linnington had the habit of counting his steps when he walked. He had made his way between the two destinations so often he had memorized the number of paces. When he reached the corner, he was careful not to trip at the curb. He was thankful for the newly installed gas streetlights. It was a help to have at least a faint glow even though the lamps resembled the moon attempting to be seen behind a veil of leaden clouds. He could not see his gloved hand a yard in front of him, and the heavy atmosphere was making it hard to get his breath. Occasionally, he would call out, "Mrs. Williams!" He passed a man going the other way and realized he had not even made out the shape of the fellow until they were almost abreast. He called again.

"My lord?" a voice rang out in the distance.

"Mrs. Williams, is that you?"

"Yes, sir. I am so glad to hear your voice. I was afraid I had lost my way."

"Stay where you are and keep speaking to me." Relief and urgency filled his words.

In a few minutes, he was close enough to see a dark shape, and he reached out, found her hand, and tucked it into his arm. "Let me guide you."

He carefully pivoted 180 degrees so he could begin the count toward the house. At the curb of the last street, she stumbled. Not satisfied with her hand, he put his arm around her waist to guide her the last three-quarters of a block. Nearly there, he had to stop, overtaken with a spasm of coughing. His lungs were blazing; the aching in his limbs was more intense. He was sure now of the fever.

Linnington finally caught his breath. "Forgive me. I seem to have a rather bad cold."

"You sound quite unwell, sir. You should be abed."

He didn't answer, only put his arm around her and started for the house.

They proceeded, but by the time they reached it, he was certain he was too unwell to make it to Whites, even if he could find a hackney and make it through the fog.

Olivia took her key from her pocket, and instead of him helping her, she held his arm until they were both in the hall and she could close the door.

Partridge was waiting there and immediately took Linnington's coat.

A wave of fatigue overwhelmed him, and he sat on the stairway. "Partridge, I'm decidedly unwell, and not sure I could make it in this weather to the club, even if I were in health. I shall spend the night here in the dressing room and stay the morning. By tomorrow afternoon, both Jeremy and Owens should have returned. Send for them when they arrive from the country, if you will."

"Very good, sir. You go on up, and I will bring your valise."

He pulled himself up by the balusters and mounted the stairs. Olivia followed closely as he swayed a bit from dizziness. He went directly to the dressing room door.

"Oh, my lord, I'm so sorry you found it necessary to come after me. You should be home."

He turned around and gave her a small smile. "I couldn't have you lost in the fog. My house would never have been completed for me to sell, I'm afraid."

"Is there anything I can get you? Some supper? Tea perhaps?"

"No, thank you. Nothing. I'm going straight to bed."

He closed the door.

***

Sometime before dawn, a shout awakened Olivia.

"To your left, men!"

Something hit the wall behind her head.

"No, Ferguson, no!"

Incomprehensible babbling followed. She arose hurriedly, pulled on her dressing gown, and stopped just long enough to light the candle on the stand next to the bed. She opened the adjoining door to see Linnington, bolt upright on his cot, waving his arms.

"Your flank, men, your flank."

He was delirious. "My lord! My lord!" She reached to shake his shoulder when, instead, he grasped her arms, pulling her down to sit facing him.

"Geoff? Is that you, Geoff?" An agonized expression passed over his face. "Geoff. For God's sake, man, speak to me. Speak to me. I can't stop the bleeding. Don't bleed out, Geoff. I can't stop it." He caught his breath then suddenly buried his head on her breast.

All Olivia could think to do was put her arms around him and croon to him, as if he were a child. He wept bitterly, but she was aware his forehead was hot and dry. She also became aware the Ps were standing at the door and she assumed had witnessed all this. Any awkwardness was lost when Linnington burst into a paroxysm of coughing. Olivia gently pulled away his hands and stood up.

"Mr. Partridge, would you happen to have any brandy on the premises?"

"Wouldn't he just," remarked Mrs. P with asperity.

"I do, Mrs. Williams, I'll get it." He turned to go up to their quarters.

"And I'll fetch honey from the kitchen."

"Let me get it, Mrs. Person. You stay and watch his lordship."

Olivia hurried down the two flights and returned with the honey pot and a spoon. By the time Partridge returned, holding the bottle of brandy, Olivia found a glass on the washstand and Mrs. Person busied herself mixing the honey and brandy. By now, Linnington was quite feverish and not seeming to comprehend much. The coughing silenced his ramblings and he lay weakly upon the bed.

Mrs. P held the glass to his lips. "Here, my lord. Take this." There was the sort of command in her voice Olivia imagined she used in ordering the cooks and maids in Crossfields' kitchens.

She had to smile when the gentleman meekly obeyed the order. Mrs. P got enough of the medicine down him, a drowsiness replaced the former agitation.

Mrs. P put the brandy, honey, and glass on the small table and pulled it within reach of the bed. "Someone should stay with him, I think."

"I agree. I'll sit with him until after breakfast and then we can take turns through the day and, Mr. Partridge, if you could stand watch in the evenings while I help Mrs. Person with supper, and I'll sit with him at night, if the plan meets with your approval." She made the remark more as a statement than a question.

After the old couple had gone up to bed, she poured what was left of the water in the ewer in her room, into the basin in the dressing room. She dampened a cloth and bathed Linnington's face. He was burning hot. She pulled the nightshirt away from his neck and bathed his shoulders and the part of his chest she could reach comfortably. Then she covered him up, putting a cooling cloth on his face. His rest was fitful, but neither did he wake or seem to slip once more into delirium.

At full light, Mr. P brought Olivia tea and toast on a tray and she took a moment to dress. Then she sat at the table with the novel Sophie had brought her to read until the Ps were through with their breakfast and could relieve her watch.

No one reported much change until late in the afternoon, but shortly before Olivia was to release her post in order to help Mrs. Person, Linnington stirred. He opened his eyes and frowned at her from across the room.

"Mrs. Williams?"

"Yes, my lord. You've been quite unwell. How are you this afternoon?"

"Not evening? How long have I been here?

"You arrived yesterday, just about this time."

"My head is splitting, and I seem to have the ague."

"I'm sure you do. Could you eat something?" She marked her place in the book and setting it aside, got up to take the glass from the little table and fill it from a pitcher of fresh water Mr. Partridge brought earlier to the room. "Here. You need to drink." She held the glass while he guided it to his lips with a trembling hand.

"I believe I am weak indeed, but I'm not hungry."

Thus began two days of battle between the women of the house and the landlord to try to get him to eat. Mrs. P made hearty broth from bones, cooked soft eggs and custard, and both ladies wheedled him into eating but he partook only a little. By the end of the third day, he was marginally stronger, but the fever had not broken, and Olivia was more and more concerned about his labored breath. In addition, on Monday there had been a heavy snow, and the family household was delayed at Crossfields, so without Jeremy, the work all fell to Mr. Partridge and to the women when he would allow them to help.

Finally, sometime after midnight on the fourth day, Olivia got up to check the patient who was restless and pushing at the covers. She discovered he was soaked with sweat.

"Thank you, God." With the prayer, she made a promise to put an extra sixpence in the collection the next Sunday. She had been praying for him more than she would admit to herself or anyone else.

She sat on the edge of the narrow bed and carefully bathed his face as she had done so many times during the week. She found she had to brush tears from her face. Watching him flounder and struggle to breathe had taken a toll on her emotions.

By midmorning, he was considerably better and had tea and toast. At noon, he pronounced himself hungry and got Partridge to help him into a dressing gown, propping him up on extra pillows. By evening, Linnington was dining heartily on the cold chicken, and salads and breads Mrs. P had carefully made and Olivia had brought from the kitchen.

"No workmen today, Mrs. Williams?"

"Things are nearly completed, except for the color in the parlor and dining room, sir. And I requested Mr. Hackman not to send the men so long as you were here. I hardly thought paint fumes the thing for ailing lungs. Besides, there has been a heavy snowfall while you were ill."

"At least it settled the fog."

"I believe Jeremy was expected the day before yesterday and we have not seen him. I'm sure he was delayed in returning from the country."

"So, without workmen, how have you spent your time, Mrs. Williams?"

"I believe I've been running a hospital, sir." She could have cut out her tongue for being so pert.

He laughed. "So you have."

The following morning, Jeremy appeared at the door. The household staff had returned, and Lady Elizabeth was expected the next day. Jeremy was under the impression Linnington must be at his club, as was his intention. When he was told of the illness, Partridge assured Jeremy the patient was definitely on the mend.

Linnington could have had Jeremy fetch Owens, but he didn't feel up to it. However, he believed he was well enough to ask Partridge to help him with his toilette, although deciding against shaving himself or asking Partridge to do it. He told Partridge the simple wash and change of nightshirt made him feel half human. Dressed in the dressing gown and slippers, he sat in the chair while Mrs. Person changed the linen on the bed, then he gratefully returned to it. He found he was still trembling at the exertion. Within moments, he was fast asleep.

Olivia took a lunch tray upstairs and, with it, a current copy of *The Times* Jeremy had brought from the house for Partridge to read, thinking Linnington would read the one at his club.

"Lunch is served, sir." She placed the tray on the table for a moment, taking the medications off the little table by the bed, pulling it close enough for him to reach the dishes when she set the breakfast tray on it. "And the newspaper if you would care to read it."

"Sit down, Mrs. Williams, and read it to me as I enjoy Mrs. Person's soup."

Olivia sat at the table, reading bits and pieces of the day's news, reading the entire article aloud when it was something catching his interest.

"I hope this isn't boring you, Mrs. Williams." He put the last plate on the tray.

"Not at all, sir. I enjoy reading the news every day, and Mr. Partridge is kind enough to give me the paper after he has finished.

"Indeed?" It seemed she read more than just the society items.

"Here is something we are both interested in." She read a rather lengthy article about a proposed bill to help veterans, especially those who had returned from the war with some incapacity. "If I may venture an opinion, sir, it seems to me this bill now before Parliament is remarkably more helpful than any proposed so far." She looked up in surprise when he gave a short laugh.

"I believe, Mrs. Williams, you are the only female I have ever known who was interested in the workings of Parliament, let alone formed an opinion concerning its affairs."

"Mr. Partridge is always most informative on these subjects." She sounded a little defensive and consciously amended her voice. "And I have my own prejudices. I find I always pay attention to matters supported by a certain Mr. Robert Peel."

"You underscore my point, madam. And just what about Peel attracts you?"

"From my limited observance, he simply seems like a very forward-looking man. So many Members seem only to talk endlessly about this and that, repeating the same rather worn points all the time. Do you agree?"

"I do, but only marginally. Peel has moments of brilliant ideas. However, I am usually inclined to the Whig cause." Curious about her opinions on other subjects, he asked, "Is there any news from France?"

"No, but there is the rare mention of hostilities in America. It is as though we English had forgotten it was going on."

"It has not been our finest hours, I believe. Especially the drubbing they gave us at the Battle of Put-In-Bay last September."

"I thought we might emulate the victorious French, including the natives on our side this time, but I suppose it was the death of their chief that contributed to the entire thing falling apart."

"I think you have the right of the situation. I believe the chieftain fell in that battle. What was his name?"

"Tecumseh, I believe."

"Ah, yes."

Not only opinions but also decidedly informed ones. Mrs. Williams has many hidden facets. What else could he uncover? As the newspaper obscured her face, he had ample time to admire her slender ankles and shapely hands.

Chapter Seventeen

Elizabeth arrived in London in the evening, too late to do anything but go to bed, but when she learned of Edmond's illness, she determined to go the next morning to check on his health, although she was assured by the staff who reported him very much on the mend and expected in the townhouse within the next day or two.

By nine thirty, she called for the brougham and was on her way to the notorious house she had heard of but, of course, never visited. It was an old house, but in a part of the city rapidly developing with new, attractive dwellings, not quite so affluent as Mayfair. Alighting, she rapped on the door, which was opened by the ever-attentive Partridge.

"My lady," was all he could manage to say, stepping aside for her to enter the hall. "May I take your cloak?"

As she took off the garment, she grew aware of voices coming from upstairs, certainly Linnington's and another one, light and rather musical. Elizabeth noticed the parlor to the right. The furniture all had swatches of material on them and other bits of fabric were piled on a table between two chairs. Each of the pieces had one sample draped across it save for a small desk between the front windows. The desk had neat stacks of papers, and some folded carefully in the pigeonholes behind an open tambour. There were patches of yellow paint on the far wall.

When she climbed the stairs, she could see into an empty bedroom.

The voices came from a small room farther down the hall.

Making her way, she couldn't help but overhear the conversation.

"Are you quite sure, my lord, the veteran's bill will not be put forward this session?"

"Eventually it will be, but I'm afraid not any time soon."

Good God, they are discussing public affairs!

"How disappointing. Especially since it seems to have such popular support."

"You have to remember how much pressure the party…"

He broke off, after the very attractive young woman, sitting at the table with *The Times* open in her hand, happened to glance at the door and see Elizabeth entering. She jumped up and made a very practiced curtsy to Elizabeth, not the bobbing she was used to with most servants.

The plain dress and stiff apron could not completely hide a most pleasing figure.

Edmond glanced over his shoulder. "Mother?" Then he added, "Mother, may I present Mrs. Williams. Mrs. Williams, my mother, Lady Linnington."

"Mrs. Williams." Elizabeth nodded.

"My lady," Olivia acknowledged, with another curtsy. "Please sit down." She pulled the chair she had been sitting in near the bed then quickly gathered up the newspaper and a breakfast tray from the table. "I'll ask Mrs. Person to bring tea."

Elizabeth noticed the tray contained along with the teapot, two cups, and two plates. Edmond had not breakfasted alone.

When the girl left, Elizabeth said, "Well, Edmond, you are quite wan and I must note, sadly in need of a razor but otherwise seem in good spirits."

"I am."

"Don't get too comfortable. Harriet is expecting you at supper on Saturday. I believe she has also invited Miss Trent."

He frowned. "Quite seriously, I'm not sure I will feel up to it. But I will return home, probably tomorrow."

Elizabeth abandoned the subject and they chatted a while, some about family business and some about their mutual friends, and then she turned to public affairs.

"I couldn't help but overhear your conversation with Mrs. Williams. What is this about a veteran's bill?"

He quickly explained the politics. "Mrs. Williams is particularly interested in the veteran's plight. She is the widow whose husband fell at Corunna. I think I may have mentioned it before, but she also has helped some of the men at St. Stephen's House with affairs concerning their pensions. She herself has had difficulty with the government concerning her own pension, so it is a subject dear to her heart."

"I see. So she also attends the men at St. Stephen's?"

"Quite. That's how I heard about it."

"Your project here seems to be well toward completion. What will Mrs. Williams do then?"

"She plans to return to her childhood home somewhere out in the West Country. In Cornwall, I believe. She anticipates being there by April, if not sooner." He said this last with a distinct note of resignation.

Elizabeth did not pursue the matter, but it was clear he had been spending part of nearly each Sunday with the young woman. No wonder they were so easy in each other's company. She also noticed his sad demeanor at the thought of Mrs. Williams leaving. If the setting had been anywhere but Edmond's dressing room in this modest house, she would have drawn an immediate conclusion. Say if all the previous communication between these two played out in the upstairs drawing room at Crossfields, she would be anticipating an engagement. She simply could draw no other conclusion than the girl had not only engaged his affection but also helped dispel his melancholy.

Instead of Mrs. Person, Olivia returned with the tea tray, replete with a plate of Mrs. P's excellent scones. She put the tray on the table, picked up the pot. "How do you take your tea, my lady?"

"Only sugar, please, Mrs. Williams." The girl had arresting blue eyes.

Elizabeth noticed the practiced serving of the beverage by Olivia as well as the well-trained silent attention to the task. In addition, the young woman didn't ask Edmond about his preference but simply poured the tea with milk and extra sugar as he liked. She gave another curtsy and backed out of the room.

Elizabeth knew her son well enough to be aware she had pressed the subject of Mrs. Williams as far as she should. The rest of the time they spent in general conversation. After forty minutes or so, long enough for a sickbed visit, she gathered her gloves to leave.

She kissed her son. "I look forward to cosseting you at home soon and shall make your regrets to Harriet."

She took a moment to pause in the hall. The bedroom door was open. The walls had been freshly painted in a lovely shade of blue, but some rather ugly green draperies hung at the window. Beneath one was a pile of matching material she took to be bed hangings that had been removed, since the tester was bare. On the table lay a rather nicely bound edition of the novel, *Sense and Sensibility*. Elizabeth touched the fine leather cover of the book thoughtfully.

This personage was hardly the mousey scullery Harriet described. She idly opened the cover of the book. To her amazement, the flyleaf was neatly inscribed "Ex Libris Sophie Talent."

Shocked but perhaps not surprised, Elizabeth replaced the cover. There was no use applying to Sophie. She clearly would say nothing on the matter. *Oh God! I may be forced to have Eleanor Whitworth to tea. Privately.* The thought repelled her and she decided to put off any such inquiry until later. Perhaps something would arise in conversation with either Edmond or Sophie. She rather doubted it.

Partridge stood waiting at the door, ready with her cloak. The carriage was outside, but she turned to the parlor where Olivia was standing, a cutting of fabric in each hand.

"Mrs. Williams?"

"Oh. Yes, my lady." Surprised, Olivia turned to face her. "May I help you?"

"I would like to tell you I took the liberty of looking into the bedroom. I quite like the color of blue. What do you have planned to finish the room, if I am not intruding?"

"No, indeed. In fact, I would value your advice. As for the bedroom, I plan simple white linen at the windows and for the bed hangings. But this room is putting me in a quandary, and I should very much appreciate your opinion."

"Certainly." Elizabeth advanced into the room. "I gather you are going to paint it one of those yellows."

"I am, and I believe I prefer the more lemon one on the left. The one in the center is entirely too pale and there seems a hint of green in the last one."

"I quite agree."

"Thank you, my lady. I am grateful for the confirmation of what I must admit was my own taste. But it's the draperies I am undecided about."

"Are those the fabrics?"

"They are."

Elizabeth took each of them into her own hands to feel the quality. One was lovely chintz with a Chinese motif of lattice, birds, and flowers. The other was a rather plain yellow-and-white stripe. "I much prefer the print."

"As do I, but it is quite expensive. I know his lordship has told me countless times I should not be dissuaded in any of my choices at the cost because he expects to recoup whatever he spends now on the sale of the property, but the print is really quite dear. I thought perhaps a compromise would be to do swags of the print and use the plainer fabric for the draperies. There are actually four windows to dress since there are the two additional in the dining room and it will be in the same colors and décor. Do you think it a sensible solution?"

"I think it sensible, but not what I would prefer. May I make a suggestion?"

"Oh, please do. I would welcome it."

"I would use the print for both. It is a small room, and I believe if I am not mistaken, you have chosen the light-green and cream stripe for the camelback sofa and a darker green for the backs of the wing chairs with the green, white, and yellow bargello for the front?"

"I have."

"Then I do not think another pattern is advisable regardless of the cost."

"I quite agree. I suppose another alternative is to use the less expensive striped fabric for both swags and draperies, but that begs a change for the sofa and I quite like the bolder striped material for it."

"If it is just cost, perhaps I can help you out of your dilemma."

"Oh?"

"A few years ago, I redecorated a bedroom in the townhouse. The original fabric was a bit old-fashioned, but I believe the things you have chosen here would complement the draperies well as they are a bit conservative. In my opinion, it would all fit very well together. If I am not mistaken, the draperies I replaced are still at the house and I would be glad to ask my housekeeper to find them. I believe there are eight sets of draperies, which would give you fabric for bed hangings. Then you need not spend more on the bedroom. Would that help?"

Olivia gave a delighted and musical laugh. "It would indeed, and I thank you for it."

"Excellent. I shall send them by Jeremy. It is a pleasure, Mrs. Williams, to have made your acquaintance. I see Edmond chose wisely in assigning you this task."

"Thank you, my lady. I am happy to have your confidence."

"Although, I must admit, I don't know how he allowed the pottery dogs on the mantle. He quite loathes the things."

Olivia laughed. "In actuality, he bought them."

"What occasioned such a purchase?" Elizabeth was intrigued.

Olivia averted her gaze in a way seeming to say she had revealed more than she meant to but continued casually.

"One day, soon after I began the project, Lord Linnington insisted I needed a desk to work from. He wanted to have a hand in the choosing, so we made a trip to the shops in Stepney to purchase my desk and some chairs for the dining room, since the original ones were quite unsightly and too large. On the way, we passed a shop with a number of pairs of dogs. After some discussion, he bought the pair we both deemed the ugliest and as a joke, I am sure."

Elizabeth smiled and took her leave. In the carriage, she reviewed the remarkable visit. This was a fascinating young lady. From things he told her, she now knew Olivia spoke French well, had excellent taste from her choices of décor, and was well spoken with a cultured inflection as well as being both attractive and intelligent enough to have caught Edmond's fancy—although Elizabeth doubted he was aware of the depth of the attraction. She, of course, had no idea of Olivia's feelings in the matter. All this had the makings of a drama, and she wasn't sure if it was tragedy or comedy. There was nothing for it. She would have to find out more about this young woman, and she suspected Sophie was well aware of the details but would not reveal them. That left Lady Whitworth.

***

After her visit with Lady Linnington, Olivia busied herself with the daily tasks, saw to it Linnington was fed, and finally retired. She tried to read her book but couldn't concentrate. She wasn't sure what she expected of Linnington's mother or even if she had thought of the lady at all, except as some vague person in his life. She did not believe Elizabeth had ever accompanied Harriet to the teashop. Surely, she would remember such an elegant customer. Olivia was not surprised at her kindness. Her son's attitude of fairness toward the servants was learned somewhere, and a mother would be a good source of such an attitude. It was Elizabeth's taking the time to seek her out that intrigued her. The effort was not at all necessary nor was the offer of help for the decorating. She could almost fancy perhaps Lady Linnington took the time in order to become better acquainted with herself. Was she perhaps suspicious her relationship with Linnington was more than one of employer? If so, Olivia hoped the offer of the drapes was a signal she was reassured on that score. Their relationship was professional and bound to stay unchanged.

She set aside the book, blew out her candle, and settled into bed. Wide awake and restless, she was acutely aware of the man sleeping just beyond the wall at the head of her bed. Lying still, she could hear his even breathing. Thankfully, it was easy and had lost all signs of the catarrh.

Finally, she allowed the thoughts she had been busily pushing away from the day they met assail her. She pulled one of her pillows into her arms and hugged it. But she didn't want the soft bolster. She wanted to go into the room next door and take the man into her arms. Yet, could such a thing ever happen? Her past made the desire impossible. She finally fell asleep, still hugging the pillow to herself.

***

In the small hours of the morning, Linnington dreamed an angel with long brown curls about her shoulders had come into the room, bent over, and whispered something to him. He awoke with the bed wet with more than sweat.

He hoped he hadn't moaned in his sleep. He lay very quietly and listened. The only faint sound from the bedroom next door was soft breathing and the possible brief rustle of sheets. *It's time I get out of here.*

As soon as there was the sound of Jeremy bringing the morning's hot water, he called and told the boy to go to the house and fetch Owens with fresh clothing for him and to bring up a tub for bathing when he returned. In short order, Owens mounted the steps closely followed by Jeremy and the bathing tub. Even with Owens's help, it took some time to divest him of whiskers and the sweaty odors of illness.

In the meantime, Jeremy brought a large package from the townhouse, putting it on the kitchen table.

Olivia and Mrs. Person immediately opened the parcel. Inside were eight generous draperies in a lovely blue-and-white resist print on very nice linen and, in addition, a candlewick bed cover. Delighted, the women went directly upstairs to the bedroom to dispose of the hated green stuff and replace it with hangings imprinted with a lovely design in shades of blue, complementing instead of fighting with the wall of the room.

Between them, they determined the window draperies, although somewhat long, could be used as they were. The bed was another matter, but one easily solved with a hammer and some tacks.

When Linnington was ready to leave, he stepped next door to see what the hammering was about. Olivia was standing in stocking feet on the bed, hammer in hand, as Mrs. P held the cloth in the right position.

"Mrs. Williams, is there nothing you cannot do?"

Thoroughly amused, he went down to the brougham Owens had

A Reasonable Lady

waiting.

Chapter Eighteen

Harriet Woolley sat before her dressing table mirror and scowled. Ignoring the ugly face it produced, she tweaked a side curl and called her maid in a querulous voice, "Heather, come here! Fix this. It makes me look like a spaniel."

The maid dutifully fetched a curling iron and restyled the curl. In reality, it did not alter the impression but Harriet was mollified.

Her breakfast tray with its dirty dishes was on the side table. She waved a hand. "Take that away, Heather."

She was in a hurry to get the day started, but she wasn't meeting Sybil Trent for another two hours, just in time go to the home of Lady Eleanor Whitworth for a private morning call. Until then, she supposed she could read a book. The new novel by whoever wrote *Sense and Sensibility* was in print and all the rage among her friends.

She spent the next forty-five minutes with her copy of the book. It failed to catch her interest. The author seemed to be making fun of polite society. The subject was no laughing matter. The anonymous author must be a man behind this piece of trash. Women were keenly aware without the traditions holding society together anarchy would surely follow. Maintaining the orderliness of things was important to Harriet.

For instance, Edmond must stop his dithering and settle down to produce an heir born by a woman of some station. She considered Sybil a perfect candidate.

Harriet had nothing but the greatest care for her own station in life. It was fortunate she'd found Malcolm. He was most compliant and didn't bother her hardly at all since Simon's birth. The situation represented to her the way things must be arranged to carry on British traditions. It was nothing to make fun of.

The hour arrived when she could summon the brougham, collect Sybil, and proceed to Lady Whitworth's. This call was important.

When the ladies arrived at the appointed hour, they were ushered into an opulent townhouse. A great curving stair rose to the second floor, a magnificent Palladian window above the landing halfway up. From there, they were conducted to a bright sitting room as overdone as the hostess with myriad chintzes, all flowers and stripes and colors.

The table had been adorned with several tiers of delicious-appearing food and the distinctive odor of tea laced with bergamot was evidently coming from a very large Royal Worchester pot. Harriet's mouth watered. This was almost worth the trip in itself.

The portly lady in a dress of many flounces rose to greet them. Greetings were made, tea was poured, sandwiches passed, and napkins placed securely over gowns. Lady Eleanor invited them to refresh their plates whenever they wished.

Then they got to the reason for their call.

"Dearest Lady Eleanor," Harriet began, "you know I have the utmost regard for my estimable brother, but upon occasion he can do things that are decidedly naïve, shall we say? A case in point is the unfortunate event of last year occasioning the departure of a foreign woman."

Three heads shook then nodded in sad agreement.

"I am quite afraid," Harriet continued, "presently he is in danger of a similar error."

Lady Whitworth visibly brightened. Her beady eyes bordered by a distinct roll of fat as well as a pronounced sag became even more alert if such a thing were possible.

"Yes," Harriet responded to the unasked question. "I am afraid he has replaced the woman in his little...love nest, shall we call it?"

Lady Whitworth seemed a bit disappointed. "And the difficulty?"

"This time, the woman is not Spanish but French, who has assumed some nondescript English name I cannot remember. But I understand her French is flawless and as we know, only the French speak their idiotic language properly. I am convinced their mouths are all ill-formed to enable them to make the sounds they do."

"In that opinion we are one." Miss Trent laughed.

Grateful for the interruption, Harriet took another cucumber sandwich. Lady Whitworth ate daintily but continuously. She had already nibbled her way through three of the things, and Harriet was afraid she wouldn't get a second chance. She eyed the lemon tarts and determined to keep ahead of the lady on that score.

"As I was saying, and I emphasize I cannot corroborate what I have heard. Formerly, the woman was employed in a so-called bakery and teashop. Its owner, a Frenchwoman and a native of that country was reported to have died and the shop closed. The speculation is the Frenchwoman is not at all dead but incarcerated for nefarious dealings. In addition, it is a probability the woman Edmond hired is not only French but paid by the French government. It is believed her residency here is but a cover for her true activities and she contrived a chance meeting. As you can appreciate, it is to her advantage to keep dear Edmond completely in the dark as to her activates."

Lady Whitworth's eyes grew as large as they could be. "Do you mean she is a spy?"

"I do. Perhaps, since we are now at peace with France, for some other force. You know the revolutionaries are still rife in such a lawless county."

"But wouldn't Lord Linnington be suspicious of her activities?"

"My understanding is he spends very little time there apart from a spell of illness he recently had while the family was out of town. He stayed in the house to enable the caretakers to tend to him. Otherwise, he comes and goes for short periods, if you understand my meaning."

She dropped her gaze and concentrated on finishing the sandwich and taking a sip of tea to let the salacious hint sink in. The knowing glances exchanged by her two companions told her the observation had hit its mark. She snagged a lemon tart just before Lady W. reached for it.

"My fear, Lady Whitworth, is if this rumor circulates my brother's name will be smeared by the revelation, if it is true, and I vow I think it is." She knitted her brow and gazed dramatically out the window.

"So, what is your hope?"

"I have imposed on your kindness to implore you to keep your ears open for any such gossip and report it to me post haste. There is no use my going directly to Edmond. I am sure he would dismiss the entire affair out of hand. I only wish to be of service to the family and to him. But you can appreciate, I would like to corroborate the rumor."

"I shall certainly let you know upon hearing anything of the matter, Harriet. I know how careful you are of your loved ones." She turned her attention to Miss Trent. "Although, I suppose if it were known, it might only prove embarrassing and perhaps make it rather urgent he sever any relations with the woman. I recall how swiftly he jettisoned the Spanish woman when her behavior became public. This way he might be encouraged to turn his attentions elsewhere." She gave Sibyl Trent's hand a motherly pat.

"Oh, I assure you, Lady Whitworth, my only care is to support my closest friend in this situation."

"Of course it is, my dear. You are the soul of fidelity and friendship."

Sybil smiled her tight little smile and toyed with the end of the green ribbon on her bonnet.

"Be assured I will help you both all I can." The lady took the last raspberry tart.

Missing out, Harriet was absolutely famished. She was ready for lunch and less talking and more eating.

They took their leave after doing away with the last crumbs.

To Lady Wentworth's credit, she had second thoughts about her implied promise. She summoned her maid to bring more tarts. She needed to think. Perhaps Elizabeth Linnington was not unaware of something on the subject. When she had time, she must make a call on her.

Chapter Nineteen

Elizabeth Linnington was no one's fool. Some ten days after her visit to the Tothill Fields house, she sat quite still in an armchair in the morning room of her townhouse. After returning from church, she lunched with her son. He did not tarry for conversation but took his leave, undoubtedly to be on his way to St. Stephen's House and a visit with the troops and with Mrs. Williams. He seemed to have recovered from his illness even though the cough had not completely gone.

Her thoughts were as gray as the rainy day, making occasional spots of water on the windowpane, reminding her of the convex glass in a mirror. She needed to think through this situation, and watching the drops slide one by one down the pane made her mindful of the passage of time.

Edmond left for the war a boy and came home a man, changed in some obscure way. He was still amiable, and just as sensible and conscientious as he had been as a boy. But the man had a dark curtain around his soul. For the past year and a half, he went about his duties at Crossfields and here in town with intelligence and efficiency. He was informed of all of the dealings in Parliament and strove to have some influence, but nothing seemed to penetrate a subtle armor encasing him—until this fall.

How different he had always been from his elder brother, Giles, who was headstrong and impetuous, happily taking his mares anywhere in the hunt, which finally took his life in an untimely fall. She had hoped Giles would marry and produce an heir before any of her fears for him materialized. It was not to be so.

But what had produced the relieving of Edmond's mind? Was it he had a way to be once more with men who shared his experiences, or was it more? She recalled it was the relaxed openness that immediately impressed her when she walked into the sick room at Tothill Fields. There was frankness, even an intimacy, in the way he argued with Mrs. Williams. And she, in turn, quite held her own. Yet, they treated each other with absolute propriety.

The young woman was well brought up. She mused on her son's theory the girl was a clergyman's daughter. Elizabeth shook her head. She was too practiced, too used to managing everything from a simple curtsy to dealing with tradesmen. Her grasp of what needed to be done to the house was finely schooled.

Then there was Sophie Talent's strange reaction to learning of Edmond's arrangement with this Mrs. Williams concerning his property, the point of which was to provide her with funds to return to Cornwall. Sophie was from Cornwall, although she had lived in London or at White Marsh Manor, James's estate in Berkshire for years and, Elizabeth believed, rarely been home to visit. Elizabeth understood Sophie well enough to know she was deeply shocked at the revelation the former teashop was closed and its attendant now at Edmond's house. Had the two kept in contact? If so, why had not Mrs. Williams, or whoever she was, applied to James and Sophie in her straits? At least they were in contact now, or the book would not be in Mrs. Williams's possession.

Elizabeth sighed. It was time to ask Lady Eleanor Whitworth to tea. She detested the woman whose only aim in life was to gossip about others and thus glean random bits of information from her current companion to pass on to the next group of her acquaintances. Elizabeth considered the woman not much elevated from a miasmic disease, but Lady Eleanor was from Cornwall, which, to Elizabeth might have been Arabia, for all her familiarity with the region. She sighed, arose, and walked to the small writing desk across the room. She sat down to compose her invitation.

My Dear Eleanor,

It occurs to me it has been far too long since you and I have had a real conversation. The times I see you at supper parties or other gatherings, I find much too many interruptions for my taste.

I find myself quite unoccupied on Tuesday next and wondered if you could come to my home for tea at about four o 'clock that day. If there is a possibility, please let my footman know by return.

Yours and in hopes of enjoying your presence,

Elizabeth Linnington

Lady Eleanor accepted the invitation to tea for the following Tuesday with alacrity. Elizabeth supposed she was eager to know if Edmond had paid addresses to Miss Sybil Trent. Elizabeth would allow her to think so and hoped to steer Lady Eleanor in quite another direction.

***

The lady rustled into the sitting room, with silk petticoats and ruffles aflutter as though she were being ushered into the presence of the king. Her lilac turban was embellished with an extravagant plume, and she had an eager flush on her face coming from more than cosmetics. She was quite panting with anticipation.

"My dear Elizabeth," she gushed. "It has been far too long." She held out both hands so Elizabeth could take them and they could exchange ladylike kisses. Elizabeth was nearly overcome by the cloud of French perfume as dense as a nimbus just before a storm.

"Indeed, Eleanor. And so I said to myself the other day after a visit from my daughter, Harriet, whom, I believe you had for tea a fortnight ago."

"We did and had a lovely cozy chat, and the subject nearly produced a note from me. It would have passed with your invitation." She took a sip of tea.

Elizabeth let the conversation hang. She assumed Lady Whitworth had come to pry about Miss Trent and Edmond's possible interest. She was astounded when it was not at all what the good lady had on her mind.

"Elizabeth, I have become aware of certain activities concerning your son, Edmond. Now, I hasten to say I have no proof of their veracity, nor could my most confidential source completely corroborate the information." A bite of sandwich came next.

"Is that so?" prompted Elizabeth.

"I am sure you are unaware of the fact, but it seems he has replaced that vile Spanish woman with another." If her words did not imply "mistress," her expression did. "Not that I have any objection to gentlemen and their pleasures, you understand. Such activity probably would be of no concern, but it has reached my ears this creature has ties to the French. I know we are supposedly at peace with the dreadful people, but not only are there still feelings of resentment, there is also, many believe, an element still wishing our dear country no good. In fact, in league to import revolution. My understanding is this woman is such a person."

"Do you mean she is some sort of agent for the French?"

"This was the suggestion, I believe, and furthermore, my informant believes your dear son to be entirely ignorant of this woman's secret intent. Men can be so silly when besotted."

Elizabeth decided to stir the pot. "Oh, dear. I indeed did not know he had taken a mistress. Could you suppose that is why he has been so hesitant to offer for Miss Trent?"

"Such is the speculation between me and my informant. I hasten to say I am told Miss Trent does not at all subscribe to any idea Edmond might have knowledge of the nefarious doing of his *inamorata*."

"Eleanor, I appreciate your making me aware of this, but I fail to see what I could do to any purpose. Edmond is certainly an adult and his business is his own. I am, though, shocked at the suggestion he might unknowingly harbor a what? Spy shall we say?"

"Precisely. I wished to warn you of all of this so you might see fit to 'put a bug in his ear' as the saying goes. I am sure he would not want any breath of scandal, particularly one possibly impugning his loyalty after he has served our dear country so gallantly."

"If this is true, he certainly should dismiss the woman forthwith."

"Exactly. Then he could turn his attentions elsewhere perhaps?" The lady simpered as she reached for another sandwich.

"I shall certainly take under advisement all you say to me today, Eleanor."

She steered the conversation into the latest gossip and then as smoothly and briefly as she could, she recalled certain events of young womanhood they shared.

"Eleanor, my dear, I believe you spent your childhood in Cornwall and didn't come to Town until you were presented. I am quite unacquainted with that part of England. Surely you had no such scandals in such a bucolic place and life was quite serene."

"Oh, indeed not, my dear." This was followed with a mind-numbing account of this and that ending with the remark, "But of course none of this was of as much account as the awful business about, Charles Constant, the Earl of Wallingford. You must remember him when we were young women? All of us were warned about him. Even then, he lived far beyond his quite excessive means."

"I have some recollection but not the details."

"Well, when he was quite banished from town he retired to Newington Hall, his estate near Launceston, there to debauch and drink himself daily into a stupor as well as continue to gamble away whatever was left not only of his fortune but the entire estate, until in a fit, he took his pistol and ended his life, a final scandal on his poor daughter."

"So, he had heirs?"

"Only the girl. Olivia, I believe was her name. They say she tried mightily to salvage something of the estate, but, in the end, all was gone including the title. What was worse for her, someone started a vicious rumor it was she who did the old reprobate in rather than suicide. I for one never credited it, although I must admit we all feared for her own safety even though she was his daughter. You know such things do happen. Anyway, she soon married the youngest son of the local clergyman, a Reverend Mr. Williams, I believe. Anyway, after that, her whereabouts were quite lost so far as I am informed." Lady Eleanor's face reflected an odd combination of sadness for the girl and delight in being able to tell this entire dreadful tale.

Elizabeth took a chance. "Well, such tales do describe an interesting part of the country I was quite unaware of. I believe, other than yourself, the only person of my acquaintance from Cornwall is Edmond's dear friend James Talent's wife, Sophie, who is so very lovely but rarely talks about her time in the country and certainly not such a disreputable story."

"She certainly would not have related *that* story. She and the daughter were quite good friends, and she was unutterably sad when after the awful downfall of the father, she was forbidden by her parents of ever seeing the daughter. Such was their revulsion at self-murder."

"I see." Elizabeth believed she saw much more than Lady Eleanor could conceive of. She ended the conversation soon after. Her mission had been arduous but, in her mind, highly successful. And she did remember Charles Constant, the Earl of Wallingford. He had been quite obnoxiously persistent in paying his attentions to her one evening at a ball. She also remembered his wife, small and pretty, but with dark hair and eyes, unlike the earl's fairer complexion and blue eyes. She especially remembered the dignity with which his wife endured the obvious ill behavior. What had been her name? Oh yes, Amelie, she believed. Elizabeth had a vague memory although Lady Wallingford was half-English, she had been reared partially at the French Court before any hostilities. That would explain the well-spoken French. Sophie, too, spoke flawless French. She once mentioned a friend's governess taught her. Elizabeth speculated that might explain Mme. Dufour and Sophie's denial of any knowledge of the teashop. But why would the two young women conceal not only Olivia's parentage but also their friendship?

"Well, well," she remarked to the empty room when Lady Eleanor had departed. One thing she did not have to speculate about was the source of Lady Whitworth's misinformation. Surely, all such nonsense was the subject discussed with Harriet in the aforementioned cozy chat. But had Miss Trent been present during the revelations to Lady Whitworth?

No matter. She had much more important things to ponder.

Chapter Twenty

The third week in January the weather was sufficiently good for Sophie to anticipate a visit with Olivia. She often took all the children but today arrived with only Caroline. Robert was with his tutor, Eugenia had sniffles, but Caroline was eager to play with Mr. Partridge's pet rabbits.

"I hope, Mama, Mrs. Person will allow Mr. Partridge to bring the rabbits into the kitchen."

Sophie was aware Mrs. P often relaxed her dictum against allowing the creatures in the house. When Caroline was there, she allowed them in the kitchen where anything they happened to drop was easily cleaned up. She was always happy to let Caroline play with the rabbits until time to call her upstairs for tea shortly before they left. Sophie was suspicious the biscuits Caroline ate at tea might not have been her first of the day. Caroline was a favorite of her "aunt" Olivia's since she had gotten to know the child from babyhood when Caroline went with her mother to have cakes and tea at Mme. Dufour's.

When they arrived, Olivia was in the parlor, overseeing the painting of the room. The painters had finished work on the top two floors and most of the woodwork on the main floor. The one wall by the fireplace was complete with its coat of yellow paint.

"What do you think, Sophie? This is the shade I prefer, as did several others. Do you think it right? Perhaps we would have done better to choose one not quite so bold."

The women discussed the color now that they had an entire wall instead of a sample to test their choice.

"I assure you, Olivia. I quite like it. Especially on a dull day, and I believe it will not be too harsh on a sunny summer one."

"I'm so glad. I am quite pleased with all my other choices. Only this one gave me pause."

The main floor was chilly with the windows cracked open to dispel the paint fumes, so the women withdrew to Olivia's bedroom. She insisted Sophie take the comfortable chair, and she brought the straight chair from the dressing room in and put it on the other side of her small table.

"What are you sewing?"

"Linnington generously gave me some extra money for Christmas, and I am making a decent outfit to wear on the coach home. It's a walking dress." Olivia had already finished the dress and it was ready to hem. "I'm so glad you came by. If I put it on, will you pin the hem? I was going to ask Mrs. P, but I would like to know what you think."

Olivia took off her apron and slipped her old gown over her head. What she put on was a dress of simple design but fashioned from fine muslin, lightly sprigged with small flowers shading from a rosy red to coral. The sleeves were long, ending in a generous ruffle and the neck high. From the armoire, she pulled a length of heavier material in a solid coral but with a dusty cast creating a subtle tint that perfectly picked up the colors of the flowers. "This will be the coat. I found some bone buttons that will go nicely, I think. The sleeves and the neck will be cut low enough the ruffles at the wrists of my dress sleeves and the high neck will show. I think the red is dark enough to stand the rigors of travel. What's your opinion, Sophie?"

"I think you have done very well, my dear. The design is plain enough for everyday wear, but the material gives it some style." She sat on the rug in front of the fireplace. "What about the length?" She turned up the hem and put in a few pins. "How is this? Do you want it shorter? This way will show your boots but covers the tops."

"Perfect."

When Olivia had redressed, they settled themselves in the chairs, Sophie working on some embroidery she brought with her and Olivia began stitching the hem in place.

"Are you still going to St. Stephen's House?" Sophie wanted to bring the subject of Linnington and thought this a good entre.

"I am. It's most satisfying to be able to be of some small service to the men even though it is a poor substitute for family and faraway friends."

"Does Linnington still go?"

"He does when in town. The men seem to take great comfort in visiting with someone who has been to war. He even has a member of his old company there."

"Really? What a coincidence."

"It's blind Sergeant Higgins, I believe I've mentioned. He was a special pet of mine even before Linnington began to go there."

Olivia had dropped the "his lordship." But she naturally did not refer to him as Edmond.

"The Sergeant has much to say about the capt'n as he calls him. Although, I must admit Higgins does embarrass me upon occasion. The first time Linnington went, he quite mistakenly thought our relationship was more than one of employer and employee. I quickly set things right." Olivia was smiling at some memory. Then she sobered. "Higgins told me much about Linnington's experience in the campaigns."

"Tell me."

"For one thing, he was with Sir John Hope when he fell. It seemed to make a lasting impression on everyone involved. Sir John was deeply respected as a commander. If I may make a personal observation, I think such a story and the fact Linnington lost his batman in the last battle he was in at Salamanca may have been the cause of some melancholy. Or at least so I thought when we first met. I believe I detected such." She raised her eyebrows inquiringly at Sophie.

"I quite agree and am glad to know some of the possible sources. James says he never discusses anything that happened in Spain. But all of us have been distressed by his low mood since he returned. You cannot appreciate the change in him, since you have only known him a short time, but as boys, James says, although Edmond was always the quieter, more studious brother, he had a wonderful smile and a rather teasing sense of humor. He was quite delightful to be around if one was a close acquaintance, although I confess, in society he has always been a bit diffident. I always thought perhaps he came to a conviction he paled in comparison to the ebullient Giles."

"But I gather the boys were close."

"They were, as brothers go, even though they had the usual falling out occasionally, according to James. By the time I became acquainted with him, he seemed to have taken a self-imposed second place to his outgoing brother. I confess, as charming as Giles was, I always found Edmond much better company. But then, as James always says, and you know, I'm bookish, too."

Sophie took careful note of the rather serene smile on her friend's face. She thoroughly enjoyed discussing her employer and learning about him. Sophie wondered which one of them had actually been lured into this conversation.

"Even though it is winter and Edmond much prefers the summer when he can be at Crossfields, we have all noted the melancholy you mentioned has quite lifted this season."

"Of course, our acquaintance is of short duration, but I think I have noticed a change when we have a chance for private conversation. He is deeply interested in public affairs."

As you have always been. Sophie nodded. "I'm surprised you have any time for conversation."

Olivia blushed. "Oh, only on our walks home from St. Stephen's House. He insists on accompanying me. I think it is a quite unfounded concern for my safety after the intruder of last fall I told you about, but I must admit, I was deeply grateful last month with the terrible fog we had. He came to be sure I was home safely as he was just returning from the country. When he found me, I was indeed nearly lost. He was not well and it cost him several days of illness, I am afraid. I felt quite guilty for putting him to the trouble."

Sophie seemed to recall James saying Linnington had been ill and luckily had this house in which to recover, since the Ps were in residence and no one was at the townhouse. In telling the story to James, Edmond had evidently omitted any particular mention of Mrs. Williams.

Finishing the hem on the dress, Olivia cut the thread with a firm snip of her scissors. "I'm sure the lightening of his mood is directly

159

associated with his service to the men at St. Stephen's House. He seems to be in better humor each time he goes."

"I'm sure he is." Mentally, Sophie rolled her eyes. *Good God, you ninnies. I don't think either one of you would recognize an attachment if it ran over you in the middle of the street.* She decided it prudent to change the subject. "Oh, I almost forgot, I brought you my copy of the new novel *Pride and Prejudice*. I know you will love it. We both quite adored *Sense and Sensibility*."

They spent the rest of the afternoon discussing books, Sophie having ascertained what she'd hoped to learn.

***

Meanwhile, Caroline was happily playing with the rabbits, Punch and Judy.

Mrs. Person was busily preparing a chicken. "You do adore the rabbits, don't you, luv?"

"Oh, yes. It's quite the best thing about visiting Aunt Olivia even though I'm always quite happy to see her, too. But she and Mama always have so much to say to each other."

"Have you always called her Aunt Olivia, dear?"

Partridge threw his wife a disapproving glance, as if to say he considered it improper to interrogate the child. Person returned his with a look that said *Mind your own business.* He resumed reading the paper.

"I can't remember calling her anything else. Mama says if my grandparents would have let her, Aunt Olivia would be my Godmother."

The Ps often laughed over what a chatty child Caroline was. Mrs.

Person persisted.

"So, your mama and Mrs. Williams have been friends for a really long time?"

"Oh, yes. Since they were little girls. As little as me, Mama says."

"But not friends with your grandparents, I gather?"

"I don't exactly know what happened, but they liked her for ever so long. They let Mama go to Aunt Olivia's house where Mme. Dufour taught both of them French and drawing and Aunt Olivia's mama taught them the piano. Then Aunt Olivia's mama and papa both died, and that's when she and Mama couldn't see each other anymore."

"But they can now."

"Yes. Mama found out she was at Mme. Dufour's teashop, and we went to see her all the time." The child broke off. "Mr. Partridge, I think Punch is being naughty to Judy. He won't leave her alone."

Glad for the interruption, Partridge put down the newspaper and picked up the rabbit. "I think if he's naughty, he needs to go in his cage." Although the male rabbit was simply preparing to do what male rabbits do, Partridge did not want an act of copulation to happen before the child. And although he would have been glad to have a nest of baby rabbits, that would have to wait. The happy day would come when he and Mrs. P retired to Crossfields, or at least somewhere in the country, and he could have as many rabbits about as he wanted.

By the time he returned, Sophie was calling Caroline from the top of the stairs. The little girl skipped upstairs, and Mrs. P followed with a tray of fresh tea and refreshments, retuning with the cold teapot.

"That was not well done of you, Emma, to question the child."

"See there? Told you she was gentry!"

For the life of him, he could not remember her ever saying such a thing.

Chapter Twenty-One

January wore on into a rather tedious February. If the month had started in the doldrums, it ended the last Sunday in the month with the explosive news Napoleon Bonaparte had escaped from his captivity on the Island of Elba. Rumor had it the "little corporal" had crossed the Alps and was raising an army as he went. Half the populace believed this and half firmly dissented.

For Olivia, the tasks she set herself around the house were being completed more or less to her satisfaction and in a timely manner. The painting was complete and gave the house a freshness it had lacked. But all the furniture on the first floor, with the exception of the dining room table and sideboard and her little desk and chair, had been taken for reupholstering. Even the slip seats on the dining chairs had been removed. She was grateful to Lady Linnington for the gift of things to complete her bedroom, so at least she had somewhere to sit in comfort and drapes to draw at night. Her days were filled with needlework and reading.

Heavy snow in February precluded her from her greatest enjoyment, her visits with Sophie and her Sundays at St. Stephen's House. She found she particularly missed those, and she at first attributed her fit of depression to the fact February was always a dreary month, and also, Higgins was demonstrably doing much worse. The sedentary nature made necessary by his other injuries and his blindness were finally taking a toll on his body, and she feared even on his will to live. She had to admit she longed to see Linnington, too.

At last, there was better weather late in February, allowing her to go to St. Stephen's House after services. She was trying to cheer up the usually happy Higgins when Linnington entered, later than his usual time. Her heart leapt, and she was sure she colored. His eyes sought her before he greeted Mr. Selkirk, and he smiled.

Higgins's gruff companion, Banks, didn't miss this exchange. "Glad to see the capt'n, are you, missy?"

"And I vow he's glad to see her, too, after this bad weather spell," guessed Higgins.

"Hush, both of you. He's my employer, nothing more."

"Rot," challenged Banks. "Anyway, he's here, so I'm leaving." He gave Higgins's shoulder a squeeze, passing Linnington without comment on his way to the door.

Higgins just smiled.

When Edmond approached the bed, after chatting with some of the other regulars in the house, Olivia arose as usual and gave him her chair. "Good afternoon, my lord, it's nice to see you." She whispered, "Higgins needs some cheering up after a long visit with Mr. Banks." She left the two of them for a private chat and sought out a young man nearly ready to return home. She had been writing letters for him.

***

"Capt'n, you going to let that lady go next month as she plans?"

"I don't think it is any of my business, Sergeant. She will be at the end of her contract and seems determined to go to the West Country."

"If you don't mind me sayin' so, sir, you're a fool to let her go.

164

Even a blind man can see how well you suit."

Edmond didn't answer. He hoped his face did not portray how forlorn he felt, even if Higgins couldn't see it."I don't know about that, Higgins, but I promise to continue my visits even without the young lady." He changed the subject.

As usual he walked her home. This time he was able to bring her good news.

"Mrs. Williams, I am happy to tell you I have determined the difficulty with your pension. It was one of those endless and inexcusable misfilings of important information by the Home Office. The authorities assure me the proper paperwork will be ready before you leave. I will get the documents to you straight away when I procure them. You can sign them, and I will return them to the Home Office."

***

A wave of relief swept over Olivia. She was resigned to the fact the matter might never be resolved.

"Oh, my lord, thank you, thank you. I'm infinitely relieved. This makes all the difference in the world to me. Now with what I have been able to save from your generous employment, I'm assured of an easier living than I anticipated." In her gratitude, she grasped his arm with both hands. He smiled down at her and covered her gloved hands with his. She was aware they looked like a pair of lovers to passersby.

For the next month, things settled into a happy routine for her. Mr. Taylor returned most of the pieces of furniture nicely reupholstered. The house began to be not only presentable but also even quite charming. By mid-March, all but the couch had been delivered, and she took a bit of her savings and bought a ticket on the mail coach for Exeter for the last Tuesday in the month. Olivia was both exhilarated and sad. She was pleased with completing her assignment, looking forward to living quietly in the country after four years and more in the din and bustle of London, but her heart ached at the thought of leaving Linnington.

To cheer herself up, she went to Covent Garden and purchased a ticket for the stalls at the opera for the Saturday night before she left. Her new traveling costume would be perfectly acceptable for an evening out if she were in the stalls. She determined even to hire a hack instead of walking the distance at night.

In addition to this foray, she borrowed a generous basket from Mrs. Person and walked to the shops along the Thames, including a hodgepodge of temporary shelters where used books and a jumble of things were sold.

The one thing still dissatisfying her was the renovation needed accessories to make the place less sterile. The parlor mantle held a battered candlestick, the clock, and the Staffordshire dogs. Hers was perfectly bare. The dining room was acceptable since she found things in the sideboard, which could be set out, including a fine china bowl for the center of the table.

These were not purchases she had cleared or even discussed with his lordship. She was determined to find a few things to brighten the place and wanted to spend as little as possible from the petty cash he gave her at the beginning of the project. The only thing bought so far for the house had been the pair of pottery dogs. She smiled.

In the shops, she found among the secondhand wares a small mirror of some indeterminate age. The frame had a chip or two and the mirror was slightly raddled at the bottom where it had gotten damp, but she could see no mold or other permanent difficulty. With this, she bought a blue Chinese ginger jar decorated with white blossoms. Its domed lid was missing and presumed broken. In addition, she found a white platter with a cobalt edge. When she tapped it with her fingernail, it gave off the dull sound of cracked pottery. She examined the piece and found only an indistinct crack barely edged in the brown of wear. Perhaps the piece was not much usable at table but would fit in quite well on her bedroom mantle with the little jar in front to conceal the crack. In one stall, she discovered a nice pair of brass candlesticks for the parlor to replace the disreputable one by the clock. The minor damage to this pair she could turn toward the wall. On the way home, she passed a flower stall. With violets still a month away, the proprietor exhibited dried flowers. Olivia bought a bunch of dried white baby's breath to fill the jar. The existing plate in the dining room, with its lovely mirror, was accessory enough there. And the Staffordshire dogs along with the mantle clock and candlesticks in the drawing room was quite sufficient.

She happily took her purchases to the house and adorned her room then hung the mirror over the little table in the downstairs hall and rearranged the mantle in the parlor.

***

The Sunday before the performance when she and Linnington arrived at the house from St. Stephen's House, she said, "Do come in, my lord, and see the result of all this work. Mr. Taylor delivered the couch on Friday, and I believe everything is in readiness for you to list the property with an agent."

"I'm sure you have done an excellent job, Mrs. Williams, and my opinion of décor would never be one to be relied on, but I should like to see the finished product."

Olivia happily showed him about the parlor and the dining room. As they started upstairs to see the bedroom, she glanced into the old mirror she'd bought at the flea market and hung above the little hall table, catching the reflection of two very happy people. She valued his approval.

After they had viewed the second floor, she accompanied him to the front door.

"So, you will be traveling soon?" he inquired.

"Yes, I purchased a ticket on the Exeter mail for a week from Tuesday. So, I supposed next Sunday will be our last visit to St. Stephen's House."

An expression of profound disappointment crossed his face. "I'm so sorry, but I will be attending my mother this next Sunday. It is her birthday." He seemed to hesitate, not knowing what to say. "I hope your stay has been a pleasant one for you. You have certainly done an estimable job. Perhaps if you stayed a little longer, you could at least enjoy some of the pleasures of the city. You are welcome to stay here until the house is sold."

"Oh, thank you, sir, but no. The arrangements are made, and I must confess I have indulged myself to a ticket for the opera on Saturday."

His face brightened. "Saturday? *The Magic Flute*, I believe."

"Yes."

"I had hoped to go. You must let me escort you."

"Oh, sir, I'm afraid it would be quite improper."

"I don't see why? Allow me to consider it a parting gift. And you will enjoy the opera much more from a box than from the stalls."

"But I couldn't. I have nothing to wear."

"You had planned to attend the opera clothed, I assume?" A twinkle in his eye belied his mock seriousness.

On impulse, she gave him a slap on his arm for his impertinence. "Of course, but the costume appropriate for the stalls is hardly evening dress for the boxes."

"Mrs. Williams, you are quite taken up with what is appropriate and what is not. I'm sure your resourcefulness will not fail you now. I shall call for you at seven thirty Saturday evening." He gave her a slight bow and went out the door.

Stunned by what just happened, Olivia had a moment of panic. He had given her no chance to agree or decline, so she must prepare. Olivia dashed upstairs, tossing her bonnet and shawl on the bed. She dug into her clothes until she found the white silk wedding dress. With it was the pair of long white kid gloves. Both had yellowed a bit but, to her critical eye, just looked creamy now, and they did match after all. She had cut up the lace-edged petticoat for the Christmas gifts, but any petticoat and shift would do. Even so, the dress was a summer one and just wouldn't do by itself.

Remembering the black silk dress with the lovely embroidery, left behind by the previous tenant, she reached for the garment. Black was not fashionable, but she had no choice. She pulled it from the heap of discarded clothes and examined it. It was much too large for her. The bodice she could cut down, but she wouldn't want to wear the voluminous skirt.

Hmm. She could wear the white silk skirt from the wedding dress. Then perhaps, if she cut the black silk bodice to fit, it would create a rather low-cut Spenser. But it would not be enough for winter if she wore only the wedding dress with it. What if she cut the black dress's skirt into a panel to be attached to the top and cut it away like the tails of a man's coat? The alteration would make enough of an overdress to serve the purpose, even though it would necessitate cutting through the embroidery. *Yes, I think I can make do.*

She hurried to supper, more excited than she would admit to herself.

***

By Sophie's Wednesday visit, Olivia had recut and sewn the bodice and pinned the top and bottom panel together. However, the top was cut indecently low for her taste. Perhaps the black lace from the fan could be fashioned into a modesty piece. She cut the half circle in two and stitched the filigree onto the inside of the bodice. She liked the effect. It covered just enough for decency and preserved the lines of the bodice.

When Sophie arrived, she brought a small bottle of perfume as a parting gift. Olivia gave her a kiss and found they were both teary at the prospect of being once more separated.

"After avoiding Tinstone all these years, I suppose I will be forced to visit my mother and take the children just so you can see them. I'm sure she will be pleased, although she never minds coming to White Marsh Manor, I find."

"I will miss you. Perhaps I can travel some, too. Linnington has procured my pension, and I am deeply grateful."

"I'm so glad to hear it. Are you both still attending the veterans at their hospice?"

"Yes, but Sunday was our last. His mother's birthday is this coming Sunday." Olivia screwed up her courage to confess, "However, something happened that terrifies me."

"What?"

"I told him I had purchased a ticket to attend the opera on Saturday. He insisted I attend with him and join him in his box. I swear I had no chance to refuse."

"Really? What prompted him?"

"He suggested I should consider it a parting gift, but I need your advice. Do come upstairs. See if what I have devised to wear will do at all for the occasion. I had planned to wear my traveling costume, but even such a nice costume simply wouldn't do for the boxes, and I am sure he will be in evening dress."

"Olivia, Jamie, and I are attending also, as are the other two whist friends and their wives, Gavin and Corinne Freeman and John and Emily Canning. With the crush of people waiting for carriages after the performance, we often find ourselves in conversation in the foyer. What if we meet?"

"Certainly, you and I must act as though we had never met, but I don't know about the other couples. Are they at all amiable?"

"They are, especially Emily Canning. I trust her to treat you with utmost courtesy." Sophie spent their time over the teapot, filling Olivia in on some of the background of the two couples she had not met.

Before she left, the women examined Olivia's handiwork.

Sophie declared the garment stunning and original.

"The only thing is, I have nothing to wear as a wrap. None of my shawls are appropriate, and my old pelisse is so heavy and so worn."

"I have a plain black hooded evening cape in velvet. It will be long on you, but you may borrow it. I doubt if James would recognize it if it was pointed out to him. You can have Jeremy retrieve it from Hannah. I'm sure he would be happy for the errand. Then he can bring it to the townhouse on Monday."

"Sophie, that would be perfect."

"All is settled, then. I shall enjoy ignoring you all Saturday evening and paying attention to the opera," Sophie teased.

Chapter Twenty-Two

As the evening approached, Sophie's nerves were causing havoc with her. She had fumbled over simple tasks, become short with her children, and prompted James to suggest she might consider a visit from the doctor. On the night of the opera, she schooled herself not to fidget on the way to Covent Garden. Once in their box, she pretended to study her program while observing Linnington's box. It was still empty. She leaned out and waved to the Cannings and Freemans who shared a box on their side of the orchestra.

Just then, Olivia and Linnington appeared. *Oh God, anyone with half an eye can see what is going on.* Olivia was radiant, and Linnington happier than she had seen him in years.

Although black was not fashionable, she had failed to appreciate the striking appearance the two of them would make all in black and white, he in evening dress and she in the gown she had fashioned, which, if not the height of fashion, appeared incredibly rich. Sophie recognized Amelie Constant's lovely pearls at her throat. The two sat down, ignoring any curiosity directed their way and began to peruse the program. The couple appeared to be discussing it and absorbed in their own conversation.

"Well, my goodness," Jamie remarked." Tonight, Mrs. Williams is an entirely different vision from the rather bedraggled waif Linnington and I rescued from the street."

"Oh, is that she?" Sophie tried to sound innocent.

"I met her briefly, but I believe it is the same young woman."

The orchestra entered the pit and the lamps at the edge of the stage were lit. Sophie was usually delighted in the wait for the overture. The rustling of silk and subdued babble of conversation, the hint of cologne and French perfume mingling with the pleasant cacophony of sound from the pit as the various instruments tuned and practiced snippets of music couldn't give her their usual thrill tonight. She just wanted the whole thing over.

Luckily, between the first and second acts, no one came to the box. Sophie dreaded whatever conversation would be made concerning the handsome couple. She scanned the audience and happened to see Lady Eleanor Whitworth arise from her seat in the front box and lean over to get a better look. Someone had alerted her to the new face at the opera. Mildly interested it seemed, Lady Whitworth peered toward Linnington's box and her expression changed. Her mouth fell open. She grasped her lorgnette for a better view. Then she sat, plopping her considerable girth into the chair. Frowning with some private consideration, she seemed in no hurry to impart her suspicions to her various companions for the evening but remained seated, still perplexed, as the second act opened.

Sophie was sure the woman's expression relayed she had immediately recognized Olivia. Sophie decided not to inform Olivia. There was no use spoiling her last two days in town, and after Tuesday, it would not matter what the woman reported. Sophie didn't know how Lady Whitworth felt about the affair of the earl's death. At the time it happened, there was even speculation Olivia had killed her father instead of suicide, so vicious was some of the gossip. If a whisper of any of this ever reached Edmond, it would be much too late to embarrass either one of them. Besides, although she was convinced Olivia was in love with Linnington, she was less sure about his affections, and James had never given her any indication he was aware of the circumstances. She was still under the stricture Olivia didn't want her history known, but she was afraid the time might come she had best tell someone and even Linnington himself.

The second intermission and third act passed uneventfully, except for Jamie bringing Sophie some refreshment. He did not report having visited with anyone, but Sophie was still on edge, nervously awaiting the end of the performance and the crush in the lobby.

During the last intermission, Gavin Freeman came by and paid his respects to Sophie. Then he and Jamie stood at the door of the box for a few moments. They whispered, but she couldn't help overhearing their conversation.

"Isn't she a pretty piece. Is that the intrepid Mrs. Williams?"

"I met her briefly and only once, but it is she."

"Well, hasn't Linnington been hiding someone's light under a bushel? You've heard the rumors, I suppose."

"I have and really don't credit them."

"I didn't, but she's tasty enough he's a fool if it isn't true."

The men laughed.

Overhearing the comment, some of Sophie's agitation, which had eased somewhat during the performance, returned with a rush. What rumors? She quickly surmised they were simply talking about the possibility of there being a liaison between the two. *Men! They can't imagine simply a mutual attraction.* However, she had not failed to note while Olivia was intent on the opera and enjoying every second of the music, Linnington spent most of his time studying the stage from a vantage point allowing him to observe Olivia's profile and creamy shoulders down to the lace and low-cut neckline all at the same time. He seemed as intent upon them as on the stage.

When the performance ended, the Talents left the box, only to be stopped by mutual friends, so by the time they reached the foyer, the Cannings and the Freemans had already assembled, the men having called for their carriage. Olivia was standing somewhat apart at the foot of the stairs, the hood of the evening cape pulled over her head and Linnington was approaching, having evidently called for his own carriage. Sophie waited with the other two couples for Jamie to signal their own footman. He then joined them just as Linnington took Olivia's arm and guided her to the gathering.

"May I present Mrs. Olivia Williams. Mr. and Mrs. Canning, Mr. and Mrs. Freeman, and Mr. and Mrs. Talent. I believe you have met Mr. Talent briefly." Each of them acknowledged the introduction in turn. Olivia and Sophie managed to be properly aloof.

An awkward silence threatened to ensue, but courtly Gavin Freeman kindly intervened. "So, Mrs. Williams, did you enjoy tonight's performance?"

"I did, sir. Particularly the Queen of the Night's aria, but I confess Papageno is always my favorite."

Before he could answer, Corinne Freeman laughed and broke in. "I warn you, Mrs. Williams, my husband has an inordinate love of the opera and can go on at length about the merest details until there is abject boredom."

"True, my love, but I happen to agree to Mrs. William's point."

The couples spent the next few minutes listening as Gavin and Olivia delved into several details concerning the performance. Then Olivia smoothly turned the subject to a more general discussion.

Sophie relaxed. She should have known her resourceful and gracious friend could handle the situation.

The carriages arrived and the couples dispersed, one by one. Out of the corner of her eye, Sophie caught sight of Lady Whitworth observing the scene, her mouth uncharacteristically shut and the thoughtful frown still on her face.

She hoped Jamie would not broach the subject on the way home, but he did.

"Sophie, I can't help but feel Linnington is truly enamored of the lovely lady on his arm tonight."

She didn't say anything, and he went on. "Of course, I have no way of knowing if any affection is returned on her part."

"Didn't I hear something about her leaving very shortly for wherever her home is? I cannot swear to it because, as you know, I try not to listen to idle gossip."

"Yes, he did confirm that, still..."

Sophie understood just how to distract her husband. She snuggled up to him and put her hand on his chest. "She can't be as enamored of him as much as I am of you, my love."

Her magic worked, and he abandoned his inquiry in favor of kissing her for the remainder of the short drive. She was simply overjoyed to have the evening concluded.

Chapter Twenty-Three

Olivia and Linnington rode to the house in companionable silence, neither of them quite knowing how to end the evening. Her heart beat a little quicker to be so close to him and the slight odor of masculine cologne mingling with the bit of the musky perfume Sophie had given her. The heady combination aroused all her senses and put her in mind of the Arabian Nights. The entire evening had been a fairy tale from the moment he remarked on the way to the opera that she looked lovely, an expected compliment from a gentleman to lady, but still she relished it.

Linnington broke their silence with an impersonal remark. "Those are particularly beautiful pearls. Are they the things of value you tried to sell?"

"Yes. They were my mother's. The pawnbroker insisted they were not real."

"They certainly appear real to me."

They sat in awkward silence for a moment. When they reached the house, he opened the door for her and stood rather hesitantly. Irrationally, she considered he might kiss her and then remonstrated with herself for having such a ridiculous thought. Honesty made her admit it had been a hope.

"Mrs. Williams, as you know, I will not see you tomorrow. But I did want to thank you for all you have done to ready the house...and for informing me about St. Stephen's House."

His impersonal and formal remarks disappointed her. She didn't want things to end this way, but she didn't know what she should want, either.

"You are quite welcome, sir. The assignment was a pleasure and your generosity has made the possibility of a new life for me a reality. And a special thank you for the pleasure of the opera tonight."

"I am entirely satisfied with your work, Mrs. Williams, and shall contact my agent on Monday to put the property up for sale immediately. Again, I thank you for it." He added, "And I enjoyed the performance and even more the company, Mrs. Williams."

"As did I, and I cannot thank you enough, my lord, for your generosity in escorting me tonight as well as the restoration of my pension."

"My pleasure, and it was repayment for a job well done." With a tip of his silk hat he said, "Good night, Mrs. Williams."

"Good night, my lord."

To her surprise, he took her hand and briefly kissed it. The warmth of his lips against her glove burned like molten metal. She held her breath, but he only turned and walked out of the open door.

What a stupid conversation! All we could do is repeat what we had already said over and over. Suddenly deflated, she took a candle from the hall table and made her way to bed, folding Sophie's cloak carefully into the box it had come in.

So much for a lovely interlude in my life. She found sleep hard to come by.

***

On Sunday, Olivia awoke at her usual time but with the sensation some incredibly heavy weight held her to the bed. All she wanted to do was pull the covers over her head and go back to sleep. The best thing for her to do was get up, get dressed, attend church, and go to

St. Stephen's House, so she tossed off the covers.

She lay still long enough to think about the evening before. It had been a joy to attend the opera, feel pretty in a new, although renovated, gown, and spend an entire evening with Linnington.

Mentally, she replayed the experience. He called for her in the same carriage they had taken to Stepney. The familiarity of her surroundings allayed any nerves she had about the evening. It allowed her to feel at ease on the way over. During the performance, they'd mostly talked about the house and about music.

It had been a thrill to be once more in a real theater with its myriad candles in the chandelier, the plush seats in the private box, sitting in the front so she could lean over the balcony both for a view of the stage and the well-dressed concertgoers. There was the smell of tallow, perfume, and excitement in the air. She had fun seeing the latest styles actually on a person instead of sketched in some periodical. And she'd been quite comfortable in her made-over gown, not even minding it was black and white instead of some fashionable color.

Together, she and Linnington had studied the program with its notes. He made comments about some of the artists he heard in previous performances. They'd laughed over the ridiculous but charming plot.

Then the orchestra's cacophony of tuning mixed with the sociable chatter of the guests. This was brought to a halt by the entrance of the maestro who acknowledged the audience and wrapped his baton on his music stand. Then the first notes of Mozart's glorious music began. It had been rapture to her.

During the concert, she'd studiously avoided looking at Sophie, afraid her face would betray recognition. Instead, she concentrated on the performance, drinking in every note since this might be the very last London performance she ever attended.

Linnington seemed to enjoy the opera as much as she. He sat with his arm resting on the back of her chair in a relaxed rather than intimate manner. Perhaps he was as aware of her as she was of his physical presence. To her it was the only solid and anchoring reality in a world of fantasy tonight. She wanted to hold on to the sense of security.

When he helped her with her evening cape, his gloved hands ever so gently caressed the points of her shoulders.

A jolt of nerves assailed her only twice. Once when an imperious old lady in a shockingly bright-pink gown kept eyeing her with a lorgnette. During the last intermission, the woman's apparent curiosity caught Olivia's attention. The woman again appeared as they'd descended to the foyer but didn't approach them, thank goodness. The old biddy was the picture of a town gossip, but Olivia did not recognize her from the teashop. There was a niggling sense of familiarity about the person though.

Any fright she had at meeting his friends vanished with their kind reception. Olivia believed she and Sophie carried off their part of the charade quite well.

Her only disappointment had been her parting with Linnington. At least he had said good night and not goodbye, sparing the finality of their connection.

Olivia dragged herself from the bed, washed, and dressed. As it was her last visit to St. Stephen's, she wore her new walking dress and coat. She had wanted him to see her in a decent costume for once, and now he wouldn't.

The day was gray and damp but not so rainy her new bonnet, with its ribbons almost the color of her walking dress and paisley shawl, wouldn't suffice to keep her dry on the way to church. She pushed away all the thoughts of the night before and mechanically went through the routine of breakfast, the familiar Morning Prayer service, and the walk to St. Stephen's House. This time neither the bells, the chattering squirrels, nor the hint of spring in the air lifted her mood.

When she entered St. Stephen's House, Higgins was particularly pale and drawn, but he smiled his usual jaunty smile.

"Good to see you, missy."

"You're looking well, Mr. Higgins."

This opening was their own private joke, since he had never seen her, nor would he ever, and when they first met, he'd made fun of the fact that looking well, or looking at all, was beyond him. She had always admired his ability to deal with his infirmity.

As the afternoon wore on, she visited with some of the other men, telling them one by one goodbye then went to sit for a while with Higgins. Thankfully Banks had not shown up this afternoon.

"So, where's the capt'n, missy?"

"I believe he had a family engagement this afternoon."

"Don't tell me he's going to let you get out of town?"

"I leave by coach Tuesday for home. I believe we said our goodbyes yesterday." She hoped her voice didn't betray her forlorn feelings.

"If it's really goodbye, the man's not as smart as I thought he was. You know, you two suit. I don't have to have eyes to see that, it's in the way you talk to each other. He never talks to anyone the way he does to you. Oh, maybe family, I wouldn't know."

"Oh, Sergeant, anything more than a casual friendship was always quite out of the question."

He was quiet for a moment. "Would you mind letting an old man touch your face?"

"Not at all, Sergeant." Olivia rearranged his pillows then sat on the side of the bed and took his hand and placed it on her cheek. He gently felt its contour then touched her forehead, her nose, and finally, the curls above her ears.

"Well, it's not your looks keepin' him away. You feel as pretty as you sound. If the capt'n ever comes again, I'm going to tell him what a fool he is."

"Oh, please don't, Mr. Higgins. I'm sure he knows his own mind."

"I'm sure he doesn't."

"I must go now. It has been such a pleasure to know you and visit you these months, and I wish you well."

"You've helped me bear my lot, missy, and I will miss you sorely."

"I'll miss you, too." She bent over the bed to kiss his grizzled cheek. Was that a tear at the edge of his bound eyes? There was definitely one at the corner of hers.

After the solitary walk home, Olivia took off her bonnet and shawl and hung them on the newel. She didn't want to be alone for a moment so went straight down to the kitchen where the Ps would be.

Their company didn't help much. The first thing Partridge said to her was, "Mrs. Williams, if I may take the liberty of making a comment, I want to say Mrs. P and I agree you looked particularly beautiful when you went out last night."

"And may I add I thought your rework of the garment was especially well done. I know you will be a success with the woman who owns the bonnet shop."

At least the mention of Mrs. Hastings gave her a chance to change the subject.

***

On Monday, Olivia awoke to feel much the same as she had the day before, but today she had almost nothing to do. To brighten her day a little, she tied up her hair with a red ribbon.

Her small trunk was packed, and the portmanteau once more held her valuables and personal items at the bottom, covered by a change of clothes for the trip. She would spend the next two nights at a coaching inn, but she was determined to secure a room and have a decent meal sent up at the Dog and Crown in Exeter. The day after, she would take the mail to Launceston and, from there, she could easily hire a carter to take her and her few possessions to the vicarage at Tinstone, a mere eight miles beyond the town. It would be an exhausting few days. She couldn't even summon the energy to take a final walk about the city.

The hours of the day crawled by, and she was glad when the light began to fade so she could abandon her room at least for the company of the Ps at supper. She tossed a bit of coal on the grate in her bedroom. It would stay warm for her through the routine of going to bed. It was not a particularly cold day for late March but Olivia shivered anyway. Picking up two small packages, Olivia carried them with her downstairs.

The odor of Mrs. Person's excellent bread filled the stairwell. Mrs. P had hastened her baking for today, just to have fresh bread for this last meal together.

She was sure to take note of this fact as they chatted at dinner.

Most of their conversation was about the growing clouds of war on the Continent. Boney was raising an army and in response, Wellington was martialing the British troops. With Linnington safely out of the fray, the three of them discussed the issue with more objectivity than they would have if he were about to go off to war. Still, the news was worrisome.

Olivia finally changed the subject.

"His lordship intends to list the house right away. What plans do the two of you have, then?"

"We will be returning to Crossfields," Mrs. Persons said rather wistfully.

"Indeed. His lordship has granted us lodging in a small cottage at the gatehouse on the property."

"I shall miss the city, and George, no doubt, will be glad for the country where he can have a vegetable garden. I suppose he will allow those rabbits to get together so that we have many more. All of whom will eat the garden and then have more offspring."

"Now, Emma. You have had two years in the city, surely it is more than enough for anyone of coal soot and messy streets and smells not nearly so nice as the country."

Olivia knew the answer but decided to tease a little, just for diversion. "I suppose, Mrs. Person, you will miss it because you grew up in the city so it seems like home?"

"No, indeed. I grew up on a farm in Yorkshire. It was Mr. P who grew up in London."

Partridge put a stop to the discussion. The set of his chin left Olivia with the impression he and his wife had been over the subject too often for his liking.

"But, now, Mrs. Williams, you are, I believe, to return to the country also."

"I am, and I confess, I shall not miss the city. My home is in the West Country, near Launceston. It is quite rural there and I believe the quiet life will suit me. I shall not miss the city, but I shall miss both of you. I want to thank you sincerely for all your kindness and help these past months. I believe the project would never have proceeded so successfully if I had not had your aid." She took the two packages from the settle where she had laid them. "May I give each of you this small token of my thanks?"

"Oh, my dear, you shouldn't have," protested Mrs. P. But she opened the package and, to her delight, found a small cook's book of recipes. In the package she gave Partridge was a scarf of the sort useful on a cold country day. He seemed just as delighted with his gift, which pleased Olivia.

"I'm afraid we have nothing to give you in return."

"Well, I do, but it won't last as long as my book. I am all prepared to pack you something to eat on your journey tomorrow, and the way you eat, probably the day after. The food is inedible at those coaching houses."

Before she could continue with a diatribe about traveling in England, the sounds of the front door opening reached the kitchen, and a familiar voice called from above stairs. "Mrs. Williams?"

A Reasonable Lady

Chapter Twenty-Four

Olivia caught her breath. Her face showed complete surprise. "Yes, my lord?"

"May I have a moment?"

She climbed the stairs. The Ps had the grace to remain where they were and let the couple say whatever goodbyes were to be said, but they did exchange glances.

When she was well out of hearing, they whispered to each other.

"I knew he wouldn't let her go with no more goodbye than a I-had-a-nice-evening thing, they were going through the other evening."

"What made you so sure?"

"Oh, come, George. You're not a blind man. You could see the fondness growing. Don't you think she deserves at least a goodbye kiss?"

"You don't seem to mind. Aren't you the one who predicted she would get her claws into his lordship?"

"That was before I knew her. It was you who always said she was gentry."

"I have always thought she was a lady of quality."

"Do you suppose he'll stay the night?" Mrs. P's face took on a distinctly dreamy expression.

"I should think not!"

"Then I shall be disappointed," she stated emphatically." If he does, maybe it will convince her to stay here. He needs her, in my opinion."

George shook his head in bewilderment.

***

Olivia found Linnington dressed in evening clothes standing in the hall. She had a sudden sense of déjà vu—this was exactly where she'd last seen him. He had something in his hand.

"I brought you a small parting gift." He held out a little jeweler's box.

She opened the leather case and nestled on the silk lining was a perfectly matched pair of teardrop-shaped pearl earrings. She stared at him and stammered something like Mrs. P had said to her. "Thank you, my lord, but it's entirely unnecessary." She was aware she sounded ungracious. "They are lovely, and I do thank you so very much."

"As I have often affirmed, you have earned all you have received, and you shouldn't wear those lovely pearls of your mother's without proper earrings. I only wish I had purchased them so you could have worn them to the opera."

She started to close the box, but he stopped her. "Please put them on. I should very much like to see them on you."

Laying the box on the hall table, Olivia put on the earrings, her delighted face reflecting in the little mirror. She turned to him. "Thank you, sir. I shall treasure them. I'm only sorry I have nothing to give to you."

He reached out and pulled apart the bow on the ribbon in her hair. "This shall do quite nicely, although I believe it is one I gave you for Christmas." He smiled, took off his gloves, and slipped them into his coat pocket. With both hands, he pulled apart the knot and

189

dropped the ribbon on the hall table then pulled the pins from her hair until it fell around her shoulders.

The intimate act was so sudden, all Olivia could do was stand rooted to the spot. He placed the pins with the ribbon beside the box on the table and took her face in both hands, weaving his fingers into her curls. For a moment, he did nothing but allow his eyes to examine every part of her face. Then, with no more hesitation, he bent his head and kissed her.

Olivia had the sensation her body was possessed, moving of its own volition. She put her arms around his waist and retuned his kiss. The first kisses deepened, resulting in a tighter embrace.

"I tried to stay away," he whispered, "but could not let you go without seeing you one more time."

"I'm glad. I was afraid I would never see you again."

He stepped away a half pace and regarded her speculatively. "So, you are as loathe to go as I am to let you."

"I am." A wave of sadness at the thought brought tears to her eyes.

He did not answer but swept her into his arms and mounted the stairs. Though well aware of what was coming, she could not force herself to resist or even care to. He kicked the door closed and laid her on the bed. After quickly shrugging out of the tight-fitting evening coat and pulling off the cravat, he reached to unlace her dress, baring her breasts.

The next few moments were a blur of caresses and discarded clothing until they were both quite naked and on the bed in the most intimate of embraces. Olivia knew from her marriage the signs of a man's desire and when it was satisfied. For him that night the satisfaction came quickly. A part of her mind wondered what he would do now. He had dressed for some occasion. She didn't want to face the awkwardness of his simply dressing and leaving.

To her surprise, he pulled down the bedcovers. "Here. You'll catch a chill." Then he took her into his arms.

Olivia, still aroused, willed herself to lie still, but she couldn't suppress a small, involuntary press of her belly against his hips.

"Give me a moment."

"What?" She looked up at him, fearing she had made some misstep.

"Give me a moment, sweetheart." His voice held amusement, which increased her confusion. She forced herself to lay rigidly still.

Every nerve in her body trembled. Olivia could not remember ever initiating cohabitation with David. She never resisted, and he was a gentle man, so it was all pleasant enough but not like this. This was incandescent. All she wanted was more and more of Linnington, a feeling not only unfamiliar but slightly embarrassing. Participating in this sort of lovemaking was foreign to her.

Then he kissed her as she had never been kissed and touched her where she had never been touched. Fire consumed her. He rolled onto his back and pulled her on top of him, guiding her hips. Whatever caution she had planned to employ completely dissolved. She moved as she would never consider moving with a man until her body exploded in a sensation not totally unfamiliar to her but not one experienced with any man.

She was mortified!

He murmured, "Yes," and rolled both of them over, quickly taking his own pleasure.

Once more, he simply gathered her into his arms. Olivia was compelled to say something, to apologize for her behavior. "You must find me very wonton, my lord," she whispered.

"I find you delicious."

He thinks this is funny! At a stab of anger, she pulled away a little, prompting him to prop himself on one elbow and pull her chin up to face him. "That's what is supposed to happen."

"Oh?"

"Did you never have such an experience with your husband?"

"No."

"That's the point of it all, sweet one." This time his laugh was accompanied by her chagrinned smile. "And do you think, considering the circumstances, you could call me Edmond?"

"Yes," she whispered.

"Say it."

"Edmond." The name was honey on her tongue.

Afraid of acting like a schoolgirl, she gathered her courage to ask, "So, it was..." She searched for what she wanted to say. She needed to know he was pleased and she had acted appropriately. She chose simplicity. "All right?"

"Oh, my dear. You are everything any man could want." He added quietly, almost to himself, "And not just in bed, my love." He pulled her down to lie in repose, tucking her head on his shoulder. "Now go to sleep."

Any more speculation drew to a close as he promptly took his own advice, falling asleep, breathing deeply and evenly.

Olivia lay awake, reveling in simply being able to touch him. Her fingers found the ridges of scars she had suspected when he was ill. She remembered his body when she was holding him in his delirium and nursing him. She reveled in the intimacy, but that had been all on her part. At that time, she could freely tend him without expecting any intimacy in return. This had all been so very different. She did not expect such mutual passion. The combined musky odor of their lovemaking was intoxicating to her.

In the quiet, the brougham pulled away, probably with Jeremy as well as the coachman. Everyone in the house was now aware of exactly what had occurred. She could not muster a single regret. Tomorrow, she would leave and not ever to see any of them, and she would not exchange a moment of what had happened for her usual aversion to scandal in any form. She would treasure this night.

After a while, her bones melted into a deep, satisfied sleep.

***

She was awakened at first light by an uncomfortably full bladder.

Damn. She always hated this part of living with a man, taking care of all the necessary bodily functions. There was nothing for it. She slipped to her side of the bed and as soundlessly as she could, pulled the covered jar from under the side rail, and removed the lid. As she slid down, the bed shifted, and the sound as bare feet hit the floor. He left the door open to the dressing room and began to relieve his own needs. She wanted to shut her ears!

She replaced the jar and reached for the shift discarded in their haste the night before.

"No, no." He slipped into bed and pulled the garment away. What followed was a truncated but satisfactory repeat of the previous night.

Afterward, he pressed her to him, and, for a while, they lay there, both reluctant to let the moment go.

"Olivia, don't go. Don't leave me."

She caught her breath at the sound of her name. She had longed to hear him address her in this familiar way, but did he share her feelings? What was he asking? The thought of a marriage proposal briefly crossed her mind.

"Stay here. You have made this your house. You are part of it. Stay here with me, and I promise I will make your life as comfortable as anyone should want."

Not a marriage proposal but a proposition that, to her thinking, whether he'd meant it or not, was not far from the arrangement her employment had displaced. A thousand thoughts raced one upon the other, how much she wanted to say yes, followed by the thought of being sequestered alone in this house while he made memories on every occasion involving his family. And he would have to marry and to produce an heir, which, after her barren years with David, she could not provide anyway. Failing him would cut her heart out.

She pulled away so she could look at his face. She put her hand on his cheek, the morning stubble a sweet abrasive on her palm. "I cannot, Edmond. Don't you see? It would never be the same. We suit well, but even fondness grows familiar after a time, and you know you would have to marry."

She left all the other thoughts unsaid, but his serious demeanor told her he understood. He pulled her hand to his mouth and kissed the palm then abruptly got out of bed, unselfconsciously gathered all the evening clothes he had discarded the night before and went into the dressing room. This time he closed the door. Was he angry?

A Reasonable Lady

The sound of Jeremy leaving the pitchers of the morning's hot water had penetrated her consciousness somewhere in the last hour. The household was awakening to its usual routine. The door into the hall creaked as Edmond retrieved his pitcher of water and called out, "Jeremy, would you go and ask Owens to bring me some street clothing?"

"He's already here, sir."

The ever-attentive valet mounted the stairs. The sounds of a man's toilette could be faintly heard, the strop of the razor and it's click against the bowl of water, all familiar to her from her marriage but feeling alien and forlorn now.

She opened the door to get her own water for a good wash with a bar of almond-scented soap she bought at the shop next to where she purchased Mr. Partridge's scarf. This bathing had to last the long journey ahead. It saddened her to wash away the fragrance of their lovemaking.

Mechanically, she put her clothing from last night in the top of her trunk and closed the lid. She buttoned herself into her new walking dress and coat. She had wanted him to see her in it, and now he would. In the act of taking off the earrings, she remembered the box was downstairs. She would leave them on. Perhaps too fine for travel wear but no matter, her bonnet strings would cover them most of the time.

Sitting at the dressing table, she pinned and tied up her hair and was just putting the last of her items into the portmanteau as Edmond came in from the dressing room, clad in perfectly pressed street clothes. There was always something of military precision about him.

He stood behind her and put his hands on her shoulders.

"You're sure, Olivia?"

"I am, Edmond."

The familiar closed expression settled on his face, but he bent and kissed her neck just below the pearl earring. Then, without a word, he left the room. Every instinct told her to run after him, to toss away all her scruples about being a kept woman, to accept gratefully the part of his heart he could give and not lust after the whole.

Olivia rose halfway as his firm footsteps proceeded to the steps and out the front door. She sat on the bench. She had made her case for leaving and he accepted it. She almost wished he had pressed the point.

Evidently, he had decided not to say another goodbye. *Probably best.* At that moment, an early robin perched on her windowsill. *How ironic. The first sign of spring when I don't believe I shall ever feel anything but the bleakness of winter from this moment on.*

Jeremy appeared at the door.

"May I take your trunk, missus?"

"Thank you, Jeremy, it's ready." She arose, turning to face the boy." And thank you for all your excellent service during my stay."

"It was a pleasure, missus."

"Will you be returning to your regular duties?"

He beamed. "No, missus. Milord has procured a place for me in Reading to apprentice in woodworking."

"Congratulations, to you. I know how you love the trade."

He shouldered her trunk. "Travel safely, missus."

"You, too, Jeremy." *Sophie may soon have to find a new lady's* maid.

Downstairs, she gathered up the jewelry box and the pins from the table and dropped them into the portmanteau. The ribbon was gone.

The Ps hurried up the stairs for a last farewell, Mrs. Person with a package of food wrapped in brown paper. "We shall sorely miss you." Tears shone in her eyes.

"And I, you."

Partridge shook her hand and opened the door for her, and she could see Edmond had not left at all but apparently waited on the porch for the carriage. Now, he stood by its open door ready to assist her. Her heart soared to know he had not left without saying good-bye. Buoyed by the prospect of even a few more moments with Linnington, she thought she heard Mrs. Person remark under her breath, with a sob, "Poor lambs!"

It was a short drive to the coaching house, but Linnington volunteered nothing.

"Have I made you angry?" she ventured.

He took her gloved hand in his and pressed the back of it to his thigh, but he didn't raise his eyes to her. "Of course not. How could you?"

She was relieved her refusal had not completely alienated him. It was small comfort.

They exchanged their final goodbyes in the coaching house courtyard. He assisted her from the brougham and took the portmanteau from her as he had the day they met. Jeremy saw to the stowing of her trunk.

Before Edmond handed her into the mail coach, he briefly kissed her hand. "Goodbye, Mrs. Williams."

"Goodbye, my lord."

He helped her into the coach and handed her the portmanteau. He didn't look back but got into the brougham, and it immediately pulled away. Olivia hugged the portmanteau and stared out the window, hoping the tears hovering on her lashes were not obvious to the portly woman sitting across from her. Her heart was shattered.

The streets of London quickly gave way to hedgerows. At least she was going to the country where perhaps long walks would help her wear away her sadness. Tinstone was a place so dissociated with him, perhaps she could forget. But so much would always make her thoughts return to him.

As the coach lumbered down the street, she couldn't help but compare the musty coach and heavy haunches of the horses pulling the mail coach with the fine brougham and pair of grays. She clearly recalled the feeling of ease and comfort she experienced the day she first rode with him on the trip to Stepney. It wasn't only the vehicle and pair; it was the sense of his presence. The lurching of the mail made the separation all the more painful. Her time at Tothill Fields had changed her, profoundly. Without a doubt, she would never be the same.

Chapter Twenty-Five

Olivia's trip proceeded as she'd anticipated. She spent the first night at a coaching inn, fully clothed and sharing a bed with her portly traveling companion, who, thankfully had not pried into her business and only snored lightly. The second night was spent marginally in more comfortable circumstances, a shared room but a bed of her own. The third night was sheer luxury in Exeter at the Dog and Crown, where, in the privacy of her room, she could drop the mask of amiability and the press of making light, impersonal conversation with her traveling companions. Alone, she cried herself to sleep.

The next day, she caught the mail to Launceston and, from there, went by a cart belonging to a farmer from Tinstone who had delivered his produce in town and was making his way home.

Expecting her, Mr. Williams helped her into the vicarage with her belongings. Her room on the second floor was on the west, sunny and bright. The casement opened onto a view of the countryside instead of the town. The room was comfortably furnished with a generous bed and enough room for a very small sitting area.

She shared the second floor with Mrs. Todd, the vicar's housekeeper. Olivia remembered her as one of the townspeople most disapproving of her father. The woman had not come to greet her, so there was no encounter until supper, where Mrs. Todd kept an ominous silence through the meal and a scowl on her face. Olivia quickly realized this was going to be something she would simply have to endure. She sensed there was nothing she could do to alter this woman's opinion of her or of her family.

Her father-in-law was delighted to see her and have her company. At last, he had someone to share news of war and the writings of David Hume. She was equally delighted to be in his company.

While her life seemed to settle into rural tranquility, occurrences in London were anything but pacific. The actions and reactions of several people would eventually make their way to the West Country and upset her life. To cap it all, it was the same week Napoleon chose to go on the march.

***

The day Olivia left, Linnington did exactly what he'd intended. He went directly to White's and, except for a short respite to eat supper, drank steadily through the day and into the evening, something he had not done since his days at Sandhurst. At nine o'clock, John Canning happened into the club, having finished with business at Parliament.

John suggested a game of billiards but soon realized his good friend was in no shape for such an activity or much else. Trying to be helpful, he inquired if there was anything he could do, upon which Linnington put his head in his hands. "There's nothing anyone can do. It's all over. She's gone."

"Who is gone, Edmond? Is something amiss with your mother?"

"Of course not. It's Olivia who is gone."

"Who is that?"

"Mrs. Williams, you dolt."

"You mean the pretty little doxy of yours you took to the opera and who is rumored to be a French spy?"

Powered by grief and an excess of alcohol, Linnington took hold of Canning by his lapels and shoved him against the wall. "She is no doxy! And who in God's name ever thought she was some French spy? She's"—he seemed to search for a word—"perfect."

John, with his sturdy Scots blood, was not a small man. He managed to loosen Linnington's grip and get him to sit down. "Tell me what's going on, Edmond."

"Nothing to say. She's gone. Wouldn't stay. I begged."

"That's a shame, my man, but I believe it is time to get you home to bed."

Between Canning and the doorman, they managed to get Edmond into John's carriage. When they reached the townhouse, he half carried Linnington inside the house and, with Jeremy's help, up the stairs and into bed. Linnington did not go quietly during this endeavor, but fortunately, his babbling made no sense. Sturdy John, then aided by Owens as well as Jeremy, managed to get his lordship divested of boots, vest, cravat, and trousers and into bed where he quickly passed into oblivion.

***

The men left Linnington's room as quietly as possible, but the ruckus awakened Elizabeth. She recognized the state of affairs, more familiar to her in her older son, but through experience, she was convinced tomorrow would be painful for Edmond. She did not expect to see him until possibly late afternoon, when he could get past the headache and be able to keep food down.

She had enough to worry about after receiving a note from Lady Whitworth the day before. Briefly, she wrote she had some important news to impart to Elizabeth, which wouldn't wait. She would presume to call at two the following afternoon, begging Elizabeth to return a note to her by her courier if it was quite impossible.

Elizabeth answered in as brief a note she received, saying she would expect the lady at the appointed hour.

Promptly at two, Lady Eleanor entered like a battleship under full sail. After the initial pleasantries had been dispensed with, Lady Eleanor got down to the real business of her call.

"Dearest Elizabeth," she began, "as I emphasized to you on the last occasion we had to talk in private, I could not vouch for the veracity of the scurrilous rumors I reported to you concerning your son's employee, Mrs. Williams. I have with my own eyes confirmed they were indeed false. I am sure I have no idea who put abroad such tales, nor why they should have thought it necessary."

After taking a sip of tea and a bite of scone, she wiped her lips. "Much to my amazement, what I have to relate to you had to do with the later part of our last discussion. Do you recall my telling you about the unfortunate young daughter of Charles Constant?"

"I do, Eleanor."

"Well. Last Saturday, I attended the opera. You may or may not be aware your son also attended and escorted a young woman to the performance."

She paused for emphasis and a bit of food.

"I believe he mentioned he was going but did not inform me more."

"This time, I am reliably informed, by whom I cannot say, the young woman was the very same he employed to refurbish the house he kept for Mrs. Fernandez, in order to ready it for sale."

"I confess I did meet his employee briefly during the time she was there. I'm not sure when we met I was aware of her name," Elizabeth lied smoothly. "Otherwise, I would have been able to set you right at the time. She had none of the demeanor of either a spy or a loose woman. And this is as much as I know at this moment."

"Let me enlighten you." Lady Whitworth reached for a sweet, took a bite, and chewed daintily, the suspense of her revelation building. "I am convinced the young woman is none other than Lady Olivia Constant whom I referenced that day!"

"Really?" Elizabeth feigned surprise. "How did you come to such a conclusion?"

"First with my own eyes. I recognized her right off. I had no concourse with the awful man, but being in Cornwall at the time of his demise, I felt obligated to attend his funeral. Thus, my contact with his daughter was years ago. To be certain the lady he escorted was this former employee, I applied for details from the wife of an acquaintance of your son's. When she revealed the lady's name, there was no other conclusion to come to when I found she had once been associated with a teashop run by a Mme. Dufour. The name and the fact Olivia's governess, employed from France by Lady Wallingford was none other than a Mme. Dufour."

Lady Eleanor shifted her bulk with an air of satisfaction for her own cleverness in searching out the details of the affair.

"I do not believe Edmond is aware of this. Further, Mrs. Williams has departed for Cornwall, with the intention, I believe, of taking up residency there permanently."

"So, I take it their relationship was purely professional."

"So far as I am aware."

"Then he is free to offer for Miss Trent if he wishes."

"If he wishes," echoed Elizabeth with no inflection.

"I find all this too, too droll. Do you have any objection to my mentioning it abroad?"

"I see no reason not to, Eleanor. It does not reflect on anyone anything other than an interesting tale."

"I wonder why Olivia has for so long avoided the public knowing her history?" Lady Eleanor mused.

"I have no explanation."

"I suppose she is still shadowed by all the bad business before she married David Williams. She really shouldn't credit it. It's been so long ago and her father was a horror."

Elizabeth was rather touched by this woman who thrived on the misfortune of others and her rather gentle attitude toward Olivia Constant. It was a credit to Olivia's character.

Lady Eleanor brightened and immediately reverted to character by once more inquiring into Edmond's intentions toward Miss Sybil Trent, now the subject of Olivia had been disposed of. Elizabeth simply stated she had seen no change in his attitude toward Miss Trent. Lady Whitworth seemed satisfied and took her leave.

Secretly, Elizabeth was relieved and happy the old harpy would set the information circulating in the gossip mills about Olivia's true identity, so Edmond would hear it and relieve either Sophie or herself the task of informing him.

Elizabeth was disappointed when Lady Eleanor did not appear at all that evening at a supper party Elizabeth attended with Harriet. Elizabeth was hoping for an early and thorough airing of the rumors.

A Reasonable Lady

The following day, jostling in importance with the momentous information Bonaparte had indeed taken Paris and intended to march north and that Wellington was in the process of forming a military alliance to deter the self-proclaimed emperor, was the news Lady Whitworth had, the evening after her *tête-à-tête* with Elizabeth, suffered a fit of apoplexy and succumbed shortly after.

News of her demise was all the talk of the evening at a small party Elizabeth attended but was soon decisively overshadowed by definitive news Britain was once more at war. The interest in the information about Mrs. Williams's past and possibly Edmond's affections towards her was lost, along with the lady.

***

On Wednesday evening, the men gathered at White's for their usual game of whist. Edmond was uncharacteristically late, which gave John Canning a chance for a private talk with the other two friends.

He described in some detail his encounter with Edmond on Monday evening.

"You mean Edmond got physical with you?" asked Jamie.

"He did indeed. I confess I brought it on by casting a bit of an aspersion on the lady in question. I mentioned to him the rumors circulating about her. I don't think he was aware of them."

"What rumors?"

Freeman told him he and Canning had heard the woman in Linnington's house was in reality a French spy as well as his mistress.

"That's ridiculous."

"Agreed," said Gavin, "and what is more, my Corinne thinks the rumors were begun by Miss Trent and Harriet Woolley."

"If so, they are beyond silly. All it does is cast a cloud on Linnington."

"Quite so, but it all made him furious." Canning straightened his cravat, remembering the force Edmond exerted in this very room to disturb it.

The men sat in contemplation for a moment. Freeman spoke up. "From all you have told John, I gather he really is smitten. She certainly is pleasant and quite attractive in my opinion and certainly cultured if her acquaintance with the opera is any guide. What would keep him from simply offering for her? He has no need to marry anyone for either title or property? Do you have any further information?"

"From what he said, I gathered it was the lady's choice to leave London despite any feelings of his. I must say what upset me the most was his resigned assertion when we got him home, he was babbling there was nothing for him but to offer for Miss Trent. So, I thought it best not to enlighten him about the suspect source of the rumors. He was angry enough at me and my opinions of his lady friend as it was."

"Oh God," said Jamie, "He can't marry that woman. He would be miserable. Sophie and I both think her shallow and devious."

The other men confessed their wives were much of the same opinion.

Their private conversation ended when Edmond appeared, with apologies for being tardy.

The rest of the evening between hands was completely taken up with speculation about what Wellington and Blucher could be planning in the way of a campaign, with the exception of some discrete teasing about his being so foxed the previous Monday. The teasing revealed Linnington had absolutely no memory of the altercation or any of his conversation with John Canning. The friends were hesitant to enlighten him.

***

The group of friends in London, concerned about Linnington's fate, was granted a short reprieve. In April, Edmond abandoned the town for two weeks at Crossfields. As he had done concerning the fall harvest season, he returned to oversee the spring planting. He reveled in his duties on the estate and this year not only was the lambing quite successful, but a pretty mare he had bought the year before successfully foaled a lovely colt. He wasn't sure why he had purchased the animal, since she was a bit small to support his frame for any great length of time, but he now found himself stroking the mare and indulging in the fantasy she would exactly fit someone like Olivia, who appreciated good horses.

The gardeners were busy cleaning winter debris from around the roses, and in the other garden, early daffodils had replaced the impetuous crocuses. The forget-me-nots bloomed next to the lake edge, and banks of white and lavender phlox spread all the way from the confines of the garden over rocks nearly to the drive. He hated to leave. Crossfields always soothed his soul, and it needed some surcease. But he couldn't stop thinking about Olivia and reliving their time together. Here, life without her was somewhat bearable in the familiar sights and sounds denoting to him the essence of home.

He needed to return to London and did so only in time for the very end of the season, where he escorted Miss Trent to a number of occasions. His friends did not think he seemed overly excited about this, but his attention to her was sufficient to cause the gossips to speculate when an announcement would be made.

By the first of May, Linnington was preoccupied with his mother's preparations to depart to the country for the summer and settling things with his man of business for the months he planned to be in the country. On Sunday, he accompanied her to church as usual and, after luncheon, went to St. Stephen's House. He wanted to check on Higgins one last time before he left.

When he arrived, Mr. Selkirk informed him he had arrived at a good time, since the old sergeant was not expected to live through the day. Edmond sat with him, not knowing if Higgins was conscious enough to be aware of his presence or not. Late in the afternoon, Higgins stirred a little, roused by a quiet conversation between Linnington and Mr. Selkirk, who had come over to see how things were.

"Sergeant?" Edmond said softly.

Higgins put out his hand, searching. Edmond took it in both of his.

"Capt'n, you here?"

"Yes. I'm right here."

"You find that girl!" He seemed once more to lapse into unconsciousness.

Somewhere near six in the evening, Sergeant Higgins died.

Edmond took long enough after pulling the sheet over the man's face to inquire about burial arrangements. Selkirk informed him all was in readiness at the military cemetery in Chelsea. There would only be an interment, and it would be on Tuesday morning at ten.

Only Linnington, Banks, Mr. Selkirk, and the priest attended, the priest at the head of the casket, Selkirk at the foot, and Linnington on one side, ignoring Banks, who was glaring at him from the other. He had neither time nor patience to waste on the man, so after each of them had thrown their handful of dirt on the lowered casket, he expressed his thanks to Selkirk and the priest for their attention to Higgins and left before any more conversation.

He could not help but reflect with sadness, both on the loss of an old comrade, and at the memory of Higgins's last words to him. He desperately wanted to at least send a letter to Olivia, informing her of Higgins's demise, but since she had pointedly omitted any direction on a note to him, saying she arrived safely and expressing her appreciation for the salvation of her pension, he was forestalled. Linnington longed for any contact with her other than the cursory little note. Obviously, she did not feel the same, or she would have made her whereabouts known to him.

***

His friends were relieved when the Linnington household departed for the country without any announcements of engagement.

Not many weeks after, Linnington received notice from his man of business affirming the Tothill Fields house had sold at a handsome price. This necessitated a trip to London to finalize matters. Edmond had Jeremy follow with a cart.

They returned with the business completed and Mr. and Mrs. P in the carriage with Edmond for the trip, while Jeremy followed with the cart full of their personal possessions. All he had left of the Tothill Fields house was her desk and chair and the silly dogs they purchased the day they shopped in Stepney. This pitiful collection, two personal notes, the handkerchiefs she gave him at Christmas, and one other keepsake was all that remained, along with a broken heart and some profound regrets. Perhaps if he had approached her staying differently, things would not have ended this way. Could he have offered for her? Would she have accepted? In honesty, he admitted to himself the idea had not occurred to him.

Edmond lingered just long enough at the cottage to see to the unloading. He wandered slowly to the main house, stopping long enough in the hall to put some items in the little desk when Jeremy brought it into the house. Then he went to tend the estate accounts in the library.

***

In the second-floor parlor, the sounds of Jeremy and another of the footmen bringing things up the stairs reached Elizabeth's ears. Curious, she looked out of the sitting room door to see the men at the open door of the blue bedroom, adjoining Edmond's chambers, evidently rearranging furniture.

After they finished and left the room, she stole inside to see what had been delivered. By the windows facing the gardens was the little tambour desk and its chair. She went to it and opened the tambour. It was empty of everything, but in the drawer, she found two linen handkerchiefs, finely stitched and with his cypher in the corner. On top of them lay two notes in Olivia's well-schooled feminine hand. The first with no mark and the second one postmarked Launceston. She was tempted to read them but refrained. Beside these items lay a length of scarlet ribbon.

She closed the drawer and laid her hand briefly on the satiny surface. As she turned to leave the room, something captured her attention. There, on the mantle sat the pair of Staffordshire dogs.

Oh dear. Oh dear, my poor, sweet boy!

Chapter Twenty-Six

April found Olivia comfortably settled at the vicarage with only two clouds on the horizon. The first was Mrs. Todd who seemed to harbor a deep resentment toward her. For the most part, they were civil to each other, but Olivia found the tension of maintaining that civility difficult to live with after the amiability of living with the Ps. Father Williams, as she called him, referring to their relationship, not his status as clergy, made up for much of this discomfort. They fell into an easy camaraderie with discussions of public affairs, books, and an occasional game of chess. Most of the conversation at meals was about the growing state of war on the Continent, a subject of interest to each of them when at the table.

The second cause of distress concerned her health. She was feeling decidedly unwell each morning. Although sad upon awakening to another day of adjusting to a life never including Edmond Linnington, she finally determined this was indeed physical.

Toward the end of April, her worries added a third. Along with the continued feeling of dislocation, with her emotions hovering somewhere between London and Cornwall, the worry about her ailment grew intense. At first, the slight nausea passed after she was up and breakfasted only on tea and toast. Food did not appeal to her. As the days stretched into May, the nausea increased until she found herself retching into the basin almost every morning. The urge to vomit persisted through much of the morning.

This situation did not long elude either Mrs. Todd or Mary Hastings, the milliner. Mrs. Todd said nothing but seemed to treat her with even more disapproval. Mrs. Hastings was solicitous. She was concerned about Olivia not eating and began to provide her with tea and a cream cracker in the midmorning. Olivia at first tried to pass off the condition as something she had eaten that disagreed with her, but it went on long enough she abandoned the excuse. Olivia would become heavy eyed with sleep in the afternoon, a fact that did not escape Mary Hasting's eye.

"Olivia, my dear. I don't think you are at all well. Should you see Dr. Taylor?"

Olivia blanched at the suggestion. "Oh no, it is nothing so serious, I assure you."

Mary stopped inquiring, but Olivia would notice her concerned frown every once in a while.

Other than this infirmity, she enjoyed both her work and reestablishing some acquaintance with the town. For the most part, its residents retained not the least interest in what the "old earl" had done and was quite satisfied with the distant relative who had acceded to the property and title. She made no attempt to contact the present occupant of Newington Hall, nor did they reach out to her. The situation seemed to suit both parties. She did note the present earl had not only kept Mr. Williams in his living at All Saint's Church but was quite generous with the parish as a whole. She took little notice of the family at Sunday services and they took no notice of her, but they seemed kindly disposed to the town's people and for that she was grateful.

By late May, with the Hawthorne's blooming, she could no longer ignore her situation.

A particularly beautiful Sunday morning just after dawn, Olivia lay upon her bed and finally allowed herself to assess the situation. For a while, she avoided considering her symptoms in detail. She lay listening to the busy birds, chattering in their own languages, probably hard at the task of nest building. Through the open casements, she could hear the turtledoves had returned. She had seen a barn swallow flit about the eaves of the church the day before. Early this morning, she heard the sweet call of the nightingale. As the breeze gently lifted the curtains, she could see the lilacs in full bloom.

Thankfully, the nausea had abated, but something about this rosy dawn brought tears to her eyes. She rolled onto her back and stared at the ceiling, watching the light reflecting from the brook dance on the gabled surface of the room.

She knew exactly what was happening to her. She had now not bled for two months, and, from her experience with other officers' wives, the signs were familiar. Her body was ever so slightly swollen and her breasts tender. She had to acknowledge she would continue to increase in size until the loose garments she wore could no longer conceal the truth. Perhaps she had another two months, but by late July, her condition would be apparent to the world.

A rush of revulsion swept over her, not for her condition but for herself. What was it about her that attracted scandal like a magnet? Here she was, about to bring more shame on her family even though they were gone. She must have committed some terrible sin to bring all these calamities upon herself. Yet, her mind refused to relegate the joy she had known with Linnington to the dustbin of venality. At least on her part, it was love allowing her to accept, yes decidedly encourage, his advances.

She did acknowledge to herself this present scandal was brought on by her own actions.

In trying to assess her portion of guilt resulting in her pregnancy, Olivia allowed herself to plow the old ground of her father's death. She had confessed nearly the entire story to Father Williams before she and David were married but never related some details to him nor to Mme. Dufour or even Sophie. It was in June, the summer just before she was eighteen.

For more than a year, she had tried to talk some sense into her father, whose business was not entirely hidden to her. Finally, his man of business and his solicitor told her the extent of ruin her father had brought down upon their heads. The more she pled with him to change his ways, the more aggressive her father became in his defense. Even worse, in the depths of his cups, he spoke to her in the abusive way she imagined he might speak to the women he hired or coerced to share his bed. For her own sake, she could not give in to her terror. The day he died, he finally made the overt actions she dreaded. She had gone to the library to once more attempt to talk to him. She did not realize how drunk he was since it was only late afternoon. As usual, she tried reason. She remembered the conversation vividly.

"Father, please. Don't you think it time you had something to eat? You have drunk quite enough, I believe."

"You believe? You don't know what you believe."

"I know I would like for you to take some time to tend to our affairs."

"Affairs. Yes, indeed affairs. At your age that's all you want. Like your mother, you'll be all kisses and sweetness until a wedding and then full of humors and headaches. At your age though you're randy as any goat. I should show you what's it's like. Break you in."

He put out his hand and gripped her shoulder. She pushed it away.

"Play coy, will you?"

He kept advancing on her. She could smell his rancid unwashed body and the smokiness of Scotch whiskey. She was repelled. With both palms, she gave his chest a push, making him stumble. Regaining his balance, he came at her in a rage, seizing her by the arms.

The result was he pushed her against his desk, tore the bodice of her dress, and was fumbling about both her body and his. Frantic to escape, she managed to aim a ferocious kick at his shin. He howled in pain and gave her just enough space to give him another shove, and this time he lost his balance but retained a grip on her arm. With her free hand, she reached into the drawer of the desk for the loaded gun he kept there. Taking him by surprise, she threatened him with the weapon.

Stunned, he backed away.

Olivia was overcome by the realization she could not pull the trigger, yet she desperately wanted to. All the feelings of fury over the way he treated her mother and his determination to ruin them completely overtook every part of her reason and all of her emotions. In horror at her own actions and feelings, she brandished the weapon at him.

In a rage she screamed at him, "You drunken old beast. You have ruined us and have no way to remedy the situation. You killed my mother and you don't deserve to live."

An expression of abject fear transformed her father's countenance. This in turn changed her rage into terror at what she knew she was perfectly capable of doing. She threw the weapon on the desk and fled to her room in hysterical tears.

Through the heavy closed door came the distinct sound of a single gunshot. She went completely numb, and, disregarding her torn dress, rushed downstairs both knowing and fearing what she would find. The sight of the bloody mess and scattered pieces of bone, flesh, and brain turned her stomach. She automatically removed the pistol form her father's hand just as the butler Billings—the only servant in the house at the time—walked into the room. He took the gun from her and laid it on the desk.

"I didn't do it. I took the gun out of his hand. He did it." She found herself stammering.

Her torn garment was obvious to Billings. "No matter, my lady.

That was his only remark. She'd always believed Billings was convinced she had not been the one to pull the trigger, but somehow, enough of the facts circulated to cast a shadow of doubt with some in the town. To her, it didn't much matter. She had taken the weapon out of the desk. She might as well have handed it to him or even pulled the trigger herself.

Olivia certainly considered herself as fully culpable now with her pregnancy as with her father's death. David's death was another matter. She was in no way responsible for a war. Yet, she'd agreed to marry him, knowing he would go into danger.

After the horror of realizing she was carrying a child and the thought of the inexorable progress of pregnancy came a peculiar sense of satisfaction. She wasn't barren after all. Whatever grief she experienced by not giving David a child vanished like morning mist. At least she would have this small part of Edmond to keep. But the prospect of an unmarried mother in a small town was daunting. Silent tears ran down her cheeks. She put her hand on her belly, and an overwhelming sense of protection swept over her for this tiny creature inside her.

Presently, there was no way out of the situation, other than a resolve to keep this in her heart and wait for the proper time to confide in someone. It could not be Sophie. She was sure Sophie would insist Linnington be told, and Olivia was nowhere near being able to face such a prospect. After she arrived in Cornwall, she sent a note to Sophie, telling her she was safely in Cornwall and also sent one to Linnington, thanking him for his assistance to her. She included no direction in either, Sophie didn't need it, and she purposely posted the letters in Launceston to conceal their true origin, not wishing him to think she was expecting any more contact. Perhaps it was a mistake to write to him at all. At the time, Olivia believed she only wanted him to know of her safe arrival and give him the information she was settled in Cornwall and expected nothing more from their acquaintance. It did not occur to her it might also signal she had no more interest in him.

Perhaps Mary Hastings would be the one in whom to confide. She got out of bed. She didn't have to decide any of this today.

***

The next eight weeks passed uneventfully, the attention of everyone drawn to the progress of the war. The news the third week in July of Wellington's victory at Waterloo penetrated quickly down to the West Country, and the fourth week in July was one of celebration. Olivia was as elated about the victory as anyone and just as distressed at her own condition. The nausea had abated, but on

Sundays, she had difficulty buttoning the Spenser around her bosom.

One day, Olivia caught sight of Mary Hasting's daughter Anne whispering to her mother at the entrance of the shop. Both of them gave Olivia a surreptitious glance as Mary hurried Anne out of the door.

By midweek, the celebration over the victory subsided, and in the afternoon, after attending to an important customer from Launceston, Olivia went into the workroom to trim a straw bonnet. Pulling a handkerchief from her pocket, she began to cry silently.

Mary Hastings was a kind woman and genuinely fond of Olivia. In years past, she had provided the countess with many a *chapeau* and bonnet and even sold Olivia her very first one. Olivia became aware Mary had seated herself opposite her, the shop now quiet. Mrs. Hastings took both of her hands and held them tightly.

"Now, luv, tell me what is going on."

Olivia just sobbed harder.

"Are you sad about your condition, my dear?"

"So, you know. As I suppose everyone else in town does."

"I confess Mrs. Todd seems to have made it her business to spread suspicion."

"I don't understand why the woman dislikes me so." Olivia was avoiding the real subject of the conversation.

"Oh, my dear, it has nothing to do with you. I am sorry to say it seems when she was a very young girl, she was badly used by your late father."

"Oh, I see." Olivia had no reason to question any further and was at least slightly relieved to know this only had to do with the fact she was the earl's daughter.

"So, tell me, how far along are you?"

"Not quite four months, I believe."

"And the father, if I may ask?"

"A gentleman in London when I worked there." She finally added, although she regretted it, "My employer."

Mary Hastings frowned. "I must ask, did he force himself on you?"

"I have to admit, he did not."

"Then do you love this man?"

"I find I do, with all my heart."

"Does he return your affection?"

"I believe to a certain extent but not so far as marriage, I am led to believe."

"Still, don't you think he should know?"

"The last thing I want is for him to feel obligated to make any permanent arraignment against his will or to bring any shame on his good name. He is a man of character and I am afraid he might offer out of a sense of duty. I could not do such a thing to him, regardless of the consequences."

"Still, I think any man should know about his paternity. Olivia, I think the first thing you must do is tell the vicar."

"I am devastated at the idea of bringing shame upon him and his house. I had thought of asking you if I could take rooms above the shop here."

"I will help you anyway I can, and I assure you, your employment is secure, but for now I think telling Mr. Williams is imperative."

She gave Olivia a quick hug. "Now, dry your eyes. I hear the bell.

Someone needs to be waited upon." She hurried into the front of the shop and Olivia began to regain her composure and get to work.

She couldn't face talking to the vicar this evening, but the next afternoon, she left the shop a little early and found him in his study.

"Father Williams, have you a moment?"

"Come sit down, my dear." He came from behind his desk to sit opposite her, much as Mrs. Hastings had done.

Olivia poured out the story. "I'm so sorry to bring this shame on you," she finished.

Like Mrs. Hastings, he took her hand. "My dear, you don't think you are the first young woman to sit in this room and tell me what you have related?"

"I suppose not."

"More than you would imagine."

His advice to her was much like Mary Hastings's. In the end, she promised to write to Sophie and ask not only for advice, but if she or James had some idea of Linnington's feelings.

In addition, once the subject was broached and she acknowledged her pregnancy, she became aware of how general the knowledge was. She'd spent so much time denying the fact to herself, her physical changes made her condition apparent to many of the women in the village and some of the men.

After church the next Sunday, Henry Goddard requested permission to see her home. He was a man somewhere between the rustic farmer he was and the country squire his acumen and industry had made him. He was quite a presentable fellow, with a charitable as well as straightforward attitude toward everything in life. He began by saying how much he had always admired Olivia.

He had gallantly ended by offering to do anything he could to be of service to her, including marriage, if that arrangement was something she would consider. She was deeply touched. This kind man was willing to provide an avenue for her to gain respectability. She needed to know how Linnington felt before she could give him an answer.

She immediately sat down at her desk to write to Sophie.

Chapter Twenty-Seven

Elizabeth found herself uncharacteristically on edge. She had been pacing about the drawing room at Crossfields. The house was silent, except for the ticking of the ornate brass mantle clock. Edmond was in London for a few days. She had insisted he go. James was also there on business, as he had informed them the last time the Talents visited. Perhaps an outing with his male friends, some vigorous exercise, and a game of whist accompanied by brandy and cigars might lighten his mood.

She was aware he had plunged once more into the black place he had been when he first returned from Spain. At the time, she believed grief over Giles might have heightened his moodiness, but time elapsed and he grew no better. It had not escaped even the attention of Harriet his dark mood had lightened and he was much like his old self during the winter. Harriet speculated the presence of the lovely Miss Trent at social occasions had drawn him out. Elizabeth, however, thought it was due to quite another attraction. The night before Mrs. Williams left, not only had he not kept his appointment at Mrs. Summer's ball but had not returned home for more than a day and a half until he was helped there by John Canning, having spent most of the intervening time drinking at Whites, as Owens had confided in Rose who informed her of the matter.

It was time she wrote to Sophie. She had tried to stay out of her son's affairs, but she could no longer sit idly and watch him descend and stay in his present black mood.

Elizabeth repaired to her bedroom and sat at her escritoire, writing—

My dearest Sophie,

I hope this finds you, James, and the children well.

My dear, I am going to presume upon your good nature and delve into a subject of the strictest privacy. I assure you I have said nothing of my suspicions in the matter to Edmond and do not intend to, unless not only am I correct, but you also agree to any action on either of our parts concerning this matter.

Sophie, after a conversation with that fount of all information, Lady Eleanor Whitworth, before her untimely demise, I believe perhaps there is a possibility you might have information concerning a certain Mrs. Williams, who, as you know, Edmond employed to ready his house in Tothill Fields for sale. From things Lady Whitworth related, I wondered if Mrs. Williams was, before her marriage, one Lady Olivia Constant, daughter of the late Earl of Wallingford. If this is so, I hasten to add I am aware of the unfortunate circumstances surrounding this young woman's fall from grace. I am also reasonably certain Edmond has no idea of her true background. However, I do have the feeling he formed more of an attachment to her than he will admit to himself or anyone else, except perhaps James.

If you have any thoughts on the subject, please write to me. If you do not, or think it best to abandon the subject completely, I shall understand.

Yours fondly,
Elizabeth Linnington

An answer came nearly by return post.

My dear Lady Elizabeth,

I cannot express to you my relief at your letter. This entire matter has weighed on my mind until I am quite distracted.

Your suspicions are completely well-founded. Olivia and I grew up together. The very Mme. Dufour who owned the teashop where Olivia was employed was her French governess. Lady Wallingford was most gracious in allowing me to participate in all the lessons at Newington Hall, and it was she herself who instructed both Olivia and me on the piano.

However, to my great distress, after the unfortunate death of the earl, my parents forbade me to have anything to do with Olivia. The town was quite divided in its attitude toward her. Consequently, when she was left completely without resources, David Williams, the son of our local vicar and a lovely man, asked for her hand. She was grateful for his generosity and, I believe, loved him solely for that reason.

As time elapsed, I came to London where I met James, and Olivia and David were billeted somewhere in Yorkshire. Over the years, we completely lost touch with each other until, one day, about two years ago now, we encountered one another by chance at a bookstall near Westminster Bridge. Since then, I made it a habit to visit the shop, usually early in the morning, so we could visit after the baking was done and before customers arrived. I am happy to say we renewed our close friendship, and I was pleased to take the children upon occasion so she could know them.

Olivia wanted to keep her true identity a secret. I believe her to have been badly scarred by the treatment of the townspeople. She seems to live in fear if people knew who she was, some would treat her in the same way, or at least pity her beyond bearing. She is in many ways quite a self-sufficient creature, and I think she considers her identity as just Mrs. Williams much more suited to her present status in life. So long as she was at Mme. Dufour's, I thought it probably appropriate she not advertise her status of birth. I was less agreeable when she was particularly insistent Edmond not be aware of her background. She wanted to preserve the relationship of employer and employee. I urged her to tell him the truth.

On this last delicate subject of their attraction to each other, I have come to much the same conclusion about how the relationship has changed. I found it especially noteworthy Edmond insisted on escorting her to the opera. Since our box is directly across the theater from yours, I detected during the evening the sort of easy intimacy people form when they are truly in love, thus the source of my own distress at the downturn in Edmond's view of life.

I await any further thoughts you have on the matter.

Fondly,

Sophie Talent

Elizabeth kept her answer short and to the point.

My Dear Sophie,

I am both relieved and distressed with your confirmation of my assessment in this matter.

What I did not relate in my last letter to you was the fact the importunate Lady Whitworth also attended the opera. It appears she espied Lady Olivia and recognized her, or thought she did. The

*following Monday, the day before Olivia was to leave town, Lady
Whitworth insisted on coming the very next afternoon to call.
Surmising I suspect, my original invitation and quizzing her at tea
reflected some suspicions on my part, she was eager to confide the
fact this certain Mrs. Williams was indeed Lady Olivia Constant. She
pressed to know the extent of Edmond 's interest in Olivia. I assured
her whatever the relationship, to my knowledge it has always been a
professional one and, in any case, was not strong enough to keep
Olivia in London as she had departed for Cornwall to live. I implied
Edmond was in all probability still interested in Miss Trent. I
confess I purposely did not show much enthusiasm for the prospect
of Miss Trent, rather hoping Lady Whitworth would make her
knowledge about Olivia known and that it would reach Edmond 's
ears forthwith, saving you and me from the conundrum of whether
or not to tell him ourselves, you because of your promise and I
because I had no idea at the time what were Olivia 's feelings.*

*As you know, the unfortunate Lady Whitworth was stricken
with apoplexy that very day. I confess I was somewhat saddened
when the Season ended with no whisper of her discovery.*

*As for Edmond, I am at a loss as to what you and I can do. I do,
however, encourage you to inquire subtly of James as to Edmond 's
mind on the matter and if he has any intention of pursuing a
relationship with Olivia, and please do keep me informed.*

Yours,

EL

Near the first of August, Sophie's next letter crossed with
Elizabeth's. Elizabeth opened it with a sense of foreboding.

Dear Elizabeth,

Earlier in the spring, long before I received your last letter, I received one from dear Olivia. She had written me when she was settled in Cornwall to tell me she was lodging with the vicar, her father-in-law, so I would know her direction. She also informed me she had secured a position with Mrs. Hastings, the local milliner, and to express her deep gratitude to Edmond for securing her long-delayed widow's pension from the government. She said she was writing to thank him but made no other mention. I assume she did not give him any direction for a return of correspondence.

Then I received yesterday a letter from her written in the greatest distress. It is also with deepest distress I inform you of its contents. Olivia is now nearly four months gone with child. She left no room for conjecture. She wrote to ask my advice.

As you can imagine, she was sorely loath to reveal to Edmond the entire length of her deception. I have some feeling for the circumstance, since her secret is the only one I have ever kept from my own husband and I am ashamed of the fact. On the other hand, she feels it not fair for Edmond be kept unaware a child of his is coming but is convinced his feelings would only be ones of obligation, and she does not think she could bear it.

There is, however, an alternative in her mind to the unbearable prospect of leaving the child without a father. The local farmer's son, a Mr. Goddard, whom I remember from girlhood as a very decent sort of young boy, has offered to take on her responsibilities. As she put it to me, she is quite tired of having to be rescued at the last moment by some helpful man, first David, then Edmond, and *now Henry Goddard. She confessed she was more than half a mind to simply go her own way. It seems Mrs. Hastings and another one or two of the townswomen have supported her in this. And, I add, some have not.*

I am at a loss to know what to do. James has gone to London and will return tomorrow, but we are immediately to go to Harriet's house party for the weekend. I am more than half a mind to break my promise to Olivia and tell him all if I can find the proper time. It seems to me things are quite beyond anything you and I can manage. Perhaps James could do better.

I shall stay in touch.

Yours Fondly,

ST

Elizabeth experienced a moment of horror at the opening lines of Sophie's letter until she read of the approaching birth. She found herself staring out of the diamond-paned parlor window at the rose garden in full and fragrant bloom, smiling at the prospect of this grandchild's arrival. All she could do now was pray about it, which she immediately began to do. Time had taken all matters out of their hands.

Things might come to a climax much sooner than she expected them and, she hoped sort themselves more quickly than she feared. Also, she hoped the resolution would be one of satisfaction to her and Sophie. But there were clouds on the horizon in the form of the gallant Mr. Goddard and Harriet's obsession with marrying Edmond off to the odious Miss Trent. Edmond was scheduled to go to Harriet's for the house party that very weekend and the aforementioned Miss Trent was to be there at Harriet's invitation. Elizabeth suspected both women intended to push Miss Trent's advantage.

She could only pray something would intervene to keep the two scheming women from accomplishing their goal this weekend. She was afraid if Edmond offered and was accepted, he would feel honor bound to stay with the commitment. She had done all she could do for the moment. Harriet had not included her in the house party, nor would she expect to attend since it was all young people. However, if things progressed without event, she was determined to take matters into her own hands and disclose all to Edmond on his return, unless some better solution could be found.

When Edmond returned from London, he was taken up with business details and hurriedly packing for the weekend at Harriet's. If Elizabeth had wanted to, there was no chance to inquire about anything. She managed to ask if his visit with James was pleasant, and he added it was, with no further comment. Whatever her part was, it would have wait until after the weekend. The prospect of his being at Harriet's with Miss Trent frightened her.

Chapter Twenty-Eight

The only thing lightening Linnington's dark mood was the victory at Waterloo. *The Times* quoted Wellington as declaring, "That was a near thing." The citation made chills run up Linnington's spine as he recalled the battles he had experienced that had indeed been a "close thing."

By August, the public celebrations had given way to more private expressions, so the Woolleys took the opportunity to invite the Talents, Cannings, and Freemans to a weekend house party at Belle Meade, their estate just beyond Oxford. Edmond suspected Harriet had, of course, also invited Miss Sybil Trent. Friday and Saturday were to be spent in games and dancing as well as partaking of Harriet's ample table. The women planned to return to their homes after services and luncheon on Sunday, with the men staying to ride on Monday and then take their leave the next day. Although not athletic, Malcolm loved to ride and exercise his considerable kennel of foxhounds. The men intended to run the hounds and perhaps challenge each other to their own private point-to-point race if the weather was not too hot for the horses.

Linnington prepared for the visit, with a certain resignation about the first part but anticipation of the second.

He traveled by carriage, with one of his favorite hunters tethered to the rear of the vehicle. He preferred to travel on his larger roan gelding, Max, but considering Monday's outing, he chose Hector, a better jumper.

The weekend began pleasantly enough, except he had the feeling

Miss Trent was attaching herself to him much as a leech would do, and he found it made him rather uncomfortable. Every time he turned, she was there with her insipid smile and simpering, it took all his politeness to refrain from being rude.

On Saturday morning, he went for a solitary ride on Hector. He needed to clear his head. His sister was determined he make a match with Miss Trent to whom he was clearly not attracted, but often physical desire was not the point of marriage anyway. She seemed amiable enough, although he had to admit after a considerable time in her company, he didn't know much of her mind or her disposition. He couldn't help but compare her to the ease and intimacy he enjoyed with Olivia, but that was not the point. Miss Trent was attractive in a rather chilly way, but of good family with ample resources. He could see why society would consider it a good match.

He had given his own behavior toward Olivia much thought. Their last night's lovemaking had been prompted by an overwhelming desire for her on his part and certainly returned in kind by her. He had made a fatal error, however. He should have offered marriage. He couldn't help but speculate a proposal might have produced a different outcome.

He was aware, of course, their difference in station would be remarked on, and it was the first time in his life he could remember ever being constrained by what society might think. He couldn't help but believe his impulse to offer her the "proposition" had come from some latent feeling about how marriage to a simple war widow would appear to the Ton. He was ashamed of himself, but since what was done was done, he had to look to the future.

Olivia sent him a short note after arriving in Cornwall, thanking him for his help and assuring him she was well settled. The note was postmarked Launceston, which told him nothing about her whereabouts and she had not offered a direction. He took the fact to mean she had put an end to whatever their relationship had been. His feelings for her had not changed, but he had enough pride to know when something could not be salvaged.

With a sigh, he turned toward Belle Meade. He supposed it was time for him to come up to scratch and get his life in some semblance of order.

Saturday evening was taken up with dancing, Linnington mostly partnering Miss Trent. The evening was hot, and sweat was pooling in his armpits, dampening his linen coat, so it was with both relief and trepidation he complied when Miss Trent declared herself nearly faint with the heat and suggested a turn on the terrace.

After the first lazy turn, the lady got to the core of her purpose in getting him alone.

"So, Linnington, you have shown me quite a lot of attention at the end of the Season and this summer. I am most grateful for it, but I am wondering about your intentions, if I may be so bold as to inquire."

"It has been my pleasure, madam," he temporized. She stopped their stroll and turned to face him.

"Have you considered matrimony, sir?"

"I have," he answered honestly.

To his astonishment, she simply smiled. "Then it is settled, Edmond. I accept and am most happy. As I may have mentioned, my parents accompanied me and are in lodgings with friends in Oxford, and I am sure it would be convenient for you to call upon my father on Tuesday morning on your way to Crossfields after you finish with your hunting Monday."

Linnington stood aghast. So, it had happened. The decision had been taken squarely out of his hands, and it appeared he was now engaged.

"You may kiss me." She held her face up and closed her eyes.

He bent and kissed her briefly on unmoving lips. It was like kissing a dry fall leaf. *My, God, what have I done ?* He had little time to ruminate. She took him by the arm and led him inside, a self-satisfied smile on her face.

It didn't take much time for the news to circulate through the women. He could tell by the smile of accomplishment on his sister's face. Blessedly the company soon broke up and went to bed.

***

Sophie relayed the news to her husband when they retired on Saturday night. She was deeply distressed, overly so for some reason James could not fathom. They were both undone by the revelation Edmond had finally done the deed.

On Sunday, the women departed in their several carriages without any overt reference to what was happening, but the men managed to express their dismay briefly to each other. At least Talent, Canning, and Freeman did. Yet, none of them had been brave enough to raise their doubts to Edmond.

Monday was taken up with sport. Racing through the countryside on horseback gave them little time to consider the news. After dinner, Malcolm excused himself to bed but encouraged the other four to continue to a game of French billiards in the game room.

James was at a loss to know whether or not to broach the subject of a pending engagement. Canning, however, had no such compunction. Seeming occupied in lining up his shot, he said to Linnington without looking at him, "So, Edmond, from what Emily tells me, you have made the move and offered for Miss Trent."

"I believe I have," he answered.

"I must say, I'm rather, surprised, my man. Of course, it is none of my business, but I find you a very forgiving person, considering Miss Trent was the source of the rumors about Mrs. Williams, for whom I think you had some regard."

James recognized the flash of anger on his friend's face. "What are you saying, John? What rumors?"

John Canning calmly took his shot, banking it well. He turned and faced Edmond directly. "Edmond, you say you do not remember anything at all of our encounter at White's the day Mrs. Williams departed London?"

"I confess I was so drunk, I do not remember nine-tenths of it. Owens did inform me you were friend enough to see me home in my condition."

"Well, that night, I told you about the rumors, and it made you exceedingly angry. Does any of this jog your memory?"

"I'm afraid it doesn't."

Canning repeated the story.

"That's ridiculous. To what end would someone make up such a tale?"

"Possibly, my friend, for fear you were overly fond of the lady. Our wives concur in our assessment of the source of the rumors, I might add." The set look on Canning's face indicated he was going to see this situation through.

"But it could serve no reasonable purpose except to cast calumny on me," persisted Linnington.

"I'm not sure in these affair's reason has much to do with it," added Freeman.

All three of the friends stared at Linnington.

He slapped the palm of his hand furiously on the table, upsetting a wineglass. "If all of you knew this and suspected I didn't, why the hell didn't you speak up sooner?"

"As for me, I had endured your wrath once on the subject and didn't care to repeat it. Had I known you had any real intention of offering for the silly girl, I would have chanced it."

"Good friends you are. The damned lot of you!"

"Please, Edmond," James pled earnestly. "What's done is done. You cannot, however, go through with this marriage. You simply aren't suited, no matter about Mrs. Williams."

Freeman finally put his oar in. "Oh, I think Mrs. Williams matters."

The silence of the other two indicated their agreement on the subject. Finally, Freeman cleared his throat." Come on, friends. None of us is in the mood for a game. Sleep on this, Edmond, and make a careful decision. You have a chance to cry off in Oxford tomorrow if you so decide. That way, you can be assured the story will have minimal circulation beyond the group here and none of us are inclined to further any information."

As they walked toward the stairs, James stopped Linnington. "Come into the library for a moment, Edmond." Without waiting for an answer, he ushered his friend into the room.

235

James took time to pour them each a healthy portion of brandy and sat opposite his oldest friend.

"I'm not going to dally about this. I know you well enough, Edmond. You're besotted by the lovely Mrs. Williams, aren't you?"

"I am. She occupies all of my thoughts."

"Then you cannot marry Miss Trent in any case. It is not fair to either her or you."

"I know you are right. I will make my apologies to her father and to her and cry off tomorrow before this progresses any further."

"I don't envy you the task, but more importantly, what are you going to do about Mrs. Williams?"

"I implored her to stay, and she refused."

"Did you offer for her?"

"Not exactly, but I did implore her to stay." Linnington gave James a sheepish grin.

"Good God. A proposition, then?"

"I suppose it was."

"If she feels the least about you as you do about her, such a suggestion was hardly an inducement, do you think?"

"Probably not, but it can't be helped now."

"Would you marry her if she consented?"

"I would."

"Then go find her, man, and ask her."

"How do you propose I do that?" Linnington was decidedly cross. "I received a note from her saying she was settled but with no direction as to her whereabouts. It was postmarked from Launceston, but such a large community cannot be the town she described to me. I can hardly ride out to Cornwall and stop in every hamlet enquiring if a Mrs. Williams of her description lives there!"

"For God's sake, Linnington, ask the servants! Haven't you discovered the truth? Servants, and I might add, wives know things we don't dream of."

Linnington's face immediately cleared. "Do you suppose the Ps would have any information as to the name of the town?"

"It's worth an inquiry."

"James, you are brilliant and just the sort of friend every man should have."

James stood up, gave his friend a manly hug. "Then all is settled. Off to bed and best of luck tomorrow."

Chapter Twenty-Nine

The men met the following morning for breakfast before each of them departed in opposite directions. Both Canning and Freeman would have two days of travel before they reached their estates in the North and East of the country. For James and Edmond, it would only be a good day's ride, Edmond east toward Crossfields and James south by approximately the same distance to White Marsh Manor.

Edmond would have a long day, since Miss Trent had informed him before she left her father would receive him at 10 a.m. She provided directions to her parents' friends' home. She certainly seemed to have all things under control without his help. The fact rankled Linnington.

His carriage with Owens and Jeremy departed on Sunday when the women left, so he stowed the small bit of traveling gear he had behind the saddle on Hector and prepared to meet Mr. Trent dressed in the same casual riding gear he had worn the day before, except for a clean shirt. He hoped he was presentable enough, but then perhaps if he presented a less favorable appearance, it might make it easier for the gentleman to accept the slight he was about to bestow on the daughter.

On the way to Oxford, he rethought his approach and after he had dismounted at the house and been admitted, he introduced himself to Mr. Trent and then requested his indulgence to meet Miss Trent in privacy a moment.

He was shown into a small parlor and after a few minutes joined by the lady.

"Miss Trent," he began, "I come to you with profound apology. I am afraid I have misled you concerning my attention, and I take full responsibility."

He paused to take a deep breath and was interrupted by Sybil Trent, an unmistakably incredulous look on her face. "You're not crying off, are you, Linnington?" There was a distinct edge in her voice.

"I fear I am, madam." He was aware he was making something of a hash of all this. Her eyes narrowed and nostrils flared. "I simply have come to the conclusion we do not suit."

"Do not suit? Is that it, or is it something to do with your little French strumpet making you feel you don't want to go through with this?" The woman was now in a state of complete rage, her voice had lost all moderation, and the tone reminded Edmond of Carmelita Fernandez when she lost control.

"The lady you mention is neither a strumpet nor French nor the cause of my decision," he said coldly, now more than ever sure he was doing the right thing.

His words only enhanced her mood, and she shouted at him, "You dog. I've wasted two years on you and not without your encouragement to my mind. Get out of here, you horrid man!" It was an order she punctuated, like Carmelita, by grasping a china ornament from the mantle and hurling it at his head. He ducked, through long practice, and the piece smashed into the wall behind him.

"I bid you good day, Miss Trent. You have made your point." Turning on his heel, he left the room. In the hall, he stopped to offer his apologies to the speechless father, saying he regretted any pain he had caused either the daughter or her family. He didn't wait for more conversation but left and continued his journey to Crossfields, feeling lighter and happier since Saturday.

He did not arrive until late afternoon. His first stop was at the P's cottage. They were surprised but delighted to see him.

Partridge began by congratulating him on his upcoming nuptials, the news having spread like wildfire through the staff.

"I'm afraid, Mr. Partridge, there has been a change in plans."

"Oh, I'm sorry to hear of it, sir."

"Or not. I have come to inquire from either you or Mrs. Person if you can recall anything Mrs. Williams told you during her stay in London about the name of the town in Cornwall where she planned to return?"

The Ps both stood silently for a moment then exchanged rather knowing looks.

Mrs. P took the lead. "I do not recall any specific reference to it, my lord." She hesitated, exchanging another glance with her husband, and Edmond's heart sank. "But I believe if you inquire of Mrs. Talent, you may have some success in finding out what you want to know."

"Sophie?"

Partridge took up at this point. "Sir, we are not at liberty to tell you more, but I think Mrs. Talent will be able to satisfy any questions you have."

The couple stood tight-lipped and unsmiling. They were not going to reveal any more, leaving him no option but to seek out Sophie.

He thanked them for their help and took his leave, hoping the fear and trepidation he felt did show.

With this mix of emotions was an enormous curiosity. If Sophie was acquainted with Olivia, he was certain she had not confided in James. Otherwise, the conversation at Belle Meade would have been different.

Instead of mounting the bay, he led the horse up the long drive, hoping the exercise would clear his head a little. By the time he reached the house and handed the animal to the groom, he had made his plans.

When his butler opened the door, he said, "Benson, please be so kind as to send Owens and Jeremy to my chambers immediately."

"Very good, my lord."

Linnington mounted the stairs two at a time and went directly to his dressing room, stripping off his coat. The men arrived, and Linnington issued rapid-fire orders. "Both of you, I need to prepare for a rather lengthy journey. Jeremy, please inform the coachman I need the traveling carriage prepared for an extensive journey. You, the driver, and Owens will leave directly tomorrow morning for Exeter. You should be there with good weather sometime on the third day. Jeremy, procure lodging for yourselves and the driver as well as stabling for the horses. Owens, engage the best room available for me at the Dog and Crown in Exeter. I will make a journey to the Talents and then meet you in Exeter, probably a day after you arrive. I shall be taking enough clothing, Owens, on Max to see me though a day at the Talents and however long it takes me to travel directly from White Marsh Manor to Exeter. I shall spend one day there and then all of us will proceed to Launceston for the next part of our journey. I have no idea how long this journey will be, so prepare my things and yours for at least two weeks, much of it traveling. Before I leave, come to the office and I shall provide funds to keep all of you until I arrive. Are there any questions?"

"I don't believe so, sir," said Owens. "Jeremy?"

"No, sir."

"Get to it then, men."

Elizabeth stood in her bedroom doorway, blatantly listening to all.

"I need a word, Mother."

"Shall we move to the sitting room?"

Edmond followed his mother into the upstairs sitting room. He had been confident barking orders to the men while quailing at the thought of informing his mother about the purpose of his journey.

He cleared his throat.

"First, I am quite sure my sister will inform you of an occurrence this weekend at the house party. It seems there was a brief misunderstanding between Miss Trent and myself."

His mother remained impassive, but some emotion flickered in her eyes.

He couldn't read her expression, so he persisted, "I realized after she left, through a series of circumstances, I could not go through with the engagement. Her parents happened to be visiting in Oxford, so I took the opportunity to call on Miss Trent there and cry off as well as offering my apologies for acting so badly toward her."

His mother remained silent, her face reflected relief, so he plunged ahead.

"Mother, I believe you remember Mrs. Williams who assisted me with the Tothill Fields house?"

"Indeed."

Her expression still did not change, so he wasn't sure what she thought about this opening gambit. He wished she would give him some hint of her feelings.

"I find I have fallen quite in love with her, Mother, and I intend to go to the West Country and ask her to be my wife. I am aware she has neither name nor fortune, but having met her, you know she presents quite a pleasing appearance in all aspects of her behavior."

"And I believe I heard you say you were going to stop by the Talents?"

"I am. It has come to my attention Sophie has some information about Mrs. Williams's whereabouts. This is a surprise to me, but I am going to the manor first to make inquiries. All I know is Olivia took the mail to Exeter, so I know that will be a convenient spot to reconnoiter."

There were surprises all around for him. First, his mother had shown no astonishment at his announcement. Second, she was smiling.

"Edmond, you do appear to make this adventure sound like a campaign rather than a wooing."

"You don't know the lady. I may have to treat it as a battle to make her accept."

"And you believe Sophie has information you need?"

"So Mr. and Mrs. Partridge led me to believe."

"Then Sophie is the one to enlighten you if she can. And, Edmond, I assure you I have complete faith in your judgment, if it relieves your mind in any way."

"It decidedly does, Mother."

"Then Godspeed, my son."

With relief, Linnington arose and gave his mother a kiss on the cheek and was about to leave when she stopped him.

"And, Edmond, if I may make a suggestion, take the landau instead of the traveling carriage. It is built for travel and much better sprung. More comfortable for a lady." *Especially one expecting a baby.*

As he turned to the door, she stopped him. "And do be sure Owens packs your new blue coat. You are quite handsome in it."

Linnington promised he would do both and, in that moment, remembered Jamie's comment about how women, as well as servants, knew everything. Suspicion briefly crossed his mind. His mother acted remarkably unsurprised.

***

After he left the room, Elizabeth went to her desk and began a letter. This time it was not to Sophie but to her cousin, Clive Heath, who just happened to be the Bishop of Exeter. She smiled a little too broadly for a gentle woman as she wrote:

Dearest Cousin Clive,

It has come to my attention my son, Edmond Linnington, may be in need of a special marriage license, and since his prospective bride lives in Cornwall and he intends to stop in Exeter on the way, it occurred to me he might intend to see you when in town for this very purpose.

I rely on him to tell you of as much of the details as he deems pertinent, but if you have any hesitation in this matter, I wanted you to receive this assurance from me he has my complete blessing.

Yours with affection,

Elizabeth Linnington

Chapter Thirty

James Talent rode home to White Marsh Manor both relieved and disturbed by what had happened. He was sure Edmond would follow in his determination. He needed to talk all this out with Sophie. Her good sense in these matters, he believed, was far superior to his. After giving his mount to the groom, he ran up the stairs to divest himself of the riding clothes and wash away some of the grime from the trip. Harris, his valet, helped him, but he insisted the man leave him with the final touches and go inquire if his wife had time for him to talk. Harris returned, saying Mrs. Talent was awaiting him in her sitting room.

Walking in, he gave Sophie a quick kiss as she patted the spot next to her.

"Come sit beside me, my love. You look like you have much to tell."

He related as much of the happenings after she left as he deemed fit for a lady's ears. However, when he finished by telling her about his advice to quiz the Ps as to Olivia's whereabouts, she unexpectedly burst into tears.

"What did I say that makes you so unhappy, my sweet?"

Instead of answering, she slipped to her knees on the floor, clasping both hands, as if in supplication. "James, I swear to you, what I am about to reveal is the only secret I have ever kept from you in our marriage. If it were not someone else's secret, I would have long ago told you all. I swear it and please, please forgive me."

"There's nothing to forgive, but I am overwhelmingly curious about what you know of this matter. I assume it is about Mrs. Williams?"

She got up and went to her desk, returning with two letters in her hand. "Here is a letter from Lady Elizabeth. She sets the matter out better than I could, so you are free to read it."

She sat patiently as James read the letter in astonishment.

"Good Lord. Why did she keep it such a secret?"

"You cannot appreciate how wounded she was by the vicious things rumored after her father's suicide. My own parents forbade me to see her, and it was only when by chance I met her several years ago at a bookstall we were able to reestablish our deep friendship. I confess I used to take the children to the teashop and I swore them to secrecy. It was very bad of me, I know." Sophie regarded her hands intensely. Shame tinted her cheeks, but James shook his head as if to dismiss all this. "I think Olivia, after losing everything, was happy to dispense with the title Lady and simply be Mrs. David Williams. As for David, he was a lovely fellow, and I know he cared for her deeply. She was a loyal wife, but I often suspected her affection was firmly rooted in gratitude." Then she added, "But, James, there is more." With this, she handed him Olivia's letter, which he read with much less satisfaction.

"My God, Sophie," was all he could think to say when he finished.

"It's imperative Edmond get along with this business."

Jamie laughed. "If I know Edmond, he has gone completely into controlling this situation. I'm sure the first thing he did upon arriving at Crossfields was to question the Ps, and the next thing he will want to do is see you for details. Let's see," he mused. "Today, he most assuredly disposed of the Trent matter and got to Crossfields. By my calculation, he should show up here sometime around tea tomorrow. I think you are quite safe to inform the staff of his imminent arrival."

"When he comes, do you think it would be a good idea to inform him of the circumstances the way I did you?" asked Sophie.

"I believe Lady Linnington's letter a good way to broach the subject, but perhaps I should present Olivia's letter myself, in the privacy of the library. I can devise a way to get him there."

"Excellent," she agreed.

"You know, Sophie, what a tragedy in a way. If the old earl had not acted in such a reprehensible way, she would have come up to London with you to make her come out. They would have met there and not gone thorough all they have endured, but in all probability, simply taken the more direct route you and I did."

"Oh, James, no. You know them better than that. You and I were completely absorbed in each other and would not have cared a whit about seeing to our friends while they would have acted as each always has. Can't you see them? They would have been properly introduced by someone, and then every time they met at Lady Farthingale's ball, Mrs. Dumpling's rout, or Almack's, Linnington would stand at one end of the room with his arms folded. A forlorn expression on his face, he would be thinking, 'What a lovely girl but she is the daughter of an earl. She couldn't possibly see anything in the second son of a minor baron, bound to be a soldier.' Olivia would sit demurely at the other end of the room, pondering, 'What a handsome man. What could he possibly see in a country bred nobody from the West Country?' As it is, James, it has taken all of us pushing, you and your whist friends and even Lady Elizabeth, to get things this far."

He laughed at her rendition of the facts. "I'm sure you have the right of it." After a moment he laughed out loud. "Oh, Sophie, if things work as we hope, I swear I would sell my soul to see Harriet Woolley's face when she realizes her country bumpkin, shopgirl sister-in-law far outranks her!"

Sophie laughed and clapped her hands at the delicious thought.

Chapter Thirty-One

Exactly as Jamie had predicted, Edmond arrived late the next day from Crossfields.

"I apologize for this abrupt visit, James, but I find I must make some inquiries of Sophie."

"She is upstairs in the sitting room, and I believe she does have quite a tale to tell you. But before we go up, Edmond, I swear I had no knowledge of what she will have to say before I arrived home yesterday afternoon. I must say, we have been expecting you and, indeed, hoped to."

Without more preamble, he ushered his confused friend up the stairs to the sitting room where Edmond greeted Sophie.

"Before we begin, Edmond, please be seated, and would you like some tea?"

"I prefer a glass of wine," James offered, and with Edmond's agreement, the three sat down for the awaited wine before the discussion. As she had the evening before, Sophie handed Edmond his mother's letter. Edmond's face turned from curiosity to astonishment.

When he finished, he laid the letter aside. "But why wouldn't she confide this to me?"

Sophie went through her feelings on the matter as she had with James the night before. In addition, she filled in many of the details of her long friendship with Olivia as well as much of her feelings about what had happened, both in Cornwall and the years Olivia and David were married.

"But, Edmond, all that is in the past, and now your future must be considered."

"I assure you, I plan to secure her hand as soon as I can make it to the West Country. I have already sent the landau to Exeter and plan to meet it in two to three days. I must try to call on my mother's cousin, the bishop for a license. Unfortunately, I may not arrive until Saturday, so I will have to wait until Monday to see him and proceed to Launceston, if poor Max is not done with carrying me around for most of the week." His radiant face reflected his delight in all they had told him.

"I'm afraid there is more, Edmond." A worried look replaced the happiness. "Come with me to the library and we will secure another glass of wine. Sophie has a letter from Olivia rather complicating the picture."

The two men repaired to the library, where James poured them each a portion of brandy instead of wine.

Then he reached into his pocket and handed Olivia's letter to Linnington.

With trepidation, Edmond opened it. There was no question from his expression when he got to the part about the child. He stopped reading and gaped at James. "Oh, my God, Jamie."

"There's more. Read to the end."

When he finished, Linnington carefully folded the letter and handed it to James." I suppose I should be grateful to one, Mr. Henry Goddard, but I intend to make as much haste to Tinstone, Cornwall, as I can manage to forestall him. Moreover, I have no assurance she will accept my offer. I could not persuade her to remain with me in London."

"But, Edmond, things are now entirely on a different foot. By your own admission, you gave the boot to your chances by not making a direct offer."

"I may have a devil of a time convincing her I am sincere in my offer and not simply acting out of guilt or a feeling of duty for the coming child."

James regarded him thoughtfully. "We cannot know anything on that score until you speak to her directly, but, Edmond, I hope you are happy about the new arrival?"

Edmond grinned. "I find I am. Quite over the moon, actually." He sobered. "But I assure you, Jamie, there was much affection, I now realize, but only one occurrence of passion." He shook his head. "Just the once. I never imagined."

"Well, I'm happy you are happy. I assure you, children can be a nuisance, but they are also a great joy."

James took a sip of brandy, content the news had been imparted and ready to engage in a long rumination about domestic life, a subject about which he was wont to talk at length.

Edmond interrupted, "Somewhat on that score, I have an intimate question to ask you, James."

"Yes?"

"I have always thought women considered the most intimate part of a marriage to be somewhat of a burden. I hoped it would be a distinct pleasure for whomever I married. Is such a thing possible once a marriage, properly sanctioned, is consummated?"

"Let me put it this way. As is obvious, Sophie and I have produced three children, and if I'm not mistaken, a fourth may be in the making. She has never objected to any part of the procedure for this to happen. I must say, quite the opposite. Does that answer your question?"

"It does, and thank you."

"Good. Now, let us prepare for dinner. I believe Sophie planned a small celebratory meal, which may be the only prenuptial feast you get, old man."

Linnington left bright and early the next morning after both the Talents wished him well.

Chapter Thirty-Two

In the August heat, it took him the entire three days to complete the journey, being sure Max had enough rest, water, and stamina not to delay the trip for any great length. He arrived late on Saturday. He earnestly hoped to secure an audience with his mother's cousin the bishop to have him prepare a special license. If Olivia accepted his offer, he wanted no delay for bans to be read and such, now particularly considering the pregnancy.

Since the next day was Sunday, he lost no time in attending services at the Cathedral. When they were over, he loitered until most of the congregation left then approached the bishop who stood in the narthex, conversing with the departing guests and members of the parish.

When the red-robed gentleman's attention turned to him, Edmond held out his hand. "Your Grace, you may not remember me, but I am Edmond Linnington, your cousin Elizabeth's son."

"Ah yes, Edmond, how good to see you in this part of England."

"I was wondering, sir, if it would be possible for you to make a few moments tomorrow for me. I am sure you have a very busy schedule, but if I could inconvenience you, I have a personal matter of some urgency to discuss with you."

The rotund little man gave Edmond's shoulder a pat. "No inconvenience at all. With Sunday's so busy for me, I like to keep Monday's rather light of duties. Let me see, shall we say around ten o'clock?"

"Indeed, it would fit my plans admirably. I am deeply grateful."

"Then I shall look forward to seeing you." With that, he turned to greet another of his flock.

When Edmond entered the Bishop's study the next day, the portly gentleman in scarlet robes and heavy gold chain and cross did not rise but held out a welcoming hand with its massive ring, to his cousin. "Sit down, dear Edmond, and tell me how I can help you." With a mischievous smile on his face, he laced his fingers together and laid them on his ample belly. "What can I do for you?"

"Your Grace, I'm on my way to Cornwall to attempt to persuade a young lady to marry me, and I find, because of circumstances, it would be helpful to obtain a special license if it is at all possible."

The bishop shifted a single piece of paper on his desk.

"Is this a godly young woman, sir, and are you easy in forgoing all the good counsel which would proceed such a match?"

"She is, and I am, sir."

"I must confess, I am not completely unaware you might be applying to me for this. I received on Saturday, from your young man, a note from your mother saying you might apply to me and assuring me in such case I was to know you have her blessing."

"I am gratified to hear it. So, you have no objection, then?"

"All I need is the lady's name." He pulled the paper closer and, taking pen in hand, dipped into an inkwell.

"Olivia Williams."

The bishop looked up in surprise and slowly lowered the pen. "Olivia Constant Williams?"

"Yes, sir." Edmond wasn't keen on the bishop's expression. A sense of foreboding washed over him.

The bishop replaced the pen in the well. "Before we continue, I must ask you some questions, Edmond. I preface them by saying, as you probably know, her father-in-law is vicar at All Saint's Church, Tinstone. The parish is in my See, and Thomas Williams and I are very old friends," and, with a twinkle in his eyes, he added, "since we are both very old indeed." He continued in a much more serious voice. "In addition to being a friend, he has been a loyal colleague over the years in many of my battles with clergy and laity here. I am also well acquainted with the trials endured by Lady Olivia. I confirmed her as a girl and conducted her father's funeral, much to the displeasure of some of my flock. I say all this in preface to telling you Thomas came to see me recently. I can be frank with you. I believe I know all the circumstances surrounding this situation. So, before I do your bidding, I want to be quite sure where your affections and your conscience lie. I hope you are not on this mission purely because of her condition. If you are aware of what I am saying, you must have been involved. Am I correct?"

"You are, Your Grace. And I assure you of my profound regard for Olivia and my very deep love. Had I approached her in a better manner, I hope I could have persuaded her to remain in London and marry me months ago."

"I sincerely hope such is your motivation. The poor girl has gone through enough in her life and deserves whatever good fortune you can bestow on her."

"I quite agree, sir."

"In that case..." He took the pen to complete the instrument. "There you are." He handed the license to Edmond. "And I wish you both happy."

In parting, the bishop gave Edmond directions to Tinstone, instructing him to take the Truro pike out of Launceston. Before he reached Bolventon, he would find Moorfield Road, branching to the left. From there, after a few miles, he would be able to see the square tower of All Saint's Church and the vicarage was next door. "If I know Thomas, you will find him either in his study or tending his roses. Most likely the latter."

Edmond thanked him for all of his help and took his leave.

Regardless of the late hour, Edmond gathered his entourage to make the trip to Launceston. He contained his eagerness by riding in the slower landau with Maximilian tethered to the rear of the carriage.

They arrived late, but Edmond managed to secure a good room at the Ship Inn and have a decent supper.

The next morning, he carefully dressed in boots and breeches donning a broad-brimmed hat to ward off the summer sun. He then decided to dally in Launceston, since it would only take him a scarce forty-five minutes to get to Tinstone, and he assumed Olivia would be at the millinery shop until close to five. Although he anticipated speaking first to Mr. Williams, he really did not relish spending the entire afternoon with the gentleman, nervously waiting for her to appear.

He lunched in the garden of the inn and poked about the considerable shops until midafternoon, finding nothing he wanted to buy. He spent another nervous thirty minutes at the pub for an additional glass of ale, vacillating between extravagant hope and fear of an abyss of disappointment. For the hundredth time, he consulted his pocket watch. When it neared four o'clock, he gratefully mounted Max for the final leg of the trip. At least things would now be settled.

He had no trouble finding the pike to Truro but was forced to stop a farmer in the field to assure him what direction was Moorfield Road. The man confirmed it was the correct byway.

As he neared the village, he could see the tower the bishop described, but more interesting, he came upon a vista revealing an enormous manor built in the Georgian style of gray stone. The sweeping lawns and fine gardens were immaculately kept. In the distance, he could hear the baying of hounds being run for exercise and training. This must be Newington Hall. She had lived a tough life since Newington Hall, but what a glorious home to grow up in.

How different was the aspect of Crossfields. There, the grounds were equally well kept, but it was nothing so grand as this. His house, although commodious in his estimation, could only be half this size. For the first time, he considered Olivia might be disappointed.

He shook off the feeling and proceeded to the village; from what he had been told, she was glad to be rid of her life at Newington Hall.

Tinstone was not quite what he expected. It was certainly more than a hamlet and less than a town but smaller than he anticipated. As he neared the church, a charming bridge lay before him where he could hear a running stream. A single street of shops lined Moorfield Road, just beyond. The church and vicarage were on this side of the stream.

From horseback, he could see a gentleman in black vest and white collar in shirtsleeves among a particularly lovely rose garden. He was surely in the right place. He dismounted, leaving Max tied to a fence post. Walking toward the man, Edmond took off his hat.

The vicar paused in what he was doing and waited.

"Vicar Williams?"

"I am."

"May I introduce myself? I am, Edmond, Lord Linnington."

The vicar briefly shook Edmond's offered hand, giving him a serious and very straight appraisal. He made no inquiry as to Edmond's purpose but rolled down his sleeves and secured his cuffs. "Perhaps, my lord, we should go inside to my study."

They made their way into the house. "Mrs. Todd, please bring tea for me and his lordship in the study." A rather plain woman with a sour expression nodded to him from what must be a kitchen door. The vicar's study was a mass of books and papers, but all seemed to have some interior order. He indicated a chair for Edmond then sat behind his desk, removing his glasses.

"If you don't mind, I should like to wait for the tea before we begin our discussion."

Edmond had the same feeling as he had with the bishop. The vicar was precisely aware of the purpose of his call.

A short time later, the woman brought in a tray and put it on a table. "How do you take your tea, milord?" Her tone was snappish.

"Milk and two sugars, please, Mrs. Todd," he answered, making sure he acknowledged her, since he wanted no more opposition in this affair than he already anticipated.

When she had served them and withdrawn, the vicar opened the conversation. He got right to it. "I may assume, sir, your visit may have something to do with my daughter-in-law?"

"It does, sir. I hoped to apply to you for permission to ask for her hand."

"Are you completely aware of her circumstances?" The query was delivered with directness.

"I believe so, sir. The wife of my dearest friend, Sophie Talent, and also a friend of Olivia's from childhood, has apprised me of all I believe there is to know."

"You are the father?"

"I am. Quite assuredly, Vicar."

"Well, that establishes your interest in Olivia. I must inquire as to your feelings for her?"

"I was certain I loved her before she left London. All I know now is life for me has become unbearable without her."

"And how do you feel about this impending birth?"

Edmond could not conceal a delighted smile. "I quite anticipate it, sir."

The vicar's face also relaxed into a smile. "Well, then. You have my blessing, although I don't believe it is required. However, I do wish you well in convincing our dear Olivia you are in earnest."

"Knowing her, sir, I appreciate your good wishes."

The vicar glanced at the clock. "She should be along any time soon. If you will take a seat in the parlor across the hall, you can await her there and I shall send her in directly."

"Thank you, sir. You have been most kind, and I particularly thank you for your attention to my beloved these last months. It cannot have been easy for her."

The vicar regarded him kindly. "As I also love her dearly, it has been my pleasure and my hope I may have been some comfort to her."

Alone in the parlor, Linnington was too anxious to be seated. He paced about for what seemed an eternity until a figure in a white dress and straw bonnet emerged, crossing the bridge over the stream. The window was open to enjoy the breeze, carrying a slight sweet smell of roses. She stopped at the fence to admire Max, putting out her hand to see if the horse would accept a bit of petting. Max poked his nose close to her hand and let her pat his neck. She seemed to be talking to him, and Max gave her face a nuzzle. This was a remarkable thing, for Max was a rather particular horse, who preferred his master to all other humans.

Yes, that little mare will be a perfect gift for my bride and new mother. At the same time, he was aware the hard part lay in convincing Olivia to marry him.

Olivia's voice came from the hallway. "Good evening, Father Williams. Are you alone? Someone has tethered a beautiful horse by the lichgate."

His answer was simple. "There is a gentleman to see you, my dear."

She did not respond. The door to the parlor opened. Olivia had taken off the bonnet, but if Linnington hoped she would rush into his arms, he was mistaken. Instead, she closed the door, and stood with her back pressed to it.

"My lord?" She wasn't going to make it easy.

Linnington had no other gambit but to plunge in. "Olivia, I have come to ask you to be my wife. And I suppose to apologize for any offense I gave you at our parting. I should have offered for you directly then."

She took a moment. "Your apology, I suppose, was for your proposal I stay in the Tothill Fields House?"

"It is. I confess to not being of completely sound mind the morning you departed."

From Olivia's skeptical lift of an eyebrow, he concluded she considered this a weak excuse. She continued acidly, "May I surmise then, your change of heart concerning our relationship has nothing to do with now being apprised my father was an earl?"

Linnington was horror-stricken. "Assuredly not." If she was growing angry, she was not the only one to suddenly be confronted by their resentments. "Since you reference the subject, why in the world did you conceal all of this? Had I known..."

"Had you known, your attitude toward me would be different, I presume."

"I never intended to imply such an idea, but I do find it difficult to accept you withheld a truth from me."

"You mean I lied, at least by omission."

"I simply fail to see the reason behind it."

She cooled a bit. "You might consider I had no wish to trail my scandalous past into your life and the lives of your family. Besides, by the time we met, I was most comfortable simply being Mrs. Williams."

"I understand your reasoning, but since the scandal attached to your father and not to you, it all seems to me beside the point."

"Suffice it to say, it doesn't to me."

Edmond was still smoldering over this conversation. "While on the subject of veracity, I fail to see what it profited you not to let me know your whereabouts, since you took time to write to me. Did you not think I might, upon reflection, regret our parting?"

"I did." She bristled. "And that is precisely why I did as I did. I had no desire for you to think I was pressuring you into further connection."

"You might have left the decision to me," he countered.

"So long as we are clearing the air, may I be assured your offer is not simply because of my condition? I assume Sophie confirmed what I am sure is obvious to you that our intimacy has had a consequence."

"And I assure you, my surprise at the news was overwhelmed delight." He couldn't help but smile and hoped he didn't appear too foolish. "And are you pleased?"

"In all honesty, there have been moments I have had regrets, but in general, I, too, am happy." After a long moment, she added, "Since you have apologized for your behavior, I must ask if there was anything about my actions that night which gave you pause. Had I asked you to stop, I am sure you would have complied."

"I cannot be entirely sure. But I hope you feel, despite the passion, I treated you with tenderness and respect."

"You did, although, I would not expect you to express such feelings in the confines of marriage."

"Good Lord, woman. What do you think it means in the marriage service when I will promise, if you let me, 'with my body I thee worship'? In addition, Olivia," he went on, now decidedly angry, "I am quite tired of this colloquy. It seems I cannot reason you into an answer; I am reduced saying simply that I love you to my own distraction and have been miserable without you. If that is to be my fate, then tell me so and at least put me out of the misery."

To his surprise, she laughed. "When I was a little girl, I remember my mother telling me never to marry a man I had not had at least one good row with."

"So, for God's sake, does this suffice, then?"

"I believe it does."

"And your answer is yes?"

"Yes, Edmond. Yes, yes, yes!"

As he had done on the day he first saw her, he covered the distance between them in a bound and, this time, gathered her into his arms instead of taking her hand. For a moment, they simply reveled in holding each other close until she raised her face for a kiss.

After another series of kisses, he continued to hold her close. His fingertip sought the small space between her hipbone and where her rounded belly met his. He gently ran his fingers its length. "May this be the only sort of thing ever to come between us my love."

"Edmond, there is something I forgot to tell you." She was all seriousness.

A moment of terror assailed him. "What?"

"I forgot to tell you I love you." With this, she stood on tiptoe and initiated her own kiss.

Chapter Thirty-Three

After taking Olivia to the local inn for a quiet supper, Linnington returned her to the vicarage, giving the special license to Mr. Williams, who agreed to officiate in two days instead of three weeks. Linnington would have preferred to do the deed straight away, but Olivia, having agreed to be a bride, declared it would take her at least a day to make proper arrangements for the ceremony even though it was to be private.

Linnington was relegated to wandering about Launceston in a fit of anticipation the entire next day. He planned never to have her out of his sight this long for the rest of his life. He considered purchasing her a wedding gift and could settle on nothing in the shops. Belatedly, he remembered to go to the goldsmiths and buy a ring. He chose a plain band with a small blue stone the color of her eyes. He tried it on his little finger.

"It should fit a lady with slender fingers, sir," the goldsmith offered. "If not, I shall gladly alter the size."

Linnington made the purchase and stowed the ring in his watch pocket.

With nothing to do, he was staring out the window of his room in the late afternoon when Owens rapped at the door and informed him there was a man downstairs asking for a moment of his lordship's time. Grateful for any interruption, he told Owens to show the man up. In short order there was a knock at the door.

"Come."

A large, well-dressed man in country clothes and the hands of a farmer entered shyly, hat in hand.

"Lord Linnington?"

"Yes."

"My name is Henry Goddard."

Linnington immediately held out his hand. "Mr. Goddard. You are a longtime friend of my bride, I believe."

"I am, sir."

"How may I help you?"

"I have been fond of Lady Olivia since we were children. I offered my good wishes to her and wanted to offer the same to you. After talking to her, I have her permission to presume to ask a great favor."

"Yes?"

"I believe you are accompanied only by your valet and man servant?"

"I am."

"Mrs. Mary Hastings has agreed to stand witness for Lady Olivia. If you concur, I would be honored to stand witness for you, tomorrow, if there is no one else you have in your plans."

Edmond was touched by this homely offer.

He held out his hand and the man took it. "I would be honored, Mr. Goddard." Still clasping the hand, he added, "I also want to thank you for all the care you offered my beloved when she needed a good friend, and you have my deepest gratitude for your attentions."

Henry Goddard smiled in relief. "Thank you, sir, it was sincerely meant. I look forward to seeing you tomorrow." With that, he bowed himself out of the room.

***

Olivia had been busy. The first thing was to inform Henry Goddard of her plan. She was gratified by his sincere congratulations and like Edmond, touched by his offer. She encouraged him to inquire of his lordship.

The next thing was to go directly to the shop to tell Mary Hastings what had occurred. Upon hearing the news, Mrs. Hastings fetched a white straw bonnet.

"Here, Olivia. At least you must have a bridal bonnet. Without a veil, I suppose, but what about a trim of blue silk ribbons. Would that suit?"

"It's lovely, Mrs. Hastings, and I would adore it. Blue is perfect."

Her daughter, Anne, came by as was her wont, and enthusiastically joined in plans for the ceremony. Olivia intended to gather as many roses as she could from the vicar's garden to adorn the altar, and Anne insisted on creating a nosegay for her to carry. Anne fished a sixpence from her reticule and gave it to Olivia.

"I shall happily wear it for luck, Anne, and return it after the ceremony." Even small coins were scarce in the family. Thus, the women had completed all the necessary tasks folklore prescribed for a happy union.

Olivia had a perfectly serviceable plain white gown of nice material she made earlier in the summer and it would have to do for bridal wear, but with the lovely bonnet, it would suit her quite well, considering the lack of time to prepare. And of course, she would wear her pearl necklace and the beautiful earrings. Lacking a new pair of white gloves to wear, she bade farewell to the women and stepped into the shop next door in the hope she would find a decent pair. The rest of the day she spent packing her well-worn trunk. She planned a luncheon for after the service the next day. Hoping there was a way Mrs. Todd could be persuaded to prepare the meal, she went to the kitchen to see. Otherwise, she would use some of her slender recourses to order a meal at the local inn.

To her relief but without enthusiasm, Mrs. Todd agreed and they decided on a menu, festive enough for a wedding but light enough for midsummer. Mrs. Todd might be unpleasant, but she was a better-than-average cook and took great pride in her work. To Olivia's relief, the woman offered to set five places at the table in the shade of a trellis in the garden, thus indicating she had no intention of joining the wedding party. She said she would prepare enough to feed Owens, Jeremy, and herself in the kitchen.

Olivia slept reasonably well with all the arrangements made.

***

Linnington slept wretchedly, overcome as many bridegrooms were by the realization he was in truth about to take on the responsibility of a wife, and in short order, a family.

Ten o'clock found him standing at the altar of All Saint's Church, Tinstone, dutifully dressed in the blue coat his mother had advised he bring with Mr. Goddard at his side. He was glad he had given his bride the time to make arrangements.

The altar was lovely with its abundance of flowers. There were even a few guests, townsfolk who were especially fond of Olivia and probably one or two out of sheer curiosity, Anne Hastings, with her handkerchief in hand to catch any tears, and Owens and Jeremy sat in the front pew.

Then his lady appeared at the door of the narthex in a charming lace-trimmed bonnet, flowers in hand. The sight her rounded body

267

was to him the most beautiful thing he had ever seen. If he harbored any doubts about her willingness to enter into this marriage, they vanished when she lifted her face surrounded by the lacy bonnet.

The description "blushing bride" came nowhere near describing the fresh eagerness of her countenance. To him, she was surrounded by an aura announcing *I love you, I trust you, and I give my entire body and welfare to you.* Vanishing with these doubts were his own about his ability to care for her and their children. With Olivia at his side, he could do anything.

The vicar began the familiar words, "Dearly beloved..."

Linnington had not thought ahead to the passage, "Who giveth this woman...?" After the words were spoken in an unusual act, the vicar himself announced in a clear voice, "I do."

The vows were exchanged in a blur, and the only other thing the groom could remember was Olivia's secret smile when he got to the "worship" and "body" part and fumbling with the simple ring. Thankfully, the band fit, and he was pleased when she spread her hand to admire it.

He was in a sweat until the vicar gave the final pronouncement, and they knelt for the blessing.

When he escorted her down the aisle and out the door, the open air was beyond relief.

The luncheon after the ceremony was cordial, and the five of them lingered over the table until midafternoon. Linnington had taken the one and only suite of rooms in the little inn, quite unimaginatively named, The Tinstone Inn. It was clean and a cut above a local public house and quite adequate for the newlyweds to spend the night before travelling to Exeter. All Linnington cared about was having a private place to take his new wife in his arms and show her how much he loved her.

***

Linnington had a surprise gift for Olivia from James and Sophie. Just before he left White Marsh Manor, James had taken him aside.

"Look here, Edmond, you do need a honeymoon and with the Continent still quite at sixes and sevens, it's no time to travel abroad. Sophie and I have a seaside cottage at Lyme Regis. It's not at all grand and not large enough for a staff, but Sophie and I take the children there for a few weeks in the summer. We hire a local woman and her daughter and son. She acts as housekeeper and cook. The daughter helps and does anything Sophie needs doing, and the son takes care of the heavy work and attends me if I really need it. You are both quite used to caring for yourselves, and I can arrange for the help if you and Olivia would like to repair there for a few weeks on your own."

"And you had not planned to use it in the coming weeks?"

"Not at all. We spent several weeks there in early summer."

Edmond was delighted at the idea, and James promised to have all in readiness within the week.

Olivia, a bit apprehensive about her welcome at Crossfields, was delighted to have her husband all to herself for a while as she screwed up her courage to face her mother-in-law and particularly, Harriet Woolley.

The next morning, they paused long enough to say a private goodbye to Vicar Williams and began the trip to Exeter to spend the night. They discussed going the long way through Plymouth and following the coast road, but both decided they were exhausted by all the drama of the past few weeks, so they would take the shorter, overland route. Lyme Regis was only another day beyond Exeter for the landau.

As they left Tinstone, Linnington signaled the coachman to pull up at the place he had halted viewing Newington Hall.

"Why are we stopping?"

"I wanted you to take a last look. You will, in all probability, never see this house again. I wanted to be sure there was nothing about it you would miss. I love Crossfields, but although it has been built onto, it is still just a very large Tudor estate. Much more old-fashioned than Newington Hall and not nearly so grand."

"Your description makes me long to see it, Edmond. And I assure you, there is nothing about that cold, evil house I shall miss. It holds only death and unhappiness for me."

"Then may I press one other point? Can you also leave behind with the sight of the place, the burden of memories you still carry?"

She regarded him solemnly for a moment. "I can try. I may not be able to forget what I saw and experienced there, but I can concentrate on whatever new life you and I will create together, but only if you promise me one thing?"

"What would that be?"

"That you, in like form, will try to put away your memories of the war."

"I gladly promise, my love."

"Then we can drive on." As the coachman urged the horses on, she never looked back.

Chapter Thirty-Four

At Exeter, Linnington sent Jeremy directly to Crossfields on Max. The coachman and Owens accompanied Edmond and Olivia to the house in Lyme Regis before they returned with the landau to the estate. The couple had no need to be transported, since everything was within easy walking distance. The landau would return for them sometime after the first week in September and they would begin the journey home.

The cottage was built of stone adjoined by a neatly tended garden and a terrace with a spectacular vista of the bay. It was a bit away of the town proper but with good access to the beach and the strand.

The house's adequate but limited facilities reminded them both of the intimacy of the Tothill Fields house, so it perfectly fit both their present condition and their temperament. The sea air with its hint of salt and fish, the sunny summer days, and the exercise of walking melted away some of the tension each of them carried. They both made an effort to keep to the promises they made when they left Newington Hall, and all of this combined began to put whatever ghosts had obsessed them, firmly in a closet.

Most of their time at the beach was spent in sleep and exercise, but since there were a few fashionable shops in the seaside town, catering to the ladies of leisure who summered there, Olivia had time to replace most of her well-worn wardrobe. She had added to it since London with new bonnets from the shop, and she took time early in the summer to stitch a few new frocks, particularly with an eye to the fact they needed to be fashioned to be of use as she expanded in girth.

She also had kept the walking dress she made for the trip to Cornwall in the hope it would fit her once the baby was born.

Linnington replaced her battered trunk with a new one slightly larger than the one he happily discarded, along with the tattered portmanteau. He found her quite a smart bandbox to carry her more personal items and jewelry.

The landau returned with the coachman and a footman named Harold, Jeremy having left service to take up his apprenticeship. Harold was formerly second footman but seemed to fit into his new role as comfortably as Jeremy.

Edmond and Olivia laughed at the thought that Harold would, in all probability, never be put to the test of keeping such secrets as the reliable Jeremy had kept.

The morning they were to depart, Olivia found herself reluctant to leave the bed. Physically, she was well enough, and it was true she longed to have their idyll go on forever, but what really worried her was how Elizabeth would receive her. Lady Linnington had been perfectly pleasant to her when they met in London, but that was before there was any suggestion Olivia was to become her future daughter-in-law. And then there was Harriet. Olivia had no idea what she would have to say about the marriage.

When they met at the house, Elizabeth had been gracious, but how would she feel with a bride almost six months pregnant by the time they reached Crossfields. Here, once more, was the prospect of scandal in her life, and this time it was in the future. Word of their marriage would make it into the gossip mills, and such a news item was fine with her. It was the impending birth announcement giving her concern. It would be impossible to miss the discrepancy of dates between marriage and the birth of their first child. She had promised not to dwell on the mishaps of the past, but what of the future?

When she broached the subject, Linnington dismissed it." Let the biddies count on their fingers if they will. I only hope for a healthy child and a relatively easy lying in for you."

His sentiment was all well and good and she was glad of his feelings, but she had no idea what would be the reaction of the rest of the family. She also didn't wish to be snubbed by society for his sake and the child's.

Lying in the bed would not stop these things from coming to pass. She sighed and pulled herself to her feet, feeling quite ungainly, now. Resolutely, she made herself ready for travel.

They took the road north in easy stages, stopping along the way for some sightseeing at Stonehenge and in Salisbury. The last leg of the journey they spent in Reading, so on Saturday, they had only scant days' journey. They planned to arrive at Crossfields shortly before teatime. She lay awake long after Edmond was asleep at the inn in Reading. She couldn't shake her anxiety.

Some of her anxiety was allayed the next day as they neared the house. He was all eagerness to show her the approach to the estate and recount its history and its points of interest. It was a lovely place, and its dignified warmth a far cry from the cold gray eminence of Newington Hall reassured her, boding well for their happiness.

She put her hand on her stomach. The baby was most active today, perhaps all aflutter at arriving at a new home. Here was the house in which this child would be born.

Olivia smiled to recall Edmond had formed the habit of speaking directly to this child in utero each morning to wish it a good day.

He attempted to hide his feelings, but it was obvious he hoped for a sturdy son and heir. She wanted a girl. Sophie's little girls were the only ones she was close to. With each of Sophie's visits, Olivia watched as Eugenia grew from infant to laughing cherub. Secretly, Olivia hoped to have a little girl with Eugenia's sparkle and Caroline's sweet, biddable temper.

They would neither get their wish.

***

Elizabeth had carefully planned the welcome. Arriving Friday afternoon was the entire Talent family, including baby Eugenia. Harriet and Malcolm were also in attendance, and she had persuaded them to furlough their son Simon from school in Oxford for the homecoming.

On Saturday afternoon, she gathered them all in the upstairs sitting room, except for James and Sophie, who waited at the front door to be first to greet the couple. Elizabeth chose the sitting room, not only because it was her favorite room in the house, but also the lattice opened directly out on the drive with glimpses of the highway beyond.

They all kept themselves occupied. Robert stood sentinel at the window, Caroline played with her dolls on the carpet, Simon shoved the pieces about in a solitary game of chess at a table, and Eugenia insisted on trying to walk as Nanny tried equally hard to keep her still in the corner. Malcolm dozed on the couch, Harriet sitting grimly beside him. Elizabeth would miss Robert's visits when he would go off to school like Simon. She had to admit he was her favorite—bright, outgoing, and quietly competent with the other children.

Today, he was excited. "I think I see the carriage," he announced.

Only Elizabeth got up and joined him at the window. At last, the landau came up the drive, and the couple alit.

"Are you anxious to meet your new aunt, Robert?"

"I am, Lady Linnington. Mama told me she had a surprise for us."

Just then, Olivia happened to look up at the house so her face was clearly visible to the boy. Robert caught his breath and turned to his sister. "Caroline, it is Aunt Olivia!"

"Did she bring the rabbits?" Caroline piped in her childish voice.

"Of course not, silly. Who would want rabbits in a carriage?"

"Children, I believe your parents are downstairs if you want to join them and greet your aunt. Caroline, if afterwards you can get Nanny to take you and the baby down to Mr. Partridge's cottage, I think you will find the rabbits."

"Punch and Judy?"

"I believe so, and perhaps some baby rabbits, too."

At this, both children raced for the stairs, Nanny hurrying after with Eugenia.

By now, Harriet sat bolt upright. "What's all this nonsense about rabbits and 'Aunt 'Olivia, Mother?"

"I'm sorry, Harriet, I believe you must not have heard. Mrs. Williams and Sophie have been friends from childhood. Sophie's father's property bordered Olivia's father's estate. Before her marriage, I believe she was Olivia Constant, daughter of Charles Constant, Earl of Wallingford."

Harriet's jaw dropped. Her expression changed, and she shook her dozing husband. "Malcolm. Malcolm! Rouse yourself. We must go down to the hall and greet our new sister-in-law."

With a grumpy frown, Malcolm hauled himself up to standing. "I thought you were going to give her a cut," he complained.

"Not at all. I'm sure I never said such a thing. Come along now, I believe they have finished greeting the servants and are about to enter the hall. Come along, Simon, leave that silly game and come with us."

She bustled out of the room, tossing an accusatory glance at her mother. Elizabeth had no doubt her daughter suspected the pertinent information had been withheld on purpose.

So it was, James missed the moment of revelation, but Elizabeth enjoyed it immensely. *So much for a mere Miss Sybil Trent!*

Elizabeth willed herself to sit in her chair. She wanted to see the couple alone. As Simon stoically followed his parents out the door, he had closed it. Even so, she could hear the progress of voices. Edmond and Olivia were undoubtedly greeting the Talents, children, and the others. Nanny's clucking at them followed the light voices of the children exiting the door. In a few moments, there was silence, and she anticipated the couple was coming up the stairs, the rest of the company having withdrawn to the parlor.

She didn't realize she was holding her breath until there was a knock.

"Come," she called.

When they entered, each wore the exact expression she had visualized—her son aglow with happiness, all trace of melancholy gone, and Olivia rosy in her pregnancy. The only variation she detected was hesitation, perhaps even some trepidation in the wide, blue eyes.

Elizabeth arose from her chair and walked toward the girl, holding out both hands. "Olivia, my dear! Welcome home!"

Made in the USA
Monee, IL
30 July 2022

10427575R00166